TAKE A BREATH

S.K. Paisley

Take a Breath
Published by Celandine
First published March 2014
Copyright © S. K. Paisley 2014

ISBN: 978-0-9928440-0-4

www.celandinebooks.com

CONTENTS

PROLOGUE 1

CHAPTER ONE 3

CHAPTER TWO 12

CHAPTER THREE 17

CHAPTER FOUR 27

CHAPTER FIVE 30

CHAPTER SIX 40

CHAPTER SEVEN 54

CHAPTER EIGHT 58

CHAPTER NINE 70

CHAPTER TEN 76

CHAPTER ELEVEN 90

CHAPTER TWELVE 111

CHAPTER THIRTEEN 116

CHAPTER FOURTEEN 141

CHAPTER FIFTEEN 154

CHAPTER SIXTEEN 164

CHAPTER SEVENTEEN 170

CHAPTER EIGHTEEN 184

CHAPTER NINETEEN 197

CHAPTER TWENTY 209

CHAPTER TWENTY-ONE 225

CHAPTER TWENTY-TWO 235

CHAPTER TWENTY-THREE 242

CHAPTER TWENTY-FOUR 255

CHAPTER TWENTY-FIVE 269

CHAPTER TWENTY-SIX 286

CHAPTER TWENTY-SEVEN 290

CHAPTER TWENTY-EIGHT 299

CHAPTER TWENTY-NINE 309

EPILOGUE 313

ACKNOWLEDGEMENTS 316

ABOUT THE AUTHOR 317

For Jamie

PROLOGUE

Pulling her mirror compact from the depths of her overflowing carrier bag, the girl began to apply gloss to her glacé-cherry lips. As she balanced on the back of the bench, her booted feet resting on the seat, she smacked her lips together with a pantomime pout. Some of the men in hard hats downed tools, reckoning up if she was old enough for their wolf whistles to pass. Her unbuttoned denim jacket delineated her blossoming bosom; her skirt was hitched high up her suntanned thighs. All make-up, glitter and sparkle, penny-farthing earrings and sweet perfume.

Her fingers jangled the coins in her pocket. The exact change for her bus. She waited, pretending to ignore the stir of excitement from the other side of the road. As she readjusted the earpiece of her headphones, the music screeched like tyres on wet tarmac. A surge of energy rippled through her and a smile stole across her face.

She was sixteen years old and knew her power. The kind of girl boys worshipped, mothers hated and fathers wanted to fuck.

CHAPTER ONE

Paul positioned himself in the centre of the couch. His hand went to his face and felt the rough bristle. Could do with a shave; he wasn't as young as he used to be. His leg started to bounce and his shoulders hiked up higher towards his ears. It had been so long, he could hardly even remember the last time.

Stretching his arms over the back of the small two-seater, relaxing his muscles, he set his knees firmly apart, taking up as much space as he could. *Act as if,* repeated like a mantra.

Already he felt better. A tingle of excitement returned to his body – a tingle he had forgotten even existed. A smile started to spread across his face and he sensed a ghost of his former self begin to settle. For the first time in a long time he felt in control.

When Annie had entered the pub earlier that night, for a fleeting moment he'd thought she was someone else. It had hit him like a punch in the stomach, knocking the wind out of him. Beneath the rain-soaked red hood of her coat he'd caught a glimpse of her chocolate curls, her olive skin, and that familiar panic had started in his bowels and risen up through his chest, into his throat.

As the hood came down he saw the hair was more chestnut

than chocolate, the skin more ivory than olive. It wasn't her. Of course it wasn't her. A snort escaped his nostrils.

"You alright?" Joe had stopped mid-sentence and was staring at Paul.

"Yeah, I'm fine. I thought I ate a bug."

Joe carried on, nonplussed. Paul's eyes followed the girl to the bar. A murmur of mischief electrified the air as grins and sideways glances were exchanged. Apart from staff, you didn't get many females drinking in this haunt. Not ones that looked like her. He searched around for the unfortunate guy who'd brought her in; it was going to be a task keeping that one out of trouble. Around pretty ladies, the punters had a tendency to forget their manners.

The pub was in one of the converted arches under a railway line, the kind of place where you were safe as long as you were known. It wasn't a palace but at least there was carpet and not sawdust on the floor. There was a railway theme throughout, which showed at least sometime, someone must have cared. Victorian pictures had been strategically positioned on the walls and some piece of polished brass machinery was on display behind the bar. Plaques celebrating past winners of the annual darts tournament hung in pride of place.

The charge-hand, a bear of a woman fondly referred to as "the Ayatollah" when out of earshot, ran a tight ship. As well as could be, the place was clean, the pints wet. No one stepped too far out of line for fear of bringing the wrath of the Ayatollah upon themselves. Paul had never been on the receiving end but he had heard the strangled scream, like razor wire, that sometimes escaped her throat. There wasn't much in life that could intimidate Paul, but the choked cry from the pit of the stomach of a woman enraged curdled his blood.

Joe was one of those who had stepped out of line. Only the week before he had incurred wrath and received a lifetime ban. Paul raised his eyes to the "Barred" list behind Joe's head as Joe regaled him with the story. *Big Malky – barred 6 weeks. Jim the Tim – barred 1 month. Moonman – barred for life. Gillian Toner – barred for life. Joe Toner – barred for life.*

"You see that?" Joe pointed proudly to the line drawn through his name. "Can't keep me barred. It's bad for business, see. This is my pub. Everyone knows this is Joe Toner's pub. I go elsewhere, the whole posse's gonna follow."

Paul, half listening, nodded in agreement.

In the background a group of men circled the girl, who had rested her arms on the bar-top. Paul's own primal instincts awakened with vigour. He watched as she squirmed, lips pursed, turning her head from their howls and jibes. He began to think that maybe she was alone, had wandered off the path.

"I mean, it wasn't even me this time," Joe went on. "It was the wife. Fattie over there threw away the dregs of her drink at close and wouldn't replace it. The wife was over the bar trying to batter her. I couldn't keep control of the wife – barred for life. That's what happens when you put a woman in charge. They take it personal."

Paul continued to watch over Joe's shoulder as the drama began to unfold at the bar. One of the younger regulars was moving in for the kill. Leaning one arm on the bar beside her, he was sliding closer. Turning her back, head down, the girl was trying to ignore him. The more she ignored, the more he pressed. The others waited, their appetites whetted. The Ayatollah watched in amusement.

Beside Paul, Joe was delving deep into his trouser leg. "I swear, one of they wee bastards's dipped my pockets."

"It's OK, Joe, I'm buying." Paul patted him on the shoulder and moved towards the bar.

Just before he reached it the girl turned and pushed through the group. The men laughed. Pulling her hood up over her head, she ran out into the rain.

Paul had left the pub a few minutes later and found her huddled in a bus shelter, the vinegary smell of piss still potent through the lighter fragrance of the rain. He stood at a safe distance, to let her know he wasn't a threat. He just wanted to find out if he could help her; he'd seen what had happened in the pub.

"There'll be no more buses this time of night," he told her.

Reluctant at first, she slowly became more receptive to the idea of help.

Paul managed to hail a taxi. He opened the door to let the girl get in first, then slipped in after her. Her red hood clung to her head; black mascara ran down her cheeks. As they drove towards her flat, her sobbing stopped. She told him her name was Annie.

"Mark." He held out his hand. She didn't need to know his real name.

They had to travel across town; Paul wasn't looking forward to the journey home. When they pulled up, he paid, then jumped from the taxi, across a foot-wide swirling torrent and onto the pavement. His upturned collar offered futile shelter from the rain. Annie followed behind him.

"Right, you be careful now."

She smiled, her key clicking into the lock. "Thanks again, Mark. I didn't know what to do, it was the wrong bus... I thought when I saw the light in the pub... Thank you for helping me."

The door opened, warmth and safety beckoned. He turned to go.

She hesitated, then called him back. "If you want to come up and dry off, wait until the rain eases..."

Paul, not sure of the wisdom of it, shrugged his shoulders and followed her in. Annie took off her dripping coat and handed him a towel before disappearing next door. He spread himself on the chintz couch and forced himself to relax. She returned a few minutes later in an oversized sweatshirt and jogging trousers, her long hair damp and beginning to frizz. She flopped self-consciously onto crossed legs on the floor, facing Paul. She seemed anxious; her eyes darted around the room, never settling on Paul, yet wherever she looked, he could tell she was watching him.

He took a cigarette out of his packet. "Do you mind?"

She fussed to find an ashtray and in its absence handed him a floral saucer from the cabinet. He lit up.

"This place was my grandmother's," she explained. "I've not had the chance to redecorate yet."

In her own habitat he could see more clearly who Annie was. Porcelain, just like her grandmother's tea set; smooth, delicate, unblemished. Vulnerable in a way that was different from the girls he was used to. Her face twinkled with youth and optimism; too fresh to have known heartache. She was sweet. And sweetness wasn't his type. He thought about leaving. But she offered him a drink. And he never turned down a drink.

The ice cubes in his glass clinked against the side; the swirl of purple juice mixed with the spirit burned his throat as he swigged it down. He talked to her; she reminded him of someone from long ago. From a time when he was a better person. For a while he imagined he was again.

Time passed; she moved onto the couch beside him. He could feel her small, cold hands stroking his arm.

"What's your tattoo of?" Her voice was too guarded to be playful, like there was some kind of performance going on for his benefit.

He rolled up his T-shirt sleeve, revealing the full glory of it. His hand massaged the muscle on which the tattoo was drawn.

"Lena? Is that your girlfriend?"

"No. She was a Russian hooker I met. It only lasted till morning but it was the most meaningful relationship I ever had."

Annie shrank away, her cheeks rosy.

"For a hundred quid," Paul went on, "she could make all your dreams come true. Took me around the world that night and in the daylight she was gone. True love; pure poetry."

"Really?"

"No." He laughed. "She was just some tart. I was young and very, very drunk when I got this. I was thinking of adding in 'Don't' – make it more up to date."

"Where is she now?" Annie asked quietly.

He dissembled indifference. "No idea. It's a good souvenir, though. Don't you think?"

Covering it up, he put it out of his mind.

Annie moved in closer.

He savoured the blush of her cheeks, watched the powerful vein pumping in her neck, listened to her breath; gentle, bleating. So full of life. It had been a long time since he'd had such close contact with a member of the opposite sex. At one time he might have reached his arm around her, and it would have been the most natural thing in the world. But his arm lay limply at his side; he was always conscious of his movements now.

He reached instead for the glass, aware that he was draining his while she sipped politely on hers. Annie had left the bottle of Smirnoff on the table so he poured himself another half glass. He didn't even bother to dilute this one. The first few swigs made his teeth grit at the potency of the alcohol, but he had a taste for it.

Her hand crawled up his chest, resting on his face, her fingers tracing the line of the scar that stretched from forehead to cheek. She reached in and kissed him, her mouth tasting vaguely of mint, her skin soft like velvet. He kissed her back, aware of his own taste of vodka and cigarettes. There was a look of something like revulsion on her face as she pulled away. It didn't bother him.

"It's nice to find someone interesting. Someone real," she said, sitting back.

"Is that what I am? I'm real?" He laughed. "I've been called a lot of things in my life but real isn't one of them."

Annie laughed too, not sure of the joke.

"Real because I'm a loser?"

He thought for a while before twisting down the collar of his T-shirt to reveal a bluish-grey hollow love heart tattooed scrappily on the back of his neck.

"Do you like this one?"

Annie reached over and inspected the amateurish effort, obscured by the stray hairs left behind after a poor haircut.

"Did you do that one yourself?"

"My cellmate Joe did it for me."

Paul remembered the burn of the hot needle dipped in ink and waited for Annie's reaction.

"So you're a criminal?"

He gave a short laugh. "A bona fide outlaw in your house, and what're you going to do about it?"

Her nervous giggle tinkled like a little bell. It faded. He let the silence linger a little too long. His gaze grew stony. She smiled again, embarrassed. Paul got the impression that smile had been used before to get her out of difficult situations, but he wasn't going to let her off so lightly.

"No, really. What are you going to do about it?"

He'd spent too long inside. He'd forgotten how to be around people.

"It's getting late," she whispered uneasily and stood up from the couch.

It was time to leave alright.

As he stood, there was a rush of blood to his head; the room tilted and his words slurred. He could hazily make out Annie, her glare seething and angry, her whole body transformed. She was no longer a lost little girl.

"Look at you." Her words were tinny and distant. "You can barely get off the couch."

He stumbled. She was right. When had he got so wasted? He hung in the air, suspended in motion.

Her bony fingers began to prod him back into his seat. He found himself inexplicably compliant. His vision blurred. For a moment he went blank. Then he felt her cold hand slap his face.

"Paul?"

When had he told her his real name?

"Paul!" She slapped him again. His eyes fought to open.

"Paul, you need to sleep now. I think you should rest." Her voice was soothing and disarmed him completely.

"I don't want to rest. You can rest when you're dead." He wasn't even sure if he spoke aloud or if the heavy sleep had already fallen.

Lena was with him. It wasn't that he could see her clearly standing before him. It was more like an impression of her; her smell, her warmth caressing his senses, making him glow. He could feel her body moving beside him. Like smoke, she dispersed and formed around him; too fragile to hold on to, yet so real it was hard to believe it was only a dream. He could hear her laugh, the sound so vivid it must have been emblazoned on his soul. Her voice like crystal.

Her laugh became shrill. Became a scream.

He hallucinated flesh, blood and tears.

CHAPTER TWO

Darkness engulfed him. He had no sense of where he was, only that he was in pain. His head was pounding and his kidneys ached from too many nights trying to drink himself into oblivion. He badly needed to piss. As he tried to stand up, his shoulders were jerked violently back. A ripping pain tore through his wrists. It took him a few moments to realise he was tied up. Upright on a chair, hands and feet bound to its arms and legs, like a man waiting for execution.

Lena? The gag in his mouth choked him, his voice an incoherent muffle. His eyes blinked with starry confusion. No, not Lena. Anna… or Annie.

He could feel his airway closing. His muscles seized in agony as they relived past imprisonments: the classroom cupboard of his primary school; his six-by-twelve-foot jail cell; and, by far the worst, the dark boot of a battered Ford Mondeo. No chink of light for comfort there, no hope of escape, just warm, stale air that wouldn't fill his lungs no matter how deeply he breathed. Cramping limbs. Stabbing fear in the bowels. A living corpse at his own funeral procession; only the prayer that when it happened it would be swift and painless.

Spasms of panic started to override his ability to reason.

•

He tried to shout but his voice caught on the alcohol-laced saliva that had built up in his mouth. As he doubled over in a fit of coughing, the restraints pulled tight against his skin. His heaving breaths throbbed in his ears. The space grew steadily smaller. He struggled for air, fog clouded his brain and he fought to retain consciousness. The sharp, frantic snorts tearing his nostrils stopped. He felt his chest muscles loosen and his body went limp. He was met by the sound of silence. That scared him most of all. When trapped in the boot of the car, he had listened to the noise of the traffic, counted the turns, the bumps in the road. It had soothed him. While he could still hear the traffic he knew he still had a chance. It was the silence that told him he'd reached the end of the road.

The shallow hiss of someone exhaling made him suddenly alert. He listened more closely and realised he was not alone in the room. Someone was breathing.

Just as it hadn't been silent, he started to notice it wasn't pitch black either. His eyes were adjusting to the dark. Daylight seeped through the heavy velvet curtains and vague shapes began to appear from out of the hazy red hue. Fireplace, table, lamp. Cabinet filled with bone china. Annie's living room took shape before him.

The breathing was coming from behind. Fainter than before, the person trying to stifle it. Conscious of him listening. In a burst of anger Paul began to rock. He screamed and spluttered through the gag. The chair legs banged off the floor. Again. Again. Each time the chair hovered for longer, ready to topple. Each time it crashed down, the bang louder than before. Feet padded quickly across the room. Two small hands tightened around his upper arms, trying to hold him down. He couldn't see the figure but sensed it was slight. It was reaching over him but not from a great height. He could smell perfume and a chill of recognition went through him. Lena's perfume.

The struggle ended when a small hand grabbed his hair, yanking his head back. His neck snapped, the suddenness and violence of the wrench stopping him dead. Nails tore his cheeks as his gag was pulled down, damp and sticky now around his neck. His hands clenched into fists. His bladder felt fit to burst.

"Don't struggle, Paul. You'll only make things worse. If that chair falls, you're staying down there." Annie's words ripped like a serrated blade across his neck. The hot sting of her breath lingered on his skin.

His grinding teeth were beginning to hurt. "I'm going to piss all over your fucking floor!"

"So piss."

"FUCKING LET ME GO!" Reverberations of his cry shook the room.

With even less care than when she'd taken it off, Annie dragged the gag back up. Pain erupted where'd she made deep scratches in his face.

His pleading went unheard as her soft feet padded off again and the door banged shut behind her. A warm stream of urine trickled down his leg, splashing onto the floor.

When he awoke with a start some time later, Annie was sitting in front of him again. He must have been asleep a while. She was sitting, staring. He hated the way she was looking at him, analysing him like a lab rat. A fucking cavity search would be less probing.

"Pleasant dreams?"

Sweat clung to his brow.

"You've got to wonder what a person's done in their life to have dreams like that."

Annie had mopped the plastic sheeting beneath him but the smell of his own piss was overpowering the disinfectant and making him feel sick. The denim of his wet jeans had rubbed away the top layer of his skin. In front of him sat a glass of water, slick with condensation. Drinking it would only make him piss again, but he was parched and needed to wash the stale saliva out of his mouth. He mumbled at her. She waited a moment before pulling his gag down.

"I need water."

She nodded, picked up the glass of water and placed it at his lips. He tried to drink, but she pulled it away before he'd had any.

"Why're you doing this to me?"

She looked at him with an ugly smile.

"Why did you drug me?"

Her smile was silent.

"Why are you doing this to me!" His cry exploded loudly.

Reaching for his gag, she started yanking it into place.

He jerked his head away from her. When her hand came close to his mouth he seized the chance and bit it. She jumped away in pain, then, harnessing the full force of her body, slapped the side of his head, leaving him momentarily stunned.

When he regained focus, Annie was pacing the room, rubbing her hand.

"How does it feel, Paul? To be helpless?"

Her pacing grew more frantic. "How does it make you feel to know I lured you here? I went looking for you. *I'm in your house. And what are you going to do about it?*" She mimicked his voice then stopped and said, "Is that what you say to all the girls?"

She came close to him, her nose almost touching his. Her face was blazing, manically charged.

"You're an animal. And you need to be caged."

She secured the gag and left the room. His head bowed as he contemplated a life full of sins and wondered for which one he was being made to pay.

CHAPTER THREE

Fourteen years ago

Deep in the park, the amber streetlamps flickered on as the soft glow of the sun began to fade. The happy squeals of spinning, swinging, sliding children had been replaced by the high-pitched screams of adolescents, inebriated and oblivious to the cool, damp evening air. Having no place better to be on a Saturday night, the dozen or so teenagers were passing the hours with stories of bravado and rebellion, war wounds and sympathy. Most of the group congregated at the roundabout, but over on the swings two girls sat slightly apart from the rest. One, a big-boned girl whose strawberry-blonde hair was scraped back in a large ponytail, frizzy tendrils escaping at the front, sat with her feet flat on the ground. The other – small, dark-haired, and with an almost boyish charm that would one day mature into real beauty - swayed slightly, uncharacteristically subdued.

Gillian, the blonde, passed her a joint. Taking a long draw, the girl exhaled and watched the cloud of white smoke as it rose high into the air and dispersed into nothing.

"You're quiet tonight," Gillian said.

Lena shrugged. "Not much to say."

Gillian wriggled uncomfortably beside her, the metal chains digging into her hips, exposing the skin on her lower back to the elements.

"Well, I've got some news that might cheer you up," Gillian began, and then waited for Lena to tease the information out of her. When she got no response, Gillian went on. "It's a secret. I've been meaning to tell you for a while."

The soles of Gillian's trainers scraped the AstroTurf beneath them. She nearly lost her balance. Unable to contain the news for long, she let the words bubble out of her like water from an overfilled kettle.

"Hughsey fancies you!" She righted herself and looked at Lena, waiting.

Lena's face remained pointedly blank. "I know," she said.

Gillian paused, thrown. It wasn't the answer she'd expected. She took a minute to go on.

"He told me to tell you," she eventually continued, her excitement ebbing. "Says he's liked you for ages."

A short distance away a skinheaded, freckle-faced boy in tracksuit and trainers stole a quick glance, his black eyes darting over the two girls on the swings. For a brief second the girls both looked at him and he knew their conversation was about him. Bursting with pride, he reared himself up and then, with all his strength, fired the trolley he was holding into the nearby roundabout, watching in wild-eyed amazement as it crashed, toppling his friend out onto the concrete. The girls turned away, ignoring the eruption of laughter that followed.

"What do you want me to tell him?" Gillian said, her voice wavering.

"Tell him nothing," Lena said tiredly. "I think he's a moron."

Gillian's round cheeks, pink with cold and cider, flushed a deep scarlet. An emotion flashed across her face. Not easily identifiable. But for a second Lena thought Gillian was going to hit her.

At that moment, two new arrivals appeared and sauntered towards the girls on the swings. The rest of the group gathered round to greet them. Dressed in jeans and shirts, they brought with them the smell of citrus cologne. Their stubble was shaved into strange, inventive shapes around their chins. They looked old enough to buy their own booze. None of the others had even seen them before.

"Dropping by for old times' sake," one of the older boys said condescendingly. "Proud to see you're keeping Saturday night drinking sessions in the park alive."

Suddenly conscious of her limbs, Lena sat back in the swing and flicked her hair while the older boys shared their joints and laughed about the depravity of their distant youth. It didn't take long for the other boys to get bored and walk away, frustrated that the newcomers had stolen the attention of all the girls in the group. Retreating to the roundabout, each of them soberly self-conscious now, they eyed their scuffed trainers. The loud laughter from the swings floated back to them like a challenge.

"If it's anything like the others, it'll be legendary!" one of the older boys boasted about the party he was going to in town. The six girls squealed like a box of kittens.

"A mate from way back," said the other, in his deep, throaty voice. Lena noticed the thick dark hair sprouting from the open neck of his shirt and wondered how old he was. Maybe as much as twenty.

"Are we invited?" asked one of the girls and giggled.

"I don't know," the older-looking of the two said uncertainly. "You never know how these things are gonna go. If something kicked off…"

"The guy's just out of lock-up," his dark-haired friend added, dangerously.

"Yeah, we used to hang about, years ago," said the first. "Little Paulie the prank monkey. Always trying to run about with the older boys, asking for ciggies. We'd be like, 'Paulie, jump off that first-floor balcony, don't break your neck and we'll give you a fag. Go nick some munchies from the shop.' And he'd be like, 'OK.' He was scabby as fuck. His da was always kickin' his heid in. We called him Scabby Do."

"He was wee but he was gem," his pal added. "Fighting the Pakis—" He stopped mid-sentence and looked at Lena. "All in good fun of course."

She noted the significance of his retraction but pretended not to. A year-round tan, her mum's boyfriend called it. A touch of the gypsy.

"Wee wide-o." The first one came to his rescue. "Rumour has it, he works for some *serious* people now though," he said and they both raised their eyebrows in demonstration of how serious.

Lena took a final drag of the joint she was smoking and flicked it away.

"We can look after ourselves," she said, feeling bold. Gillian poked her in the ribs but she ignored it. She could feel the envious eyes of the other girls on her as the boys exchanged glances and laughed.

"Yeah, we can look after ourselves," the other girls added in mistimed chorus.

"Well, I suppose," said the first boy to the other. "As long as you know what you're getting yourself into."

Lena fluttered her eyelashes.

In the end only Lena and Gillian left with them for the party. The others, full of drunken abandon, at first wanted to go but then dropped out one by one, making excuses. Gillian had tried to protest but Lena had fixed her eyes on her, cutting her short.

"OK. But I can't stay too late," Gillian said grudgingly. They both knew the trouble they'd get into for staying out past their curfew, but they put that to the back of their minds.

As they left, Gillian nodded over to Hughsey to let him know her loyalty was still to him. Lena kept her eyes ahead.

On the way to the bus stop, the boys shared their vodka. Lena tried not to think about the long journey home.

They got off the bus in the centre of town and walked down bustling Sauchiehall Street, busier now than it ever was during the day. The bright lights of pubs and nightclubs washed the dull sandstone walls with colour. Car horns blasted and motors revved. Rowdy crowds flowed between venues, faces charged with frantic energy. A feeling rippled from person to person that anyone could do anything at any time.

Lena scoped it with wide-eyed longing.

The boys led them up to Charing Cross and turned onto North Street, heading south, flanked by the M8 on one side. They passed the Mitchell Library and the street grew steadily quieter. The towers of the Anderston high-rises, their destination, loomed in the distance. As they approached them, the lights and the noise began to fade. Beyond the high-rises, a shadowy church creaked beside a deserted school yard, the faded yellow sunflowers painted on its windows defiant against the stark urban concrete. Under the tangle of motorway bridges, a pedestrian underpass led into the seedy underworld of the city's streetwalkers and kerb crawlers. Lena looked over and shivered.

It was after midnight by the time they reached the towers.

A sickly yellow glow lit the graffiti-scarred lift as it rattled all the way to the fifteenth floor. "Penthouse," the dark-haired boy said as the doors slid open. They were hit by a blast of sound and the pungent smell of skunk. "Here we go!"

"Stick close to us," said his friend. "We'll keep you safe."

Both boys bounced towards the end flat, from where people were spilling out into the corridor. They disappeared through the open front door. Lena looked at Gillian, shrugged and followed their lead.

There were bodies everywhere. Every inch of the flat was filled. A thick cloud of smoke hung in the air. The boys were swallowed by the crowd. Lena began to push through, the pathway they left behind disappearing like footsteps in fresh snow. Music blasted from a room up ahead. Colourful lights escaped, illuminating the dark hall in flashes of yellow, magenta, azure. The floor vibrated as they walked towards it. Lena's heart pounded in her chest. She drew close enough to catch a peek inside. It was packed with people milling around, dancing, being happy, beautiful.

Gillian's damp hand closed around hers. "How long do we have to stay?" she asked, her muffled voice fading into the music. They were being jostled from right to left.

"We just got here." Lena's voice carried thinly to her friend.

Gillian's grip around her hand tightened. She was shouting something else, trying to pull her back, but Lena pushed onwards. Somewhere in the struggle her hand broke free of Gillian's, but she didn't look back.

Her back streaked with sweat, her arms outstretched, Lena swayed to her own rhythm on the improvised dance floor. She and Gillian had separated almost as soon as they'd got inside, but the boys they'd come with were standing in the corner of the room, smiling over. The pill they had given her created a pleasant tingling in her belly. She felt so happy and filled with love for everyone around her and she wanted it to last forever. Her slim hips snaked in her skinny jeans and she lost herself in the light and music. Every song that played was her favourite. Every stranger in the room, a friend.

When Gillian appeared in front of her, she had no idea how much time had passed. With two strong hands, Gillian clasped Lena's shoulders. "Where did you go? I searched everywhere for you."

Lena could barely hear her over the music. She wriggled free and continued dancing.

Gillian grabbed her again, her fingers pressing into Lena's upper arms. "What have you taken?" Effortlessly, she turned Lena towards her.

Lena's head lolled and she felt Gillian's nails digging in, puncturing her flesh. She struggled to get free but Gillian pressed tighter and tighter.

"Fuck off!" Lena hissed and dragged her nails down

Gillian's hand, drawing blood.

Gillian recoiled, rubbing her wounded hand against her chest. Lena jerked free. Red marks rose where Gillian's nails had dug into Lena's arms.

"Fine," Gillian sobbed, tears welling in her eyes. "I hope you get raped."

A few seconds later she left the flat, standing on toes and throwing elbows as she went.

Lena suddenly felt sick. The room was hot and the lights were making her dizzy. Seized by cramps and nausea, she made a beeline for the toilet. Other people were in there but she managed to clear it and push shut the door behind her. The music was muted by the ringing in her ears. She placed the toilet lid down and sat on top of it, putting her head in her hands, trying to steady the dizziness. When she moved again, her legs were glued to the floor but her head floated off somewhere in space. Staring into the bathroom mirror at the black holes that had become her eyes, she unsuccessfully willed herself sober.

Splashing cold water on her face, she continued to stare, until she realised that the steady thumping was not in her head but a hand beating the bathroom door. She opened the door and someone pushed past her, diving for the toilet. Leaving them to it, she re-entered the crowd, the sound of retching behind her drowned out by the music.

Back in the room, the heat was overpowering so she fought her way to the window. She tried to open it but it was locked. Placing her forehead on the cool glass, she attempted to focus but the ground outside, fifteen floors below, wavered before her eyes. She was burning up.

"Nice view?" came a male voice from behind her. "You should take this."

A hand placed a plastic cup of clear liquid in her unsteady fingers. Slowly, she lowered herself to the ground and crouched just below the window; surrounded by legs and feet, she felt oddly peaceful. The chilled water washed through her as she drank.

"Do you want to go get some fresh air?"

She looked up but his face was in shadow, backlit by the flashing lights. His hand reached down for hers and she felt herself being pulled to her feet.

He took her up to the rooftop, unlocking the door with a set of keys he produced from his back pocket. The air felt like frosted ice against her bare skin. She was shivering from the cold but it helped clear her head. Before her, the hazy jewelled skyline danced and twinkled. She thought about her mum, out there, one tiny amber sparkle that would last through the night.

He took his jacket off and put it round her. She could feel the warmth of his body close behind her.

"Beautiful, isn't it?"

In her head she agreed.

"My own little part of the city."

She turned around and could see him now. It was hard to tell in the light what colour his hair was but he was tall and his eyes were smiling. Butterflies danced in her stomach.

"I'm Paul."

"Lena."

There was sparse golden-brown stubble on his chin, with a hint of red; it rubbed against her cheek as he put his arms around her.

"If you invite everyone you've ever met and offer enough drugs and booze, someone interesting always shows up," he said, hazily.

She wasn't entirely sure what he meant by that but it made her smile nonetheless.

CHAPTER FOUR

Annie sat on a stool facing him, a trolley of food beside her.

"You should eat something. Keep your strength up. Just nod to let me know you're not going to start screaming again."

Paul snarled through the gag and fought to free himself from his binds.

Annie burst into forced, theatrical laughter. "Oh, please! Is that supposed to be intimidating?" She bent in close. "Are you nodding?"

With resignation he moved his head up and down. She pulled his gag down and he flexed his aching jaw.

"The ropes are hurting. I can't feel my hands."

With the first show of concern he'd seen from her, she bounced up from her seat then began carefully examining his hands, which were strapped to the arms of the chair. She felt around the rope on both sides; it was slack enough for her to fit two fingers under.

"Wiggle your fingers." He did. With an air of authority, she kneaded one of his hands, like a doctor. Then she checked the rope around his ankles. "They don't feel cold."

She did another check of his hands and feet, then sat back down on her stool.

"They seem OK. See, I used hemp rope, the softest on

the skin, and the Prusik knot, which should ensure the rope doesn't tighten. You shouldn't be too uncomfortable."

"Well I am."

"Just keep wiggling your fingers and toes and let me know if it gets any worse. We don't want your circulation cut off."

He sighed angrily in protest, resigned to the fact it was pointless.

Annie resumed the feeding, picking up the bowl of soup from the trolley. She put the spoon to his mouth, steam rising before him. He shook his head.

"Eat." She forced some into his mouth. It burned his lips and he yelled in pain. Ignoring him, she dipped the spoon into the soup again.

He pursed his lips tightly. She tried to force the spoon in anyway, knocking his tooth in the struggle, pouring most of it down his chin.

"Eat."

Paul turned his head away from her.

"Suit yourself!" she snapped.

The spoon clinked against the ceramic bowl as she dropped it impatiently. She stood up, knocked her stool over angrily and marched across to the armchair, which she sank into, pulling her knees up to her chin.

Paul saw an opportunity while his gag was off. "Look, I think you need help," he said in the gentlest voice he could muster. "You need to contact someone. Is there a doctor, a friend that can help?"

"I'm not the one that needs help, Paul," she seethed. "I'm not the one tied up, sitting in a pool of my own piss."

He dropped his head.

"A grown man who allows himself to be tied up by a fifteen-year-old girl. You are pathetic, Paul."

He looked her up and down suspiciously. "You're not fifteen," he said.

"Oh no?" She smiled with satisfaction.

"Don't be stupid." He shook his head.

"Wouldn't be the first time you've had to explain the nature of your relationship with an underage girl, would it?"

He exhaled in exasperation. "What are you talking about?"

"Would it, Paul?" Her eyes bored into him.

"You've got the wrong person," he said, worriedly. "Look, if something happened to you, you should talk to someone about it."

"Don't lie to me, Paul," she hissed. "I know a lot more about you than you think."

His mind was spinning in confusion. It didn't seem like she was bluffing.

"Of course I'm not fifteen. But it's interesting to know you can tell the difference."

"What does that mean? What does that mean?" he raged angrily.

On her way out the door, she flipped the switch, plunging him into darkness again. Paul's shoulders slumped; he was too tired now to even bother shouting.

CHAPTER FIVE

Lena lay awake, her eyes fixed on the thin streams of light leaking through plastic slatted blinds that hung crookedly in a window frame she didn't recognise. She'd lain like that for some time, in a stranger's bed, not wanting to move; her body sore and dried out, her tongue thick and oily with the taste of vodka and ash. The slightest movement set the room in motion.

The light fell in stark stripes across the thick blue duvet wrapped around her. A sweet smell of aftershave lingered in the cover's fabric. She remembered waking briefly to find him lying next to her. But there was no one there now. There was no way of knowing how long ago he'd left.

Just in her eyeline on the floor beneath the bed were her trainers – the familiar white toe scuffed, the plastic seam loose along one side, the pair placed carefully together. Beside them, her drawstring bag. Her jeans and top she was still wearing. But, as far as she could see, no jacket. She must have left it lying somewhere. She guessed she would get it later. She sank into the pocket of warmth she had captured beneath the duvet. It was going to be a long, cold journey home. A small ripple of dread ran though her when she thought of the scene at home. Jason angry. Her mum worrying. It was hard to tell which way it would go: welcomed back with open arms, or full-blown neighbours-calling-the-police carnage. Both seemed equally good. Or bad.

Muffled voices carried thinly though the wall from the room next door. She wondered if his was one of them. Music too, dull and foggy in her ears, like her intake of colours and her output of thoughts. She watched the pattern of the light change, as the stripes grew and stretched and crept from the duvet to the floor. When they reached the opposite wall she decided it was time to get up and see.

Her first big move was to reach for her bag, an arm's length away. The effort of lifting it from the floor to rest on her belly above the duvet brought her out in cold sweats. Next she rummaged weakly for her purse. Enough money inside for a half fare home. Her keys jangled; beside them, a mirror. She pulled it out and unfastened the clasp. After a quick glance at her reflection – the matted greasy hair, the powdery-grey mascara stains beneath her eyes – she snapped it shut and put it back, drawing the strings tight.

She swung her legs around, her stockinged feet resting on the sodden, cigarette-singed carpet. Taking a few moments to steady herself, she slipped on her trainers, rose from the bed, then delicately made her way out into the hall. Her feet squelched through soggy patches of faggy water spilled from makeshift bongs and beer that had leaked from the trail of half-empty cans.

The hall was empty, the lights were off and there were no windows. The only light was coming from a door off to the right, slightly ajar. As she moved quietly towards it she could hear voices over music on the other side. She tiptoed up to it and stopped to listen.

"You used to be allowed to be a quiet person," a voice, local but well-spoken, was saying. "Now it's all like, 'Oh no, he's that quiet boy. He's quiet – I wonder what deep-seated issues he's dealing with.' Social skills? How about I demonstrate mine on you and next time you want to talk about social skills I poke you in the fucking eye. I blame Tony Blair, with his big-toothed smile and dynamic personality. I'm growing up in an era of all style and no substance."

"Do you think he's read any of these?" a second voice responded.

"Who? Paul? Probably uses them for roach," the first answered with flat disinterest.

"*The Seven Habits of Highly Effective People?* Eh, I don't remember the habit of chibbin' people that don't do what you want. Eh, know whit ah mean, man?"

"Maybe they hand a copy to everyone leaving prison. To motivate them to become better criminals."

"Well, you should be careful what books you give to people. Can be dangerous."

"Education. Education. Education."

Lena pushed open the door and entered. Two necks snapped towards her, one looking over the back of a two-seater couch, the other on hunkers beside a small bookshelf, one hand discreetly putting a book back between the others. Both faces were moulded into the plasticine smiles of people caught saying something they shouldn't. An awkward silence followed.

"I'm looking for my jacket," she announced and had a quick glance around the room. Her head was pounding, the cramps in her stomach wringing her insides out. Paul wasn't with them.

"Another survivor. I didn't know there were any more of us left," said the one at the bookshelf with fake joviality as he retreated to the beanbag on the floor. In his late teens, he was dressed in trackie bottoms and a hoodie littered with bomber marks where hot coals had rolled out of a joint and singed the fabric.

"You look about as rough as I feel, doll." The one looking up at her from the two-seater didn't sound as well-spoken any more. He leaned over the back of the couch and passed her the joint he was holding. Long-haired and wearing an old Iron Maiden T-shirt and jeans, he had an unappealing, plooky quality. His skin was oily, with small breakouts around his forehead and chin, and he looked as if he hadn't grown into his long limbs yet.

As she took smoke into her empty stomach, lights started flashing; everything became pale, her gut lurched. She grabbed a seat in the free armchair beside the couch. She could feel their eyes on her. The one on the beanbag patted his knees. "There's a free seat right here if you want." They sniggered. She chose to ignore them.

A third lad was sunk low on the couch. He hadn't looked up as she came in. He was small, wearing a hat pulled down to his eyebrows; thick, milk-bottle specs poked out timidly from underneath it, as if he were a turtle emerging from its shell. He didn't move but stared at her with enormous spaced-out brown eyes.

"You hook up with Paul last night?" asked the one on the beanbag.

"What?" Her ears were burning. She looked around the dishevelled room and spied what might be her jacket bundled up in the corner.

"You sure you know what you're getting into?" the plooky one said under his breath.

"Remember. Don't wear black eyes," said the timid one.

Her heart began to race as she shifted uncomfortably in her seat. "Sorry?"

He indicated the space under her eye. "Black… smudged under your eyes."

The others laughed loudly. The spacey turtle guy stared on in drugged confusion, his eyebrows and the top rim of his glasses disappearing under his hat, the hint of a grin on his face.

Lena tightened her arms around her stomach, trying to ease the cramps. The last time she'd eaten anything had been at lunch the day before. The clock on the wall said two. The game was over. It was time to go.

"If you ever fancy going out some place decent—"

The buzzer went and they all jumped to attention. "That'll be Paul."

The plooky one shot up and left the room to answer the door.

Lena held her breath in anticipation.

"Forgot my keys," boomed a voice from the hall. She recognised it from the night before.

Paul bounced into the room, light on the balls of his feet like a boxer, and placed two bottles of Irn-Bru and a bag full of chocolate and crisps on the table. "Provisions!"

A flurry of hands grabbed for them.

"Everyone, this is William."

The eyes of the room fell on the larger figure that had followed Paul into the room. Simian features and ape-like arms. He sat on the arm of the couch where the elbow of the plooky one had been resting.

Paul squashed into the armchair beside Lena and winked. The fresh smell of the outdoors that still clung to him came to her in wafts. The small finger of his right hand gently caressed the outside of her thigh.

She noticed how his presence invigorated the room. Both the conversation and the atmosphere changed. It took her a while to realise it was because they were showing off to him. Paul must only have been eighteen or nineteen, the same as them, but the rest behaved like children around him.

"So, are ya used to all the open space yet, Paul?" ventured the timid one.

"Six months? Didn't even sweat it. Fuck. Three cooked meals, Sky TV, as much PlayStation as you could handle; had everythin' I needed." Paul leaned forward on the seat, so she could see only his back and the side of his head; she watched him intently as he commanded the room. "I tell you, the best week was in the infirmary, didn't even have to get out of bed. Just rang my little bell, hot nurses came runnin'. Extra ice cream, know what I mean?" He grinned and winked, this time to the room, and she suddenly felt herself cheated.

"What were you in there for? Shanked?"

"Nah. Repetitive strain injury."

"Too much Grand Theft Auto?"

"Too much wanking. Baws like watermelons!" Everyone laughed as Paul gave a demonstration to illustrate how heavy.

Lena watched as they hung on his every word. Even as he mocked and insulted them. She pulled her knees up to her chin and waited for a good time to leave, drawing the least amount of attention to herself.

"Cunt got what he deserved though," Paul mused to himself.

"Messed with the wrong guy," the one from the beanbag said, not so confident now.

"Someone eyes up your bird, what're you meant to do?" Paul said with a thinly veiled threat, then sat back on the chair and reached his arm over the back, behind Lena.

"Hit him o'er the heid wi' a ginger bottle and shove him in front of an oncoming taxi." William's voice rumbled like an ogre's.

The room broke into uproarious laughter. Nervous and forced and resentful. Paul's eyes were a blazing burst of energy.

"I heard it was because he called you a poof."

The misguided comment silenced the group. William clamped his hand around the back of the plooky one's neck. Lena watched the colour drain out of his pimpled face. Beside her she felt Paul's muscles stiffen.

"What did you say?" growled Paul as he rose to his feet.

The plooky one tried to gulp the words back, his tone conciliatory. "Must've got it wrong."

There was an awful moment before Paul spoke. "Guess you did," he sneered. "How else could I have been fucking your maw?"

Everyone burst into laughter again, like a valve relieving the tension. Everyone except the plooky boy, whose ears were glowing red, agitation burning his face.

They started to disperse not long after. Lena found that

it was her jacket crumpled in a ball in the corner and she gathered her stuff, finding comfort in surrounding herself with the familiar, resigned to going home.

"I thought you were going to stay longer?" Paul spoke quietly, out of earshot of the others. He gestured for her to wait while he showed them to the door. "Just give me five minutes. I need to speak to William."

She hovered, unsure, then went back to her seat as they all left the room.

When he came back he placed a see-through bag packed full of pills and powders on the table. It was just the two of them and the room was quiet. He sat down on the couch and patted the seat beside him. Almost against her will she found herself moving onto it.

"Are you feeling OK?" He laid the back of his hand on her forehead. "You're pretty pale." His voice was full of concern. "I think your blood sugar's low. When did you last eat something?"

She shook her head miserably.

He got up and reached for the Irn-Bru. "Here, drink some of this, it'll make you feel better."

He poured some and gave it to her along with a packet of salt 'n' vinegar Discos. She took them. He smiled.

She looked into his face, the one she remembered staring out over the resting city. His fair hair was long at the back and formed curls at the nape of his neck. His skin was light brown, the kind that would go dark in the sun. His eyes, depending on the light, were green, brown, sometimes black. One eyelid was slightly heavier, as if one eye was open to the world while the other, narrowed, scrutinised it. Searching his face now, it was impossible to find any hint of malice. But for a horrible second in the midst of his bragging, its twists and contortions had made it a ferocious face, one she could imagine looming menacingly from a dark street corner or in the shadows at the back of a bus.

"You think I'm an asshole?"

"I don't know." She shrank back. Images of her mum waiting for her were going through her head, of Jason and all the commotion that would be unleashed when she got home.

His fingers ran though her hair. "You're beautiful."

"Don't!" She pulled away.

"What's wrong?"

She eyed him with mistrust. When other people said that, it was never meant as a compliment. The boys at school. It was always delivered with a sneer, with the expectation of something in return.

"You are," he said, and in his earnest face she found no reason not to believe him. She felt the contour of his cheek and the sickness inside her melted away.

Then nothing mattered apart from what was happening in that room. Being alone with Paul, in his flat, at the top of his tower. She enjoyed the tingle in her body, the thrill of his hands on her, the euphoria rising within her.

The kiss seemed to come from both of them.

She knew something was going to happen, but, contrary to rumours, she was not overly experienced. One frenzied fumble at school and another hopeless attempt.

They manoeuvred themselves into a comfortable position, with him resting on the edge of the couch and Lena standing in front of him. His head was cocked and he looked at her

•

in a way that made her blush. But she had learned enough from watching MTV to know that bashfulness was not a good strategy in the art of seduction and she forced herself to meet his gaze.

He had a wry smile on his face and his chest was going up and down; she felt a flutter in her that she'd never experienced before. She wasn't exactly sure what he wanted her to do, but he seemed happy enough with her knee rubbing his crotch through his jeans. He pulled her closer, his hands feeling the lines of her body. Her confidence grew as she realised he was aroused by her. She kissed his lips, combing his hair with her fingers.

Her kisses progressed to his neck, and then his chest; tentatively she undid the buttons of his shirt. Bending straight-legged from the waist, she slowly unbuckled his belt, looking into his eyes. His wry smile was now a broad grin that spread across his face. He helped her with the awkward trouser moment. At the back of her mind she heard her friend's voice repeating, *It's just like licking a lollipop.* With Paul's guiding hand resting on the crown of her head, following the gentle bobbing action, she took his cock in her mouth and did what came naturally.

Afterwards she felt like she'd given him a very kind gift.

CHAPTER SIX

Her initial confidence didn't last long, and doubts and shame began to creep in. Afterwards, Lena wasn't sure how to behave, or what to expect from Paul. She wasn't sure if she should leave, if he was going to ask her to leave, now that he'd got what he wanted from her. She wasn't sure if there was genuine warmth in the kisses that followed or if they were part of his goodbye to her; part of some unspoken ritual she would have recognised if she'd been more experienced. He broke away to pull up his trousers. She curled deep into the arm of the chair, making space between them, ready to take her cue from him. He stretched lazily, a wide smile on his face, his arm slowly lowering on to her knee.

He turned to her and she waited for his judgement.

"Cup of tea?" he asked.

Lena stayed on the couch while Paul disappeared into the kitchen. She could hear him rummaging and took the time to look around the room. Every inch was covered with junk from the party. What she could see of the laminate was so dirty with footprints, it looked like the road. The light machine still sat in the corner, but apart from that there were almost no possessions. Just a few books in a pile, a stereo and some CDs on a small bookshelf. The couch, chair, beanbag and table were the only other furniture. The woodchip walls were white and bare except for grey water splashes just above the skirting board. It smelled of stale beer and smoke.

Paul came back in with two mugs of tea and a folded black bin bag. He put the mugs down on the table and then straightened, looking at the piles of rubbish around the floor.

"I need to get this place cleaned up," he said. "Don't want you thinking I live in a rubbish dump."

He opened the bag and started to scoop up air with it until it swelled like a balloon. Then he moved at speed around the room, picking up discarded paper cups and empty cans and throwing them in. Lena took a swig of her tea then got up to help. It took about five minutes to get everything off the floor and by that time the bin bag was full. Lena threw in the last cup and looked at him.

"The hall?" he said.

They spent the next half an hour going from room to room. Lena was glad to be active. It left no opportunity for awkwardness and took her mind off the pain of her hangover. Afterwards she went for a quick shower and when she came out the floors in the kitchen and hall had been mopped. Paul was finishing off the floor in the living room. The windows were open and a cold breeze was blowing in. She was still wearing just her vest top and jeans, but was feeling a little better.

Paul saw that she was shivering. "Do you want to bring in the blanket from the bed?" he asked. "It's just until the floors dry."

Lena dragged the thick blue duvet into the living room, jumping from dry spot to dry spot until she reached the couch. She wrapped herself in it and when Paul came back in and sat down beside her she shared it with him.

He sighed, out of breath, and looked around the room. "Bit better. I'll do it properly tomorrow."

Lena felt warm under the duvet, beside him. "I like your flat."

He pulled another face. "It's just temporary, until I get back on my feet. Good view, though."

Her eyes fell on the books. She nodded towards them. "Are those yours?"

"Do I look like the kinda guy who sits around reading books on business?"

"I don't know. Maybe. Yeah."

He smiled and then said, "There's a guy over on Woodlands. Gives you half the cover price. When I was short of money I used to nick them and bring them in. Some of them I kept."

She remembered the conversation she'd overheard earlier. "I didn't like your friends, this morning."

"They're not my friends. They're my customers."

He reached over for his tin and began rolling. She watched him fill the papers with tobacco and with his fingers sprinkle on some ground-up leaves from a small plastic bag before rolling up a neat spliff. She knew she had to think about getting home, but one joint wasn't going to make much difference.

Paul passed it to her. "Spark up!"

She reached for the lighter.

They spent the rest of the afternoon on the couch smoking joints. She was wasted. So was he. Two stoners laughing, trying to fix the world's problems from a living room. Lena was too wrapped up in her own enjoyment to notice the sun going down.

"Most girls like me to be that way," Paul said with assurance.

Lena shook her head and scrunched up her face. *"Baws like watermelons…"*

Paul looked momentarily hurt by the rebuke and she was glad.

"With those guys it's like an act," he explained, his hands held up like a market trader in defence. "There's a way to be that makes my life easier. It's business. I give them what they want. Not just the drugs. It's more like a lifestyle. These guys want to be close to the action but far enough away not to get burned. They think because I was inside it makes me hard. I play up to it because it's what they want to hear."

"Do you always give people what they want?"

She was watching his face. She couldn't stop watching his face. Not handsome, she thought, not in a conventional way. Objectively speaking, there was nothing extraordinary about his face. But it didn't stop her heart racing every time she looked at it. The way he laughed and carried himself so convincingly, she began to wonder if maybe she'd got it wrong and it was the most handsome face in the world.

"Win, win. If there's something you can both gain from it, why not?"

"That guy nearly whitied." She laughed, enjoying watching him squirm at her teasing, no real concern for the guy whose rescue she was coming to.

"It does no harm every once in a while to remind them

who they're dealing with."

"Who are they dealing with?"

"Not much. I'm a lover, not a fighter."

"Why, cos it's what I want to hear?"

Paul lunged across the couch; his arms wrapped around her, tickling the breath out of her. Their laughter rang around the room.

When she was with him she felt no need to be guarded. She could say what she wanted to say and wasn't worried about hurting his feelings or that he would laugh at her. He listened to her. They had a conversation. She wasn't sure if she'd ever had one of them before. She listened to him. Not always understanding, but finding warmth and encouragement in his words. Every once in a while he articulated her thoughts and she basked in the reassuring confidence it gave her when he made them sound entirely plausible, validating her existence.

"Do you ever just think that everyone you know is an asshole?"

She said it glibly because it was the most important thing she had said all day; the most honest confession she'd ever shared with anyone in her life. The thought that ate away at her day by day.

He laughed again. "I know exactly what you mean."

The ashtray was resting on his chest. Smoke blew out of his nose. "Only I don't think they're assholes, I think they're weak."

Right, she thought. It wasn't quite what she'd meant. She had been trying to say that she was weak, for thinking like that. It worried her when she had thoughts like that. She looked at her friends and envied them that they never had thoughts like that. Or if they did, they didn't show it. She couldn't understand what was wrong with her. The world was a hostile place and she was ill-equipped to deal with it.

She sipped her tea.

"I mean, like those guys today," he said. "The one that nearly whitied."

He waited for her laugh before he continued. He was taking her with him. "I give them a couple of nine bars, some pills every month to sell up at the uni. I give them a shit deal. And they know it. But it's worth it to them. They're not gonna fight me on it because I know they aren't in it for the money. They're in it for the show. In a couple of years, when they get their nine-to-five and their house, they can tell stories of their fucked-up youth and impress their friends. But for me, this is actually my livelihood. This is my life.

"If it's what they want, they should do it. But don't dip your toe. Why sit in the corner when you can be in the centre of the action? If you're gonna do something, do it. All the way. Be it. All the time. Because otherwise you're a fucking tosser and people like me are gonna rip the pish out of you."

She thought of her friends and how she hid her grades from them. How she thought the clothes they wore were stupid but still dressed the same – just because. But it hurt when they whispered behind her back. Even the people she thought were her friends, the ones that were supposed to be looking out for her, only did it as long as she played her part.

"Most people are assholes, it's true. So what? That's their problem. But it's not gonna change who I am. I'm still gonna do what I want to do."

She took a large gulp, holding back. Not ready to believe

him. Not wanting to give up a part of herself – feeling that once it was gone she could never get it back. Because it meant going solo and she didn't know if she was ready for that yet.

"But what about when what I want is the opposite of what someone else wants? Should I just force it? I don't want to hurt anyone," Lena said.

"Sometimes you have to. That's a choice you have to make." His face was impassive.

"Like the guy you threw in front of a taxi?"

He looked at her like he'd just been mauled by a kitten he'd been petting. She regretted saying it. Wished she could take it back. The silence was strained. She wanted to return to the laughter, the soul-searching conversation. She'd ruined everything. Pushed it too far.

For a second she thought he was about to get up and leave. Then his eyebrow went up; he rocked his head, drew in a deep breath. She was surprised when he took the joint from her and started to speak.

"That was a mistake."

Then he laughed.

"Because you got caught?" she asked, annoyed.

"No," he answered quickly, sharply. "Not because I got caught."

He waited a while and then continued.

"You know I'm a drug dealer. It's a good job for me. It means that I'm not going round punting kitchens or double glazing that people don't want. I'm not working at McDonald's with some spotty-faced virgin telling me to fry chips faster, smile more at the customers. Or in a call centre clocking in and out to piss. I couldn't do that. I can't have other people telling me what to do.

"I used to think it was me that was damaged. That there was something wrong with me. That I couldn't fit in. I was called antisocial, oppositional, dysfunctional. Then one day I didn't think that. One day I realised that being the way I am isn't a bad thing. I had a couple of harsh lessons. Helped put things in perspective. I realised that when it's all taken away, there's something inside me that survives. And just knowing that, it knocks down any walls, unlocks any doors. And people are scared of that. Because it shows up their own weakness. I don't blame myself. They can't make me feel guilty for being who I am."

Lena listened carefully, sensing that somewhere in there was the key she was looking for. The tools she needed to survive a little better herself.

"When I stood in front of the judge and he told me I was getting a sentence, I was terrified," Paul said, deadly serious. He wasn't laughing or smiling anymore. "I lost control in a moment of weakness. Could have jeopardised everything. There was no choice in it. The guy provoked me. I reacted. And it was stupid. And the cost of that was six months of my life.

"It wasn't pretty. I was fresh meat in there. First day I walked in, they could smell I was different. I wasn't in the infirmary because of a wrist strain, I was there because I got into a fight. I got into a lot of fights. Sometimes violence is necessary. But it's never an easy choice. Not for me. That's why I knew I was different. I hated every minute of it.

"Do you want to know the worst part, though?" He looked at her, his mouth grim, his face dark. "Knowing I could have killed a guy. Knowing I came that close." He measured a small distance between his index finger and thumb. "Because that's one thing you can never escape from."

Lena felt a shiver and let his words settle; some she took straight to heart, others she saved for later. Her eyes fell on the clock on the shelf. It was midnight. She realised she had to go, or stay out for a second night. She sat up straight, not wanting to cut him off when he was speaking so openly, so honestly. She wanted to stay there beside him and hear him talking till morning. But a second night was pushing an already precarious situation at home.

"I have... err... college tomorrow." She avoided his eye. "My flatmates will be wondering where I am."

"Blow it off and hang out with me," he said.

She wanted to. She wanted to live with freedom and without responsibility. She didn't want to be a teenager with school and teachers and people to answer to every minute of every day. Partly she wanted to upset her mother, let her see what bringing an asshole like Jason into their house had done to her daughter. There would be havoc when she got home.

But she could take it, she thought. It was worth whatever they threw at her. She was a survivor too.

"Please," he said, with a desperation that took her by surprise. And suddenly he seemed very small in the room with blank walls, filled with little else besides loneliness.

"OK," she said.

They stayed up talking for the rest of the night and when morning beckoned, he took her hand and led her to bed.

That afternoon, when she woke up beside him, she discovered what it was to feel totally connected to another person, to the world.

This is what real life is all about, she thought. Happiness exists and it's there to be taken. And there's nothing wrong with that.

It wasn't selfish. There was nothing to feel guilty about. Why did adults make everything so complicated? Why did they fill your head with lies and their stupid ideas of how your life should be? Stupid lies their parents had told them and their parents before them. Lena had never met an adult yet who was happy, so why should she listen to any of them?

Some of Paul's words rang in her ears. *Why recognise another man's rules, the responsibilities he gives me, when you can choose your own?*

In that moment, Lena couldn't remember ever having been so happy.

A few minutes later, when the buzzer went and a heavy fist pounded on the door, it all came crashing down around her.

"POLICE! OPEN UP!"

There was a horrible moment when they both froze.

Paul whipped round and pointed to a spot on the bedroom floor. "The stash."

Lena couldn't see where he was pointing, but it was too late, he was already making his way to the door. Then she spied the transparent bag filled with pills, pellets and powders. Grabbing it, she ran to the toilet. Her fingers fumbled as she tried to open the ziplock. Another thud at the door caused her to jump. In desperation she tore her nails through the soft cellophane, spilling the contents into the toilet bowl. She watched the white dots spiral down the U-bend just as the door in the hall crashed open and a policeman's stern monotone, forceful as a juggernaut, carried through the wall.

"Paul Dalziel?"

"Yeah, so?"

She heard a tussle, followed by the sound of someone bashing into a wall.

"We're looking for a Lena Warren," the policeman said. "We have reason to believe she attended a party here on Saturday night."

Heavy footsteps pounded her way. After two deep breaths she opened the bathroom door and was met by a female police officer.

"She's here," the officer yelled back to her colleague, who pushed Paul into the living room.

Lena was ushered out of the flat, flushed with embarrassment and shame. As she passed the living room she heard Paul shout, "Fourteen? FOURTEEN!" He was with a uniformed male officer and his face was stony, his hand over his mouth.

All the way to the police station, Lena couldn't get the image out of her mind.

Lena couldn't look her mum in the eye when she entered the room. There was no sensible place to look other than down, but the physical strain of it was hurting her head. She didn't want to look at her, at the black rings under her eyes and the lines on her forehead.

She was surprised by how small her mother looked, her arms wrapped around her body like a blanket. Seeing her dispassionately, as a stranger would, Lena noted the long, unkempt hair, the thin puckered mouth, washed-out baggy

T-shirt and raggedy sweatpants. She had the face and posture of a woman much older than thirty-seven, her good looks long vanished. From her slackened facial muscles, Lena could tell she'd already been drinking.

Another woman joined them. The velvety tone of her voice marked her out as a social worker and made Lena shudder. The woman looked Lena and her mother up and down appraisingly.

During the interview Lena could sense her mum willing it to be over, affronted by the shame of it all. She was of the generation that still respected professionals and she was mortified that she'd caused a fuss over nothing, wasting time that could have been used on someone more deserving. Lena wished her mum didn't think like that.

Were you held against your will? Forced to do anything you didn't want to do? Paid any sums of money? At any point offered or given drugs? Lena could feel the burn of her mum's glare as she did her best to explain that she'd lost track of time. That she'd gone to a party. Lied about her age. No harm had come to her. No one was to blame but her. It wouldn't happen again.

No matter how earnestly she protested, though, she got the feeling they never quite believed her.

After a grilling on her home life, they were eventually satisfied and allowed her to go.

On the bus home she wanted to reach out to her mum, to say sorry or try to explain, but the wall that had been building between them was tangible now, too strong to break through. They sat in silence.

Back at the house, Lena went straight to her room and

listened to her mum and Jason arguing downstairs. Lena heard her mum telling him not to interfere, that she'd deal with her daughter her own way. Lena was grateful; it was the first time she could remember her mum sticking up for her. But she knew there'd be trouble. It was humiliating for him that the law had been laid down and she was certain he wouldn't let it go.

Lying alone in the darkness, she watched the headlights of passing cars creeping over the ceiling. Her mind was whizzing with all that had happened. Just one weekend, but somehow she felt different now. She didn't feel like she was in her own bedroom. It didn't feel like her own bed. She didn't belong to them anymore. This thought saddened and frightened her as she turned and sank her face into the pillow.

At school the next day, she kept her head down amid a storm of stares and whispers. Gillian had leaked details to anyone who would listen, talking up her own part in it, exaggerating other bits for effect. Lena obviously had some serious mental problems and as her best friend she couldn't stand to be around to watch her self-destruct.

After Lena's mum had contacted the school to say she hadn't come home on Saturday night, Gillian had held out for most of Monday before being forced to confess all – the party, the drinking, the older boys she'd left Lena alone with. Gillian was ignoring her now, annoyed that Lena had usurped her position at the centre of the drama.

The worst thing for Lena was the concern. In the female teachers it brought out their maternal instinct, while the male teachers kept a wary distance. Some pupils were admiring, others disapproving. Either way, she didn't care. She just wanted to be left alone. The only person who had any right to say anything was her mum, but Lena wasn't sure any meaningful conversation would ever take place between them again.

CHAPTER SEVEN

Left alone in the dark, Paul sat tied to his prison chair, reliving dead memories. The fire Annie had lit earlier had long since faded, but among the ashes some embers still burned fervently. As he stared into their hypnotic glow, it was the memories from those early days that kindled. It smarted and stung to remember, but even so, he found them to be a small glimmer in all the darkness. In the cold room he found surprising warmth.

*

It had been a long week, like any that starts with a Monday afternoon wake-up call from the police. He'd had to scratch together every penny he could to make up for what the girl had put down the toilet. Calling in debts, asking favours, ripping off a couple of easy targets with placebos and extra laxative powder. He'd been busy. Coming off the back of a six-month sentence, there'd have been some raised eyebrows if he'd gone crying about a lost stash. Flushed. At least she'd had the sense to do that. He deserved it for having been so stupid. Being forced to swallow the loss himself was painful, but it was better than three years for possession with intent to supply.

The rain was drumming relentlessly on the streets, the wind hurling billowing sheets of it against tarmac, brick and mortar. As his taxi splashed through the downpour, Paul tuned out the driver, who was fishing to find out which team he supported. Old Firm nights were always the same. He had never understood how, for so many, a group of men running around a pitch provided so much meaning. If they didn't get you with religion, they got you with football and somehow in Glasgow they managed to combine the two.

The club where he worked had been bouncing all night, with a lot of people out either celebrating or drowning their post-match sorrows. A good night for business. And Paul badly needed that. Finally, at around 2 a.m., dead beat, he had decided to call it a night.

The taxi pulled up outside his flat.

"Keep the change," he said, then made a quick dash for the front door to his block. Cold water trickled down his neck and fat droplets feathered his nose and lashes as he felt inside his pocket, among crumpled notes, for his keys. At least the street smell of vinegar and grime would be washed away tomorrow.

The door was off the snib. Someone had bust the lock again. He sighed.

Diving into the damp hallway, he looked around for the jake that had knocked in the door, but there was no one. Shaking off the excess water, he got in the lift then rattled towards home on the fifteenth floor.

When he stepped out of the lift, the door crashed shut behind him. Only one light, at the opposite end of the corridor, was working, buzzing incessantly.

Maybe it was the noise that unnerved him as he walked to his door. The reason he stopped before he put his key in the lock, unable to shake the sense that there were eyes on him. He had an instinct for trouble and something didn't feel right.

Out of the shadows, a hooded figure darted towards him. Paul turned and primed himself, his right hand swinging back, key clutched tightly between index and middle finger. The figure cowered from the impending blow and Paul managed to hold the punch.

Her hood fell down and she turned towards him. Ropey threads of dark hair latticed her face. She looked like a half-drowned cat hanging from the scruff of its neck, waiting for the final dunk to finish the job.

Paul slowly brought his arm down, his heart pounding. "What the fuck are you doing? I nearly fucking knocked you out."

"Sorry. I didn't mean to—"

He turned back to his door. He could see her straightening herself behind him.

"You'd better get out of here. I might yet… Do you have any idea how much trouble you caused?" he said, enraged. He'd wondered how long it would be before she showed up again. He opened his flat door and turned on the light. She was waiting behind him but he stood in the doorway, blocking the entrance. "Little girls shouldn't be out this late. Go home to your maw."

His hall light lit her face and he saw her burst lip and swollen cheek.

"Please." She swayed on her feet. Her skin was grey, her lips tinged blue with cold. She was shaking uncontrollably.

He hesitated in the doorway, not able to slam the door in her face. "You can't come in here. I can't have the polis up at my door again."

"It's only for one night. I had nowhere else to go."

He looked at her battered face and felt a dull, spreading anger.

Standing aside, he let her into his flat. Her sodden jacket dripped on his floor. His act of kindness apparently overwhelmed her and she choked back big snorts. Closing his door behind them, all thoughts of sleep and a warm bed disappeared into the night air.

"Do you want to tell me what happened?"

CHAPTER EIGHT

Paul ushered her into the living room. She sat on the couch and he brought through a dry towel. The room was warm. He sat beside her while she patted her hair down. She knew he was waiting for an explanation but when she opened her mouth to speak she was silenced by stage fright. Her thoughts were muddled and she was tired and confused; all her energy had been sapped trying to keep warm. Coming here had made sense earlier, but now that she was sitting face to face with a baffled Paul, she felt overcome with emotion and couldn't quite put it all into words. All she could do was breathe deeply and concentrate on her fingers. She saw that they were wrinkled and as she watched they began to blur with tears.

The atmosphere at home had been tense all week. When she got back from the police station she'd gone straight to her room, waiting for the showdown that never came. Next day she got up, went to school, came home. Straight up to her room again. Her resolve to avoid the two of them had lasted the whole week.

Saturday was the first day she spent any time outside her room. Her mum had a cleaning job and Jason was out at the football. With the living room to herself, she stretched out on the couch and watched daytime TV.

She knew the avoidance tactics were stupid. That she had to face them at some point. But she couldn't bring herself to do it. If it had just been her mum, the stalemate would have been over days ago. In the past they'd never slept on a quarrel. But with Jason there, everything was different. Ever since he'd moved in a few months before, he'd been throwing his weight around. And her mum let him. It was like she'd forgotten everything Lena had done for her. It was impossible to even get her mum alone.

Jason and her mum had met at the pub down the road. Jason was visiting friends in the area. It was karaoke night. While sipping a soda and lime, her mum had quietly moved the room with "One Day at a Time", a song made famous in Glasgow by Lena's namesake. According to Jason, he had brought the house down with a rendition of Robbie Williams's "Angels". They were cheering for an encore up and down the streets. The guy who ran the karaoke even thought Jason was a professional singer.

Of all the women Jason could have had that night, he chose her mum.

They'd come home afterwards for a cup of tea. Lena had been sitting on the couch reading a book for school. He took the book from her hands, pretending to study it, swaying where he stood. "Me," he said, then slapped the book with the side of his palm, "I just pick up a book and boom! It's read. That's all I do, is read."

That was how most of his stories went. Bigging himself up, creating his own legend. How hard he was. How many fights he'd won. Women he'd conquered. Lena rolled her eyes and her mum secretly smirked. At first he had been a joke between her and her mum. They laughed at him behind his back.

"He's harmless," her mum would say.

And as long as he was a joke, Lena didn't mind. It was nice to see her mum getting out and dressing up again. The last few years had been tough. After Frank left and took Annabelle with him, it had all just fallen apart.

Lena had liked Frank. He had genuinely tried to help. With Jason it was always grand gestures. Flowers. Chocolates. But nothing they actually needed. He made good money as a driving instructor but after all his monthly debts were paid off there never seemed to be anything left. He had a lot of excuses: his ex-wife bleeding him dry, his sisters cheating him out of his inheritance. There was always some tale of persecution. Things were never, ever his fault.

The first time the three of them went out together, Jason had driven them to Harry Ramsden's and then to the cinema. He had a few drinks but said he was still OK to drive because of his super reflexes.

On the way there, Jason had cut up another driver. Hitting the horn, he drove right up beside the other car and yelled at the closed window, "Watch where you're going! Ya Paki bitch."

Lena's mum had turned round from the front seat and smiled apologetically.

"Do you know, Lena, why Asian women are the worst drivers?" Jason said. "It's a well-known fact. There's only one Asian woman in Glasgow who can drive. And she does the test for all of them. With the veil on, no one can tell the difference. So if you see a woman with a veil behind a wheel, steer clear."

It must be great learning to drive with him, she thought.

At dinner he flirted with the waitresses. Lena's mum didn't notice. She looked at him with starry eyes. It was that look that made Lena start to worry.

A few weeks later his bags were sitting in their hallway when she came home from school. She went into the living room, where the two of them were sitting on the couch, a litre bottle of vodka half-finished on the table. Jason was posing and flexing his muscles. Her mum was fondling them, massaging him like he was a sacred cow.

"Lena, we've something to tell you," she said.

"I'm moving in," Jason interjected. "So I can lie low. Can't show my face in Cardonald for a while."

Lena's heart sank as he told the story.

"My ex was having problems with the neighbour. When I went round to sort it out, the cow punched my ex in the face, so I nutted her. Turns out her husband's a bit of a hard man. Wants to kill me."

Lena left the room. Bewildered at how she could have let it happen. How she'd managed to drop the ball so spectacularly. She thought it had all just been a bit of fun. But here he was, living under their roof. Just when she'd thought things were getting back on track. Just when she'd thought there was a chance Annabelle could come home. It would never happen now. How could her mum let her down so badly?

Lena heard them at night when they stayed up drinking,

stepped over them the next morning when she left for school. Jason started calling in sick to work. At first just the early-morning lessons, then all of them – either too hung over to drive or still over the limit. He went to the doctor's with depression and returned with a line to say he couldn't work. Her mum held him when he cried.

But he was still the man of the house.

At just after five that Saturday afternoon, Lena heard a key click in the door. Her shoulders tensed and her feet moved automatically to the floor. She hadn't expected either of them back for hours.

Jason came through from the hall into the living room, dressed in team colours, smelling of fish supper and beer. He didn't say anything as he walked past, just lifted the remote control from the table in front of her. He sat in the armchair and flicked over to the football results.

The *Grandstand* theme music played. A voice began to read out the scores. "St Mirren, nil, Dunfermline Athletic, one—"

"I was watching something," Lena said, but only half-heartedly. It maddened her that he got away with more childish behaviour than she did.

"And now I'm watching this."

A sigh of frustration escaped her. He sneered. It was the most anyone had said to her in a week.

She got up off her seat and huffed into the kitchen. She knew he wouldn't have done that if her mum had been there.

"Bring me in a beer!" he called after her.

In the kitchen she walked in a circle, clenching and unclenching her hands.

"I said, bring me in a beer!" he yelled again.

She went to the fridge, opened a cold beer and took it through to him, hating herself for doing it. She wanted to scream *Fuck off!* in his face, but she knew she wouldn't. There was always an unspoken threat when he asked her to do stuff, challenging her to find out how far he would take it if she said no.

There was a scoffing glint in his eye when she handed it to him. She had to look away. It burned her every time she couldn't hold his gaze.

"And in today's Old Firm match, Celtic, one, Rangers—" said the voice from the TV.

"That's right, ya fucking cheating CUNTS!" he shouted back at it, his face a strange shade of red.

Lena walked away in disgust, back into the kitchen to make a sandwich. She didn't plan on coming out of her room again that night.

And that's when it all went wrong.

She started to hum a song. Not deliberately. It was in her head. One of the football songs she'd heard the boys at school singing. The tune was catchy.

"Stop singing that fucking song," came his voice, menacing, from the living room.

She stopped instantly, then laughed a little, nervously. That song really annoyed him. She went back to making her sandwich, then started up again. It was her house and she could sing if she wanted to. It was meant to tease him. He deserved it.

"I said, stop singing the fucking song," he repeated, from behind her.

She jumped when she turned round and saw him standing there, propped against the kitchen doorframe. His tone of voice should have been a warning, but she ignored it. Why should she stop? What was he going to do about it? Whatever it was, she could take it.

"You've got your mum wrapped round your little finger, haven't you? If I was in charge…" he spat drunkenly, his cheeks branded with rage.

But you're not in charge, she screamed internally. *You're just a big, ugly, fat-headed bully.*

In a misguided act of defiance, she sang louder. All the frustration and anger she felt towards him, she poured into the lyrics in protest, until the veins were popping out of her temples.

"I said, stop singing that FUCKING SONG!"

He erupted from the doorway, fist smashing into her face, knocking her to the floor. She lay stunned as white lights flashed in front of her eyes. More kicks slammed into her body, each one knocking the wind out of her afresh. He stopped and she stayed curled in a ball, not moving a muscle, listening to the heavy thud of his feet as he stalked off to the living room. Her face ached and she was trembling so hard she didn't know if she could get up.

She lay there for a while, dazed, unable to fully comprehend what had happened. Then she heard him get up and walk to the bathroom. She heard the door shut. She waited some more to make sure he wasn't coming back before she finally struggled to her feet, grabbed her jacket and stumbled to the front door. She undid the lock and ran outside into the spitting rain. Her weekly ticket was crumpled in her pocket;

she fished it out and waved her hand at the oncoming bus. No one looked in her direction as she limped to a seat. Beneath the privacy of her hood, she forced back tears and tried to think of somewhere to go. She had only a little change. She couldn't afford a room. Gillian still wasn't talking to her. She didn't have anyone else she could go to. Utterly helpless, she put in her headphones and lost herself in the music while the bus did one circuit and then another.

Hours passed. By the time the bus had begun its third circuit, it was night-time. A different sort of crowd began to fill the seats and clog the aisle: people on their way to nights out in the city centre. Lena stared listlessly out the window and turned her music up higher, wishing for the power of invisibility, desperately trying to avoid unwanted attention.

The bus grew hot and stuffy. An overpowering smell of sour milk mixed with damp wool choked the air. The window, clouded with condensation, became a mirror in which she was able to monitor the goings-on. A blur of faces and colours. The party already started for most of them. Singing and dancing, passing bottles and phone numbers. Her eye kept catching that of one man standing in the aisle. She turned to face him, looked away and then back, but his eyes didn't move. She told herself it wasn't her he was looking at, but when the seat beside her became vacant, in her peripheral vision she saw him move in beside her. She shrank into the window, suddenly aware that his body was blocking her exit. Even before he opened his mouth, she knew he was going to speak to her. He was close enough that she could smell the whisky. He whispered, "I'm undercover police. Is everything OK?"

She turned round in alarm. "Fine."

Outside, the lights of George Square twinkled.

"Are you sure? Have you got some place to go?"

She looked at the faces around her, but no one else was watching them.

His knee drew closer and touched hers. She jumped to her feet. Her legs were stiff from sitting in one position for too long but she still managed to hurdle his legs and join the stream of people pushing out into the street. She got off the bus and straightaway was hit by the wind and the rain. She pulled her hood up over her head so that only her eyes were peeping through.

At the other side of the square was the bus she needed to take her in the direction of home. It was a couple of minutes to midnight. If she didn't get on it, she would be stranded, her ticket invalid. Cutting through the traffic, she sprinted across the square, barging past screaming girls in miniskirts, drenched by the rain, and men staggering, one in a bloodstained shirt. Voices were shouting and debris littered the ground. She kept her eyes focused on the bus, narrowly missing colliding with a bare-chested man who'd stumbled into her path. Even when the bus flashed its indicator and pulled out into the traffic, she kept on going. But then it roared down the street and out of sight and she finally she gave up, stopped where she stood, her arms flailing in exasperation, tears welling in her eyes.

The sound of smashing glass in close proximity made her flinch. She swung round to face the mayhem but instead found herself face to face with the man from the bus. He stopped still.

"I just want to help," he mouthed.

For a second she was too stunned to react. Then, after two steadying breaths, she turned on her heel and began to run. She crossed the road without stopping. Wet tyres squealed to avoid her. From the other side, she turned back to find him still there, in close pursuit. She broke into a sprint, dodging through the crowds. Passing Central Station, the lines of people standing in taxi queues, she was directionless but unwilling to stop. Before she knew it, she was in the darkest part of town, heading down towards the Clyde. The rain was battering down. There were few cars on the road, only a handful of people on the pavements. She was alone. She had no place to go. No one to turn to. There was nowhere left to run.

Slowing down, she jumped into the shelter of an empty shop doorway and searched the road behind her, her heart beating wildly in her chest. She couldn't see him. But that didn't mean he wasn't there. Every corner, every darkened alleyway was a potential lair.

An involuntary sob escaped her, a tiny plea absorbed by the night. Her eyes fell on the Anderston high-rises in the distance. An idea began to form. Not a very good one, but it was the only one she had.

If she closed her eyes and walked as fast as she could, she would reach his door in five minutes. Only the underpass stood between her and the block of flats where she had to believe she would find help. She looked at it and shuddered to think what horrors lurked beneath it. She'd never even braved it in daylight. But reaching his flat became the goal that overrode all other thoughts. She had to try.

With determination, she started along past the street walkers and kerb crawlers. She braced herself as she entered the dank shadows, too scared to breathe for fear of disturbing the dangers that lay within. Not wanting to run, draw attention. There were bodies huddled, wrapped in cardboard, but she paid them no heed and kept walking. Her footsteps crunched over glass, echoing loudly in her ears.

When she emerged on the other side, she couldn't shift the sickening thought that if she were a cat, she'd have just used one of her nine lives.

Within a few steps she was at the edge of his courtyard.

At the door she pressed his buzzer. Again and again. When she got no answer she whimpered in despair. There was nothing left for her to do. She'd come this far for nothing. In desperation she threw her weight against the door and heard it click open.

Unwilling, too ashamed to go into those details, she kept it brief.

"There was a fight and I can't go home tonight."

"With your mum?"

She shook her head and with sharp breaths the words ripped out of her throat. "Jason. Her boyfriend."

Paul put his arm around her shoulders. When she stared up at him she saw a strange expression cross his face. She mumbled some more incoherent words but he quieted her. He'd heard all he wanted to hear.

"Don't worry. Listen, I know why you came here. You don't even need to ask. OK?"

She looked up at him, half dazed.

"I'm gonna sort this for you." He smiled.

She wasn't sure what he meant, but it was exactly what she needed to hear. She didn't see how much it moved him to have her tear-filled eyes sparkle up at him, showing a trust he had never known. She didn't hear the pact he made with himself. The pact to never let anything bad happen to her ever again.

CHAPTER NINE

Paul offered to drive her home the following day. In the car, Lena stared at the passing streets so intently, she was startled when she felt Paul's hand reach down and touch hers. He briefly took his eyes off the road and smiled.

"Don't worry."

Lena relaxed her hands. She realised she'd been wringing them tightly together. Now her nervous energy transferred to her feet, which began bouncing up and down, ruffling the supermarket plastic bag filled with her damp clothes. Paul's sweatshirt and joggies swamped her, their dryness still a comfort, the chill of last night's wind still deep in her bones. She pulled the oversized sleeves down over her hands to make a pair of gloves.

Asking for help had not been easy but somehow he made her feel it had been the right thing to do.

But he was still very much a stranger to her and she felt shy in front of him. Suddenly life was very serious. He'd scolded her for walking through the red-light district, for not calling her mum to tell her she was safe. There was no joking or flirting this time. Once he seemed satisfied that, other than a few cuts and bruises, she was going to live, he told her to get some sleep; he would drive her home in the morning.

She crawled into the familiar bed and lay awake, waiting to see if he would get in too. After a while she drifted off to sleep. In the morning, momentarily confused by the strange bed, unfamiliar bed sheets, she crept next door to find Paul asleep on the couch.

"Not yet."

They'd pulled up outside Lena's house. She'd started to get out when Paul placed his arm in front of her, motioning her back. Lena followed his line of vision to two figures standing at the bus stop opposite her house. There was barely an acknowledgement as the two advanced towards them and then walked up the path to the door of her ground-floor cottage flat.

She looked closer, "Isn't that... William?"

His companion was just as hard-looking, intent on trouble.

"What's going on?" she asked, panic creeping in.

"Watch."

She saw her front door open and the two of them drag Jason out into the garden, which was shared with the upstairs neighbour. They pulled him onto the grass. Got him on his knees and proceeded to stomp and punch him. Jason was big, but his attempts at self-defence were futile against the two of them.

Lena watched in horror as her mum came into the garden, screaming. The upstairs neighbour was at the window shouting about calling the police. Lena roused herself. She flashed Paul a pleading look as she got out of the car. "Make it stop."

A horn blasted behind her and William and his accomplice

stopped the beating.

Jason was holding his face. Through the bubbles of spittle and blood which had formed in the corner of his mouth, he spat out, "You've broke my nose."

"Next time it'll be your legs if you lay a hand on her again."

Lena ran into the garden as they kicked him one last time in the face before casually sauntering through the gate. When she looked back, she saw that Paul's car had already gone.

Her mum helped Jason into the house, muttering, "No police." She flashed a look over her shoulder at Lena. "I'll deal with you later."

Lena guiltily followed the stooping pair into the house, along a trail of deep red droplets on the pathway. She felt nauseous. Jason and her mum took a taxi to the hospital. Lena stayed in alone.

That night, Jason packed his bags and left. Lena listened from her room to the muffled cries and arguments and pleadings. She couldn't bear to look him in the face. His broken face. When she heard the door close she crept out of her room. Her mum was sitting in the living room at the dining table with her head in her hands.

"Mum?" She was barely even whispering. "Mum."

"What are we going to do now? How are we going to make the rent now?"

Lena knew he didn't help with the rent, but it helped her mum to pretend that he did. She had no response for her. Nothing was the right thing to say. She'd watched his jaw shatter.

At midnight Lena sneaked stealthily downstairs. Her mum

was sleeping, curled up on the couch, an empty bottle of supermarket own-brand vodka lying beside her. Lena drew a blanket over her shoulders and gently shook her. When she didn't wake up, Lena tiptoed to the mantelpiece and took five pounds from her purse. If her mum noticed, she would say Jason took it. Then she quietly left through the front door, closing it softly behind her.

When she reached the main road it didn't take long to hail a taxi.

"The Anderston high-rises, please."

She could see the taxi driver eyeing her suspiciously in the mirror and remembered that her cheek was still shaded with a deep purple shadow, a swollen lump still protruding from her lower lip.

She took the now familiar journey up to Paul's flat and knocked on his door. From the light underneath she guessed he was home. She heard feet padding towards the door and could tell someone was looking at her through the peephole. Fingers fumbled at the lock and then came the rattle of the chain being taken off. Paul appeared, in a rumpled T-shirt and jeans, his hair dishevelled.

"What do you want, Lena?" he asked in a tone that made her defensive.

He glanced back over his shoulder. She looked too. She started to speak when a female voice from inside the flat interrupted.

"Paul? Who is it, Paul?"

"It's no one. Just give me a minute," he shouted back. Stepping out into the corridor, he closed the door till only a chink of light escaped.

No one? thought Lena.

"Is something wrong?"

"No…" She'd lost her bearings. She wasn't sure how to respond. "I just came… I wanted to tell you that Jason left."

"Good. I thought he might."

She desperately wanted to fill the silence, to prolong the conversation, even though in her heart she knew it was already over.

"I didn't get a chance to thank you. When I ran out of the car… I didn't want you to think I was ungrateful."

"I didn't think that."

A long silence lingered as Lena slowly melted inside.

"Look, Lena—"

She interrupted him, "Can I come in?"

He exhaled loudly, rubbing one eye with his hand, watching her with the other. "I'm sorry. I don't think that's a good idea."

"Paul!" the voice called from inside, more urgently than before. "Paul!" The voice grew steadily louder as its owner approached the door. She was wearing a Chinese-style dressing gown, her hair swept high in a loose bun, sparkly earrings dangling to her shoulders. Her curvaceous hips swung with attitude. She looked Lena up and down with disapproval then turned to address Paul.

"You've not started pimping while I've been away, have you?"

"Shut up! She's my little cousin." He sounded angry.

The girl eyed Lena suspiciously, a laughing glint in her eye. "She doesn't look like your little cousin." Her head nodded from side to side and she jutted out her chin when she spoke.

"Just get the fuck inside. I said give me a minute."

"Don't think I'm gonna wait all night."

She gave Lena one last disparaging look before turning provocatively like a lazy cat and disappearing down the hallway. "And don't let all the cold air in."

The strong scent of her perfume lingered around the doorstep after she'd left.

"C'mon." Paul sighed as he pulled his jacket from the hook just inside the door and slipped on his shoes. He closed the girl in and walked towards the lift. Lena had no choice but to follow. They didn't speak on the way down or when they stepped out into the cold night. The white clouds of their breath danced around in complicated swirls.

He held out his arm and as a taxi pulled up he turned to her with a smile, ignoring her wounded, imploring stare.

"You need to go home. This isn't the place for you. Make it up with your maw. She cares enough to bring the polis to my door."

He held open the door and Lena stepped inside. Taking out his wallet, he paid the driver in advance. She had nothing to say any more. She didn't care if she looked crushed. As the taxi pulled away, she swung around for one last look, one last chance to capture his image, to store every detail of him in her memory. But he had already walked away.

When she got home, her mum was still sleeping soundly on the couch. The cover had fallen off. Before going to bed, Lena pulled it back over her shoulders and gave her a kiss on the cheek.

CHAPTER TEN

Paul was sweating; the atmosphere was stale and muggy. The sun was beginning to set, casting an orangey-red hue over the living room. Annie had his wallet in her hand. She made a show of rifling through it. Whatever pantomime she was putting on, Paul didn't want to give her the satisfaction of being the participating audience. He watched mutely as she pulled out a card and twirled it through her fingers, like a magician preparing to make it disappear.

"Funny what you can find out about a person by going through their wallet. It's a bit like mind-reading. 'Criminal Justice Social Worker'?" she read aloud, holding up a card.

"Let me go," Paul said as she delved in again, taking out bits and pieces, commenting, and putting them back.

"Casino membership. RBS gold card. Bet that impresses the ladies." She smiled and raised her eyebrow. "Expired. Driver's licence…" She looked from the picture to Paul, to the picture again and shook her head. "Thirty-three. Life's been tough on you."

Next she took out a small, passport-sized photo, bringing it up near her nose for closer inspection. "And who's this?" She turned it to face him.

Paul looked at the broad, trusting smile of the boy in the

picture, almost a carbon copy of an image he'd once seen of himself at that age, except the boy had his mother's eyes. He wanted to tear it from her hands.

"Put it back."

Annie wasn't listening. She'd taken a bent and damaged picture from his wallet and was studying the dog-eared Polaroid; the image was faded and cracked, a matrix of thin white veins spreading across it. Her fingers clasped the corners.

Even though it had been years since he'd looked at it, Paul knew every line, every shade. He followed Annie's eyes as they took in Lena's nubile beauty, her cherubic face scrunched into a tantalising pout. Her arms pressed together to exaggerate her bosom. So heartbreakingly open; bewitching. In that perfect moment, her entire personality had been captured. Paul could see the photo was too discoloured to convey how bright the sun had been that day. Glasgow had shone like an emerald, the trees fat with an abundance of lush green leaves. He could see it now, so clearly, that buoyant spring day, almost two years to the day since he'd first met her.

He'd never been able to part with that photograph of Lena. She had been sixteen and full of exuberance. Back when love and life still held so much promise.

*

Twelve Years Ago

That day, scantily clad, sun-starved Glaswegians throughout the city were basking in the precious rays of the late spring sun. Paul found himself wandering through Kelvingrove Park, ducking frisbees, skirting barbeques, soaking himself in the waves of celebration that were breaking all around him. Almost every spot on the itchy fresh-mown grass had been claimed. On the pathway skateboarders flew past at breakneck speed. Paul dodged them as he meandered along it.

He wound his way up a small hill and as he neared the top fleetingly he got a sense that someone was watching him. Scanning the rush of colours before him, he noticed one face suspended in motion, turned towards him. He looked away and back again. Their eyes met and he strained for recognition. Sitting on a bench, dressed in short skirt and penny-farthing earrings, denim jacket slung over her lap, she seemed to glitter and sparkle. She waved at him and he began to approach, a lopsided grin spreading across his face as it all started to come back to him.

"Lena. Little Lena. Look at you, sitting there all pretty. Long time no see."

He hadn't seen or heard from her since that night he'd put her in a taxi and sent her home to her mother. Two years and a lifetime. Not so little anymore, he thought, as she gave him a look that said she knew some things about the world too, now. Paul noticed her newly accentuated curves, her defined cheekbones.

"Paul. Nice to see you."

Two overfilled bags sprawled beside her and he nodded his head towards them. "And you. Still causing trouble?"

She patted them and he shook his head in amusement.

At that moment they were interrupted by a scrawny, pixie-looking boy dressed in an oversized wool coat, despite the weather, and tatty boots.

"Do you mind if I take your picture?" he said in a deep

theatrical voice that seemed impossible for his tiny frame. The pixie waved his Polaroid camera at Lena, ignoring Paul.

"Who are you, the paparazzi?" Paul sneered.

With a scornful sigh, the pixie continued speaking to Lena. "I'm a conceptual artist." He produced a flier from his torn pocket and handed it to her. "I'm collecting material for my latest installation, entitled *A Subterranean Macrocosmic Tapestry Explored*. I want to make a comment about the emergence of an electronic global wasteland and the death of culture. I just saw you in that wonderful pose and thought it encapsulated all I wanted to say on the subject, and I would like to include it in my exhibition."

"Of course," Lena said and arranged herself provocatively, crossing her booted feet, tossing her long, dark hair and pouting.

The pixie took the picture and Paul leaned over his shoulder to have a look.

Agitatedly covering the image, he hid it from Paul's prying eyes. "The exhibition is on Saturday." For the first time he looked at Paul and handed him a flier. "Free champagne." And with that he flounced off through the park with a sprightly skip.

"What a fag," Paul said.

"You're just jealous cos he didn't want to take a picture of you. I personally think he had a good eye. I mean, I so obviously encapsulate the definition of macrocos-something electronic tapestries... You're just not creative enough to see it. You're not an *artist*, Paul."

"So do you fancy a Coke or something? All this hot weather's got me parched."

"I'd rather a vodka. If you're buying."

"You're not old enough for a vodka."

She looked at him incredulously and rolled her eyes. "I was born looking eighteen – you should know."

They left the park and walked a few yards to the nearest pub; a converted school, the old playground now a bustling beer garden. It was packed with students from the university. In the background, the turrets of the university buildings stood tall against the blue sky. Paul went to the bar while Lena found them a seat. When he came back she squinted up at him, the sun in her eyes.

"No straw?" she asked haughtily, ruffling her downy fringe.

He could see she was no longer the fourteen-year-old who hung on his every word. He wondered how many there'd been since.

He put the drinks down. "Get your own straw," he said, settling into his chair, shrugging her off. He wasn't so special to her anymore. Or at least that's what she wanted him to think.

"You look different," she said.

Paul smiled. "Yeah? How so?"

"I don't know." She sipped on her drink. "Your hair is longer. Your clothes… smarter."

Paul looked down at his battered jeans and T-shirt. They didn't seem so smart. "Well…" He considered. "I've started working."

"A legitimate enterprise?" She raised an eyebrow.

"I'm working on it," he joked.

His mind flitted back to the conversation he'd had a few weeks earlier. A dimly lit room: Manny Munroe sitting opposite him behind a mountainous desk, and henchmen guarding the door. From the adjacent room, the crack of pool cues striking balls had sounded like eggs being smashed, jarring his thoughts.

"I've got a job for you," Manny had said in his insidious monotone.

Paul waited eagerly.

"I'm looking for someone to help out in one of my bars. I need someone I can trust. Keep an eye on things: who's giving away free drinks to who, who's dipping their fingers into what and when and from where. But, more importantly, who's talking to who."

Paul nodded. When Manny had told him he was going on the payroll, he'd expected something more interesting than working in a ratty bar. But it was a start.

"Your shift starts at eleven. It's been arranged with the manager, John. But he doesn't know it's got anything to do with me. You need to make sure it stays that way. You're just a young guy earning money like everyone else. Report back every month or so, or if anything interesting comes up. You have my number."

Lena sniffed, bringing Paul's attention back to the present. "I thought that was against your life philosophy or something," she said sharply. "Working for others, and all the rest of it."

"Well, you know…" he bluffed. "It should lead to bigger things. It's a bar in town. The Low Road – you might know it?"

She shook her head.

"It's really cool, kind of underground vibe going on." Underground like a damp hole, he thought. Though she didn't have to know that. "And I have a son now," he announced, like an afterthought. He didn't know why he felt embarrassed telling her.

Lena's face went red.

"Ten months old. Jack. First birthday coming up. Same day as his old pop." He could see himself slowly changing in her eyes. "So I need the extra money for him and stuff."

"Congratulations," she said, but her voice was flat.

"And what about you?" he added quickly. "Shouldn't you be at school or something?"

Her glass paused mid-air. He could see the question annoyed her.

"No. I'm at college now."

"Oh, right. Well, shouldn't you be there?"

Paul watched as she sipped her drink self-consciously.

"Compassionate leave. I'm moving house today."

Paul leaned far back in his chair, mischief in his face. "Who is the poor guy?"

His laughter nipped and her eyes narrowed.

"He's not poor. He's very wealthy, actually. And he's going to be even wealthier when he qualifies and owns his own dental practice."

Paul took a swig of his pint and stretched in the sunshine. "So where is he now?"

Her attempt to sound casual came off as defensive. "He's in class, training to be a valuable, contributing member of society – something I'm sure you're going to mock because they didn't teach you it at the University of Hard Knocks."

She looked at her phone nervously.

"Does he know you're moving in?" Paul pressed, and

watched her get flustered.

"Of course he does," she spat, her face a crimson flush.

They both knew it wasn't true. Her hand covered a small hole in her top and suddenly he saw the situation for what it really was; she'd put on a bit too much make-up, tried just a little too hard. Her expectations were written too plainly on her face, along with her desperation. He instantly regretted giving her a hard time.

"Hey," he said and reached out a reassuring hand. "I'm only teasing."

She pulled away.

The tension soon eased and they talked away the afternoon. She told him about college. About her mum and Jason.

"That prick came back? When?"

"A few weeks after."

"Did he ever—"

"No." She cut him off. "No, never again."

She wanted to show him that things were going well for her now, and he was happy for her. No one knew more than him what it was like to be out on your own. Sitting among the students and elite of the city, he felt more acutely than ever how each and every small scrap he had was his because he'd carried it with sweat and blood. His resentment pushed him to do better.

Watching Lena now, with her pretty face, her two carrier bags and her wits her only weapons against the world, he remembered how hard it had been. The intervening two years had really toughened her up. But underneath the thinned eyebrows and sharpened features, he found it was still there, her softness, her vulnerability, though she managed to hide it well.

The hours passed and the sun began to set. Lena put on her jacket and the seats around them started to empty. Paul was debating whether or not to offer her a couch for the night when her mobile phone buzzed and she grabbed it quickly to read the message.

"Lover-boy?"

"Yeah," she said and beamed at him. "Says he'll be here in ten minutes."

Paul looked at his watch.

"You don't have to wait," she said quickly.

"I don't mind. Unless you're trying to hide him?" he added slyly. "Is he one of those proper students with a briefcase and oversized head and glasses? I bet he's a real snob and heavyweight intellectual? I hope so. Don't leave me disappointed."

"No." She laughed and looked at their emptying glasses. "He's normal."

Twenty minutes later the dental student arrived. Lena threw her arms around him while Paul watched, assessing the pair.

"Paul, this is Graham. Graham, Paul, an old friend."

They shook hands. Paul expected a territorial knuckle crush but there was no suspicion in his greeting. If it had been the other way about and Paul was being introduced to some guy his girlfriend had been passing the time with, it would have been different.

"Same again?" Graham said with an open-hearted gesture of friendship.

Paul knew he should be going but curiosity held him back. He took a swig of the last of his pint and nodded. Lena too. Graham disappeared off to the bar.

"Seems like a nice guy," Paul conceded. He still thought he could take him in a fight. Graham was all beach muscles. Paul liked to think of his own wiry strength as functional.

Lena beamed again.

Graham returned and the three of them shared a drink. Paul spent the time searching for the chink in the armour: middle-class guilt, an over-exaggerated Glaswegian lilt for Paul's benefit, an arrogant underestimation of Paul. He waited for the opportunity to expose his superiority in front of Lena. But the chance never came. What he found was a handsome, charming, self-aware young man of about his age, with no obvious faults and a clear affection for the girl. When Graham shook his hand and flashed his winning smile to reveal his dazzling row of perfect white teeth, Paul shrank back in his chair, reeling from the glare. He felt beaten in every possible way. Graham was everything he feared he would be, and more.

As the pair wandered off, arm in arm, Paul felt strangely defeated. He finished off the last of his pint and took off towards town, the purple dusk enveloping the fluffy pink clouds, a heavy darkness resting on the landscape.

Walking through the streets of Glasgow, he took in the scummy red sandstone tenements, the endless rows of seedy bars, the streams of volatile people. The roaming packs of feral children. He sensed imminent danger in every one of them. Real danger, not the kind you could bottle or sell tickets to like a bungee jump. Thriving, pulsing danger that wasn't regulated. He felt a thrill. People paid money to feel this alive but all he had to do was walk down the street. It was intoxicating. His chest swelled. He loved this city. And one day, he told himself, he was going to run it all.

The following Saturday, sipping his flute of warm cava, Paul sauntered purposefully around the Centre for Contemporary Arts. His well-honed air of entitlement allowed him to blend into almost any crowd. He circled the exhibition, spending the proper amount of time at each display, catching snippets of conversation, ignoring the purses and wallets that were begging to be lifted, all the while surreptitiously scanning the room for Lena.

After casing the room and finding that she wasn't there, he slowly came to a halt beside a large see-through plastic ball, about seven feet high, its floor filled with piles of raw meat. He wondered what it could mean.

Just beyond it, he saw the pixie from the park holding court over a bunch of people. The pixie was dressed in a nice suit, shirt and tie but had completed the look with unkempt hair and battered trainers, ensuring no one missed the irony of his corporate costume; the artist was still underneath. Paul bypassed him and made his way over to the exhibit behind the group. At the least he wanted to see what he'd taken her picture for.

There were lots, maybe even hundreds, of Polaroid pictures, stuck to the wall, piled on a step, spilling onto the floor. Hundreds of faces of young people, smiling, posing, pulling faces. Over the top of them was a large sign: "Lost Property: Reclaim your soul". At one side he spied the photograph of Lena. He felt a spark of annoyance and drew his eyes over the pixie, who was still busy speaking to his guests. Paul ripped the photograph from the wall and put it in his pocket. He headed for the exit. As he did, he noticed there was now a man inside the large plastic ball, along with the meat, wearing a vest under dungarees and a welder's mask. He was holding a sledgehammer. People began to gather round and Paul stopped to have a look too. When the crowd had grown quite large, the man inside the ball let out a scream and began pulverising the meat at his feet, splashing blood all over the walls of the ball. Paul watched as he pounded away while intermittently wailing until it was no longer possible to see the man through the splattered blood.

*

Annie was still holding the photograph in her hands.

"And this? Just some tart?" she asked, her voice wavering.

Paul remembered his words from the night before and watched as Annie continued to stare at the picture, her head bent. Her finger etched Lena's profile and he was surprised to find her trying to stave off tears. He recalled Annie's small, cold hand on his tattoo the night before, pressing him for details, outlining Lena's name on his skin. And a thought, a terrible thought, began to take shape.

"Did you know her?" he asked warily.

Annie's head snapped up, her eyes red. "You still don't recognise me, Paul?"

His heart contracted in intense anguish as from the back of his mind he dredged up the memory of a small child, nine or ten. Red-headed, her chubby face pale against the stark black of her funeral dress. Not Annie – something longer, less pedestrian. Annabelle, Annabella? Lena's half-sister. Her estranged half-sister. They were nothing alike, but the vaguest resemblance was there. In her voice, in the small movements of her face. He could see it now, but any tender impulses were suppressed beneath much stronger feelings of hatred towards his captor. He watched her cheeks flush, her face contort and Paul knew the situation was serious.

"What do you want from me?"

Tears transformed her blue eyes into green marbles. "I want the truth."

She got up and walked out of the room, once more plunging him into darkness.

Paul fell into a fevered sleep.

The air was still. Music was playing. Lena was swaying in time. She enjoyed the slow seduction, teasing out her movements. Briefly returned to the moment, she caught a glimpse of herself in the mirror. She walked up to it and gazed expressionlessly at the reflection staring back at her. Slowly she reached for a red lipstick and began to apply it.

"Lena?"

She continued to stare at her reflection.

"Lena?"

Paul breathed deeply.

She was with him again. Her soft, taunting laugh stung like frosted ice. Her fingers raw on his cheek.

"Paul, baby, get his knuckles rapped? All those dropping the soap rumours true? What a loser."

Her lips glistened like beads of blood. She pressed them

onto his, sucking the breath from him.

Suddenly the ropes around him began to tighten, tearing at his wrists and ankles. The cord around his chest pressed deeper, deeper. He gasped for air. She began to scream. And so did the others. All of them screaming in unison. A caterwauling chorus. Their wails deafened him.

He woke with a jolt. In front of him, on the table, Annie had left the photograph. Lena was smiling up at him now. He turned his eyes away, his cheeks wet with tears.

CHAPTER ELEVEN

In the Low Road, days and nights had a tendency to merge. It didn't matter what time Paul came though the heavy wooden doors – whether the sun was splitting the sky, the moon rising or setting – it was always just pub time. The healthy bustle of the nearby streets died at the doorway. Inside, peeling beer mats sat without irony on scored Formica table-tops, and plastic church-hall chairs lay across the floor like an obstacle course, their legs strategically placed to trip up the unwary. The lingering smell of smoke masked the more pungent whiffs which every once in a while stung the nose like a bad case of halitosis. Every shift Paul was met by the same threadbare, beer-soaked carpet and the same threadbare, beer-soaked customers.

The staff were as washed-out as the hand-written tombola posters Sellotaped to the nicotine-stained walls. And they were skinning the place alive: free drinks for friends, watering down stock, skimming off the top, drinking during shifts. They were casual in their record-keeping and even more so in their handling of cash. The owner, John, didn't seem to notice or care. When he wasn't sleeping off hangovers, he was drinking down in the office or in the snug with customers.

For the first few weeks, Paul kept his head down and

tried to get to know the business; the scams to avoid, the customers to watch, the dealers to evict. It was the ideal place to learn how not to run a pub. He saved it all to report back to Manny. He had no idea what Manny was going to do with the information, but that wasn't his concern; he was just the eyes and the ears and apart from that he just had to live the life as best he could.

So he watched and he listened and, when called upon, told his stories along with the rest of them. But he never divulged more than he needed to. Some truths, mostly about his son; people usually warmed to him once they knew he was a father and asked fewer questions about which area of the city he came from. If it came up, he was vague on specifics, hinted at a difficult childhood. People filled in their own detail and marvelled at how well he was getting on with his life, bringing up his little son. After hours, at the late-night lock-ins encouraged by John, he watched what he drank so as not to let his mouth run away with itself; always mindful. Because Paul knew for a fact what for the others was just rumour – the real money behind the bar came from silent partner Manny Munroe. And for whatever reason, Manny was watching.

At the epicentre of the gossip mill was Sheila, the miniscule matriarch and longest-serving member of staff. A whippet of a woman in her mid-fifties, she attended to the place with the devotion of head housekeeper in an English manor house. She was the only thing keeping it going, as far as Paul could see.

Just watching her work was exhausting. When she wasn't pulling pints, she busied herself with any number of tasks:

soaping the gantry, scraping syrup off the nozzles, polishing the tarnished metalwork. It was hard to imagine what sort of disrepair the place would be in if she hadn't spent the last twenty-five years cleaning it.

After a few weeks Paul was appointed Sheila's surrogate child; he had that effect on women of a certain age, who sensed some need in him for a mother. Another tool to be used. He was happy to play the wayward son in the absence of Sheila's own. She doled out advice on everything from easy women to parenting and the pitfalls of drink. It was delivered with such well-intentioned enthusiasm, Paul always smiled in spite of himself.

Usually after a late shift Paul would walk Sheila to her bus stop and wait with her until her bus arrived. Out of earshot of the pub, she reminisced about the old days. Mostly she lamented how rundown the place had got and described with sadness the fierce young man John had once been, back when he'd started out. It was hard to reconcile the energetic youngster Sheila spoke of with the pie-eyed man John had become, even if he did still have a certain red-faced avuncular charm.

Paul liked to indulge Sheila and tried not to notice her slipping tenners into his pocket. He didn't know why she thought he needed the money more than her, but it was useless to protest. She would have given away the shirt on her back if she thought someone needed it.

As the weeks passed, it became clear for all to see that John was getting worse. Paul recognised a man under pressure and had his suspicions where that pressure was coming from.

One night, after a heavy session, John broke down. The tears flowed, turned to sobs, turned to wailing.

"Bastard. Fucking BASTARD!" He slammed his fist down on the table, knocking over several glasses.

Sheila rushed off for a cloth to dry up the spillages.

His cheeks were purple, his gut hanging over his trousers. It was days since he'd last shaved. John was a big man and it took a group effort to get him up and out into a taxi, homeward bound. Paul waited with Sheila for her bus. They stood sombrely, Sheila's face twitching.

"There's something afoot here," she mumbled.

Paul held his breath. Sheila was ready to cry.

"Or someone," she added.

"Who?" he pressed, proceeding with caution.

"MANNY MUNROE!" Sheila spat his name with such contempt, her mouth sucked in to rid itself of the bitter residue left behind.

Paul winced, no longer aware of the cold; a warm cloud mushroomed inside his head.

"That's right." Sheila nodded angrily. "Not many people know this. But our little bar... is partly his."

Paul instinctively immobilised his features – an obvious tell when playing poker, but Sheila misread his hand and patted his shoulder protectively, moved by his sensitivity.

"Sweet boy. Don't worry, you'll never have any dealings with him. Munroe hasn't set foot inside the place for years. But he's been there in spirit, hiding in the background. Holding on. Taking his cut."

"Have you met him?" Paul ventured, greedy for any insight.

Sheila nodded very slightly, as if suppressing the memory.

In the distance her bus turned the corner and started towards them. They watched it approach.

"I've seen the books," she said bitterly. "Washing dirty money and goodness knows what else for that man has left behind some stains. John's slowly wasted himself under Munroe's shadow."

Paul shivered, suddenly cold again. The bus screeched to a halt in front of them, the doors hissing open.

"He's a liability." Sheila put one foot onto the bus step. "Munroe was never going to sit quiet forever." She stopped speaking and looked at him with a strange expression, as if she was only just starting to realise the storm was coming.

Paul was able to piece together more of the story over the next few days. His appetite whetted, he urged Sheila for details.

When the partnership formed, it was John who had the reputation as a hard man; his dad had been a famous gangster and in a lot of ways he used that to distinguish himself on the streets, becoming the leader of one of the city gangs. But he wasn't cut out for it and he sidestepped into business before he had time to get burned. Manny was younger and had been his right-hand man in the gang. He was known for his furious temper and propensity for violence; a robotic henchman who acted out John's instructions. Or so everyone thought.

When John made his bid for the bar, Manny offered to bankroll the shortfall, using the proceeds from a successful robbery on a post office. Manny went on to expand, using his profits to fund venture after venture. He intimidated officials into granting him licences. Used relentless violence to move in on different rackets in town. Going the extra distance, doing whatever his rivals wouldn't or couldn't. John, on the other hand, failed at everything he tried. He lost money gambling, drinking. Had a string of failed marriages. Sheila reckoned he'd finally run The Low Road into the ground: he was up to his eyeballs in debt and was about to lose the pub too.

"You want to know why I think Munroe keeps the place going?" Her voice cracked as she explained it to Paul. "I think it's so he can watch John suffer. Like everyone else, John thought Munroe was nothing more than a brainless thug. That was his big mistake. And Munroe's been making him pay for that ever since."

Every day, for a brief period during lunch, the pub was busy. Crowds of local office- and shop-workers would throng in for a cheap meal and a pint. It was the only part of the day when time flew past, usually in a whirl of miscalculations, lost orders and smashed glasses.

On the day that would be John's last shift at the pub, it was no different. Paul spent the hour after the lunchtime rush cleaning up the aftermath. When the plates were cleared and all seats turned upright, Sheila went on her break and Paul got stuck in to the row of empty glasses that covered the bar, waiting in line to be washed. There was only one regular left propping up the bar and another man in the corner popping pound after pound into the puggy machine.

Paul was hard at work when the man from the corner came over, sat at the bar and ordered a pint. He looked to be in his mid-fifties, his grey hair turning white in parts, day-old stubble on his chin. He was dressed in the cream and grey jacket-and-trouser combo of an older man, but underneath his build was solid. Wiry tendrils of hair sprouted where the top button of his shirt was undone.

"That thing ever pay out?"

"It does eventually. You need more change?"

"Nah, I'm done. Lost enough for today." Paul placed the pint in front of him. "John working today?"

"I don't know if you could call it working. He's down in his office. Who's asking?"

"Just a friend. Eddie." Eddie held out his large hand. "Nice to meet you."

"Paul." Wiping off dishwater, Paul took the man's hand, the skin rough and callused. It closed round his in a tight grip that crushed his knuckles.

"Worked here long?"

"A few weeks." Paul pulled away.

Eddie squinted at Paul as he took his pint. "Have we met before?"

"Don't think so."

"You seem familiar."

Paul looked at Eddie more closely. His tired blue eyes were sunk beneath bruised, puffy circles and the thin blue and purple thread veins scrawled across his red cheeks indicated a man who lived with stress and a fondness for the bottle. He was stocky, potentially fat, and his voice resonated with the deep echo of a priest's, as if amplified through a vaulted cathedral. Paul instantly disliked him.

Eddie shook his head in confusion. "Must be someone else. Is it OK if I head down?"

"Just let me check he's decent."

Paul phoned down and on the tenth ring John answered. He grumbled to himself for a moment before telling Paul to send Eddie down.

"On you go."

As he heard Eddie's steps descending the stone stairs to the office, Paul took out the keys and locked the front door. He hoped Sheila would come back from lunch a little late.

The regular was sipping on his pint and watched Paul with drunken confusion but said nothing, already half comatose.

"Watch the bar for me, Charlie. I'll only be gone a second. There better be some booze left on the gantry when I come back."

Paul knew a policeman when he saw one. The air was thick with the smell of bacon.

He tiptoed to the halfway point on the stone stairs, careful not to knock into anything or creak the old wooden banister. John's office was directly underneath him. He could see only the light from it, reaching across the dark hall, but even over the hum of machinery from the barrel room next door, he could hear them talking.

"Where else am I supposed to find you? At home? You've left me no choice. Bonus that I've caught you sober."

Paul stood listening, while keeping one eye on the door for Sheila.

"Carmichael, listen to me. I don't want to do this. I can't do this…" John sounded desperate, pleading with Carmichael.

Paul descended further, unable to believe what he was hearing.

"You don't have a choice."

Waiting for John's response, he heard a rattle at the door. He retreated back up the stairs. Charlie's head was under a stream of lager. Sheila was waiting at the door.

Paul walked up the drive of his two-bedroom semi-detached house in New Gorbals. He took out his key and was met by silence as the front door swung open. He breathed a sigh of relief. Stacy was probably down the road at her mother's – recently she'd been going there more and more. Tripping over laundry and baby toys, he made his way into the living room, his hip brushing the stair banister as he squeezed past.

An enormous playpen monopolised most of the floor. Dirty plates were piled on the coffee table, the smell of stale food clinging to the room. "Baby's First Birthday" cards still stood on the mantelpiece from the week before. Taking the phone from its cradle, Paul began lifting toys and throwing them into the pen, clearing a pathway to the window. He stepped over the smashed photo frame still on the floor from the night before; a large crack in the glass cut through the smiling photo of the happy trio taken on the day Stacy had returned from hospital. Leaning on the plastic sill, he switched on the phone and began to dial.

Manny's gravelly voice answered. "What do you want?"

"You said to contact you if anything interesting came up."

Paul fixed his eyes on the upturned supermarket trolley lying on his front lawn. Roots from the nearby hedge had sprouted around the bottom end of it, their long spindly fingers tightly wrapped around its rusting bars as if nature was claiming it back.

"And?"

"Something interesting came up."

"Well, don't be coy!"

Paul had been absently chewing on his lower lip and

accidently tore a small sliver off, the sudden bitter taste of blood tickling his tongue. "I think John was talking to a cop today." His voice was strained, alien.

"What made you think he was a cop?"

"I don't know. He had that look. I overheard them – John sounded pretty upset."

"Did you get a name?"

"He told me Eddie. But John called him Carmichael."

Manny was silent on the other end. For a moment Paul thought the connection had failed, then his voice came back on.

"Where are you?"

"At my house."

"Stay there. I'm going to come pick you up." With that he clicked off.

Paul was left, heart pounding, standing in his living room watching the moody grey sky turn to wrathful black.

He waited and waited, the blue glare of the television lighting the darkened room. He'd turned the volume up, way up; loud enough to drown out the pounding rain, obliterate the world outside the room.

Not long after midnight, the beams from a pair of car headlights shone through his window. He flicked the TV to mute and listened to the engine stop as the car pulled up outside his house. Stacy still hadn't come home. Probably didn't want to take the baby out in the rain. Paul left the TV on and slipped out, gently closing the latch behind him.

A pearl-grey Daimler Sovereign with tinted windows was waiting just outside his gate. The moonlight bounced off its smooth waxed body. It looked huge in the street, the cars outside his neighbours' houses diminished by its presence.

Paul took a moment to admire it before the door flew open. Manny was sitting in the back and patted the seat beside him. Paul climbed in and slammed the door a little too forcefully. The driver's light flicked off, but not before he'd caught a glimpse of the grinning face behind the wheel.

"Manny. Terry."

Terry gave a vague grunt of acknowledgement; in the five years Paul had known him, it was about as much as he'd ever heard him say.

Manny gave Paul a friendly pat on the shoulder. There was always something about his movements. Every action was a display of self-restraint.

Terry revved the engine and pulled out.

"How do you like my new motor?" Manny drew his hand down the walnut burl panelling. The smell of fresh leather and expensive aftershave teased Paul's nostrils.

"Beautiful." Paul had never seen anything like it.

"Did you see how low the suspension sits? That's the armoured plates. Kevlar 29. Bullet-proof, just like its owner."

Paul caught Terry's eyes watching him in the mirror. A shadow fell and his face loomed like a Baron Samedi mask.

The first time he'd met Terry, Paul had been a skinny sixteen-year-old. He'd shown up outside Manny's pool hall, armed only with a crumpled flier bearing its name, and had lumbered over on his crutches to where two of Manny's crew were standing smoking in the sun. "I'm here to see Mr Munroe," he said.

Buck-toothed "Bucky" Buchanan had stood toe to toe with him. He was in his mid-twenties then, small and wiry, with skin so grey it was almost blue, translucent like a fish.

His shaved head sprouted a subtle reddish glow and a thick scar reached from mouth to chin. "What would Mr Munroe want with a runt like you?"

He pressed his chest into Paul's. One of Paul's crutches slid and he nearly lost his balance.

The other heavy, Dickie Dunsmore, had laughed with the slack-jawed mania of a hyena. He was stockier, a bit older, his hewn face so badly scarred from acne it looked like it had been put through a cheese grater.

Terry had been waiting just inside the pool hall door; when he strode out towards them, Bucky Buchanan stood aside and Paul immediately wanted to run away and hide. Whereas Bucky and Dunsmore were all noise and bravado, their gold chains and impossibly camp attire just daring you to laugh at them, Terry was a wall of understated, brooding silence, with an equally terrifying face to match. One half of Terry's face was missing. Paul found out later that Terry had been caught in a bomb blast. Where they'd tried to rebuild his lip, he was left with his teeth bared, giving the appearance of a permanent grin. Together with the cavernous eye socket, it looked like one half of a grinning skull.

His mid-Ulster accent cracked with bitterness. "Who told you to come here?"

"Mr Munroe did." Paul held out the flier.

Terry's hand, thick like a bunch of bananas, took it from him. He gazed down at it. "What's your name?"

"Paul Dalziel."

Terry went to the phone inside the door. Paul couldn't hear what he said. Bucky Buchanan and Dunsmore circled him, ready to pounce.

Terry came back out. "Let him up, boys."

Grumbling, they stood aside.

Terry led him up the stairs, past the pool tables and into an office. Manny was waiting for him behind his desk. "I wondered if you'd show up," he said.

"I only just got out the hospital." Paul was shaking uncontrollably.

Manny watched him with scepticism. "Are you a smackhead or something?"

Even if he'd had a voice, Paul wouldn't have known what to say.

Manny's face darkened. "I'm asking if you take heroin?"

Better to be a reckless junkie or a liar? "I... I've never injected."

Manny digested the information. "Make sure you never do. I don't employ smackheads."

If he thought about it, that day marked the turning point. The boy he'd been then no longer existed. He looked at Manny and Terry now. He wasn't sure what the connection was between them. Over the years he had observed a loyalty that went beyond just hired muscle. Like a faithful pit-bull, Terry was always at Manny's side.

"That phone call you gave us today caused a bit of a stir." Both Manny and Terry laughed.

Paul read the road sign as they joined the motorway. "So John was talking to the polis?"

Manny nodded almost imperceptibly. "Detective Chief Inspector Carmichael. CID cunt. Likes squeezing my balls. When you're a high-profile businessman like myself it goes with the territory. Low-paid civil servants can't stand to see anyone else make a living."

The car rolled smoothly on. They were driving north.

"So what's going to happen?"

There was a moment of silence in which Manny and Terry exchanged glances.

"What has to happen when someone can't be trusted."

Behind Manny's head, Paul could see black telephone wires running in an endless stream against the night sky, the hypnotic lines loosening and slackening between pylons; closer, further, closer, but never quite close enough to meet. He kept an eye on the signs.

The leather squeaked when Paul moved in his seat.

They drove for over an hour. Paul didn't ask any more questions and Manny didn't give any more answers. He didn't need to. Paul would find out soon enough. He had an idea and it was easier not to hear it out loud. Either way, he was going with them.

They left the city behind. The further they went, the fewer streetlights there were. They were going deep into the countryside. When they finally pulled onto a dirt road, Terry flicked the headlights off and they crept along the gravel.

"I was worried something like this would happen with John. A dependency makes you vulnerable to men like Carmichael."

Paul caught sight of a darkened house at the end of the drive. A white van was parked outside, its lights switched off. The Daimler rolled up beside it and Terry cut the engine.

"OK, Paul, let's go."

Terry stayed in the car while Manny and Paul got out.

The earlier storm had carried off the clouds and the sky was crystal clear now. Manny led him by the light of the stars, past the house to a barn next door, the night sky a sequin-studded dome hemming them into the vast space.

It was dark inside the barn except for a faint yellow light to the rear of it, which they followed. As they neared, Paul could hear voices talking, laughing. He held his breath as he walked through the door.

A sickly light shone from a bare bulb hanging off a wooden beam. It cast an eerie glow over the bloodied figure beneath it; tied to a chair, head bent over, softly moaning, his chest moving lightly up and down. Dickie Dunsmore and Bucky Buchanan stood to attention.

"Good work, boys." Manny examined their handiwork with his professional eye. "Still some breath in him."
He lifted the prisoner's head. The man's face looked like it had been crudely carved out of wood, with indistinct lumps where his features were meant to be, seemingly painted with red and purple varnish. Teeth were scattered across the floor. Manny's heavy boots crunched over them. It was almost impossible to recognise in the blackened pulp, horrifically swollen and covered in congealed blood, the face of laughing, good-time publican John. But it was him. Paul fought the urge to vomit.

Manny spat on John's broken body.

"Sorry it had to end this way, old friend. But you always were a fucking pussy. Now you're a fucking grass."

Sounds started to emanate from the body. The gentle breathing changed to heavy panting. Sweat and blood dripped from his face. Strangled, choked coughs escaped him.

Manny turned to his men. "OK, go set up outside." He nodded his head towards Paul. "Give him the bat."

"What?" Paul swung round to face him.

"I told him to give you the bat."

Paul stepped back as Buchanan's gloved hand offered him the shiny aluminium baseball bat; he wore a buck-toothed grin on his pallid face and his skin was grey like a corpse's. When Paul didn't take it, it was shoved into his hand. The metal burned cold against his skin.

Dunsmore and Buchanan left the room.

Now it was just Paul and Manny alone with what was left of the whimpering John.

"I knew I wasn't making a mistake with you. What you did impressed me today." Manny moved around the room, checking its contents with bored curiosity. Paul looked down at the bat, which weighed surprisingly light in his hands. "You understand why I need you to do this?"

"Do what?" he asked in disbelief.

"Crush his skull."

Beside him John began to cry, his pleading words nothing more than babbles. A stream of urine formed a bloodstained puddle beneath him.

"I can't have people talking. I brought you here tonight so you could see what happens when they do. So you know. The pigs are going to be coming down hard on you from now on. So don't give them any hold over you."

Paul clenched his teeth and a thin film of sweat formed on his upper lip. "I can't do that, Manny." His two feet were fastened to the floor.

"You don't have a choice. I need to know I can trust you."

"You can trust me."

Manny sighed.

"Please don't make me do this."

"We don't have all night. If it makes it any easier, I told those boys out there to dig a grave big enough for two."

The words shot through Paul like an electric current. He looked at the weapon in his shaking hands, then back to Manny, who had lit a cigarette and was staring dead at him. He wasn't going to change his mind; he wasn't going to save him. Paul looked around: there was only one exit and Manny was standing in its way.

The pallid bone-white moon shone through the window.

"Go over there, take a couple of practice shots."

Paul walked limply into the corner. He began swinging the bat, softly at first, then with progressively more strength. He swivelled from the hips, the weight of his body packing power behind the swing. The bat made a loud swishing sound as it sliced the air.

"OK. Ready?" Manny said impatiently.

On unsteady legs, Paul walked up to John and measured the correct distance from his ear. He took deep breaths, the bat swaying back and forth just behind John's head.

John was braying like an injured animal; harsh, dry cries.

Paul measured once, twice.

Three times, then put the bat down.

"I can't."

Manny exhaled and nodded over Paul's shoulder. Paul whipped round, right into the cavernous face of Terry, standing silently a few feet behind him.

He backed away, bat still in hand.

"OK, Paul." Terry's words crunched in his mouth like broken glass. "Put that bat down and let's go for a walk."

He didn't say anything else. He just stood there, waiting, something like pity on his hideous face.

Paul looked up to the draughty roof, its missing rafters letting in the cold night air, then down to the brown pool beneath the dying man.

The silence seemed to last forever.

"Is this where you want it to end, Paul?"

There was something soothing in Terry's cracked and broken voice. He wasn't like Manny, who could commit extreme violence one minute and eat a sandwich the next. Terry understood the true cost of what you were taking away. Somehow that made it easier for Paul to answer no.

An odd state of calm came over Paul and he moved back towards John.

"All it takes is one good swing. Then it's over," he heard Manny say.

All his focus was on the bat in his hand. He stood once more behind John and placed the bat close to his ear. He could feel Terry's deathly presence behind him.

John's cries grew shrill.

Paul sucked in a lungful of air.

"Put the fucker out of his misery!" Manny growled.

Paul lifted the bat. Closed his eyes. Swung with every ounce of strength he had.

"You can tell a lot about a person from their shoes," John once told a group of them after hours during one of his lock-ins. "Look at me. Traditional brogues. Strong, reliable. A man's shoe. The shoe of a man. Little the worse for wear. Maybe not as functional as they used to be, ladies." Paul, not long started in the pub, had laughed along with the rest of them. "Jennifer, even in a pub you wear high heels; classy lady. You'll make a good wife for someone someday. Barney, your boots are always polished even when the rest of you is not. You used to be a military man. Sheila: comfortable, trustworthy shoes. Well trod. They're a pair of shoes that could tell you a thing or two. And Paul. Always in trainers. Is that so you can make a sharp exit? Ladies, can you trust someone who's always ready to run away?"

The bat smashed into John's skull, cracking it like an egg. His body flopped over lifelessly. Paul lifted the bat away; blood, bone, hair and lumps of brain were stuck to the shiny metal. His breath came out in short gasps, like someone crying, but there were no tears.

He looked down at his trainers, covered in blood.

There was nowhere left to run.

Manny flicked specks of blood and brain from his jacket. "That's why I get other people to do this. Can get messy."

Paul stared in a daze at the tortured body slumped in the chair. At the collapsed skull, the oozing matter.

Manny took the bat from him and patted his back. "Well done. There's a hose out back. You'll have to clean yourself. There's a change of clothes waiting for you in the back of the van."

Paul wandered to the back of the house, past the others, who, with shovels in hand, were digging a shallow grave for John's remains. The flames from their bonfire reached into the night sky. He found the hose and, like Manny had instructed, stripped and began to wash. The icy water was numbingly cold, but he didn't care. It was too dark to see the blood wash from him and down the drain. He rinsed his hair, holding the freezing stream over his head until he couldn't take it anymore. Then, reaching for the handle, he blindly switched the flow off and stood in the moonlight blinking the last of the water from his eyes.

Manny's figure appeared in the blurry half-light, standing there holding a plastic supermarket bag and, in his outstretched hand, a towel. Aware of his nakedness, Paul grabbed the towel and wrapped it tightly around himself. Manny's eyes lingered before he threw the bag at Paul's feet.

"Change into these."

Manny took another clear plastic bag from his pocket and shook it open. Then he picked up Paul's bloodstained clothes, put them in it and sealed the bag, never taking his eyes off Paul.

"Insurance," he said, before turning away. "See you in the car."

Stacy ambushed him the moment he walked through the door, channels of black mascara running down her cheeks, her hair tied messily in a bun, her body wrapped in the worn towelling dressing gown that had been her second skin since the baby.

"Where have you been? Who is she?"

The baby began screaming upstairs.

He brushed past her, ignoring her shrill demands.

"Paul! Whose clothes are they? Paul?"

He heard her crying behind him as he took the stairs two

at a time and slammed shut the bedroom door, pushing the chest of drawers in front of it.

The baby was standing in his cot, peering through the bars, tears and snot on his little red face. Paul ran over and picked him up, holding him tight to his chest, smelling his soft fuzzy hair.

Stacy's feet banged up the steps too. She beat her fists on the door. "Paul! Let me in. The baby's crying – he needs feeding. Please!"

It was an hour before she finally managed to force her way in to find Paul, babe in arms, staring out of the window.

CHAPTER TWELVE

"Curtains shut all day, all night. It used to be your neighbours would check on you if your curtains were shut all day, all night." Annie almost sang it. A slice of amber light from the streetlamp shone through as she peeped out the window. "But no one cares anymore. People lie dead for weeks in this city. Only the smell of rotting flesh and the maggots bring concern to the door."

She paced manically. The odour of captivity hung in the room.

"Is that a threat?"

"It's been twenty-four hours, Paul, and not a single person's tried to contact you." She waved his mobile in the air. "Would anyone even miss you if you were gone?"

He glared at her as she crossed the room to the mantelpiece, where she rested her elbow; her foot bobbed up and down.

"How did you find me?" His phlegm-filled words caught in his throat. The coughing that followed caused the tendons in his body to squeal like over-wound guitar strings. He waited for the snap that didn't come and the fit passed.

"It wasn't difficult. I knew you were due for release, I made some enquiries."

He eased back into the least painful position he could

find. "You knew what I was inside for and still invited me into your home? That was brave."

"Why do you think I took precautions?" she spat.

"Still…" He smiled. A weighty pause ensued before he spoke again. "I already told the polis I don't know anything."

"Liar!" Her face was scrunched like a hideous gargoyle.

She started towards him. Paul immediately clamped down, expecting her to strike him. She stopped in front of him, looming over his chair. He cranked his neck up to look at her.

"My sister was involved with a volatile thug with a history of violence. Who worked for murderers, associated with murderers. Was a murderer. She disappears the day you go into prison and you don't know anything about it? In nine years she hasn't contacted anyone, accessed her bank account, registered for employment. Missing persons ads, public appeals for information – every possible connection's been followed up, and still nothing. You don't just disappear off the face of the earth."

"People disappear every day," he answered.

The blow finally landed, hard against his head. He lolled forward, then shook off the daze. When he looked up again she was back on her perch at the window, her body resting against the sill. The curtains were pulled tight against hooks ready to snap off the rail. She gripped the windowsill with one hand, restraining herself while the other clenched against her breastbone.

"So I knew Lena," he shouted over to her. "A lot of people knew Lena." His ear burned where she'd hit him.

"She was fourteen," she hissed. "You groomed her,

led her astray."

"I led her astray?" The veins in his temples bulged. "Alcoholic mother, absent father, steroids-abusing stepfather. A sister who she never saw. What chance did she have? I was the only one who cared for her. You haven't got a clue."

"An animal like you isn't capable of love." She stood up, close to shouting. "Obsession, possession, control. That's all you know about. She was defenceless. Worshipped you. Would have done anything for you. And you destroyed her. I remember you at the funeral. I was so scared. She was scared of you. She was trying to get away from you!"

Annie was gripping and ungripping her fingers, agitatedly chewing the inside of her mouth. "The police say they've exhausted all their lines of enquiry. But I'm willing to do what the police won't," she said coldly. "I've resigned myself to the worst. It may be a confession you give. But whatever happened, I'm going to make you tell me."

She turned to check through the curtain and he could only see the back of her head.

"So you hunted me down?" His voice was low and tremulous with anger.

"That's right." She nodded, snapping back around. "Because I knew that would be the only thing you'd understand. Threats. Violence. It's the language you speak. You're a dangerous animal and you need to be caged."

"And then what?" He almost laughed. "You're going to let me go? I'm curious. Like you said, I'm a dangerous animal. A convicted murderer. What do you think's going to happen once these ropes come off?"

She crossed her arms over her chest, both feet

square on the floor.

"C'mon. Talk to me in my language. Tell me you know what you've got yourself into. How far are you going to go to make me talk?"

"I've gone this far." She wavered a little but stood her ground.

Paul shook his head contemptuously. "I've been starved before. Tortured before. You think you're going to break me? Think you're ready for me? You're not, little girl."

"We'll see."

Paul watched the determined set of her jaw, the way her small hand crept up her neck. He pictured his fingers around it. Squeezing.

"Do you though?" He imagined his thumb on her jugular. "Do you see how this is going to end? Because I do. If you don't untie me now, only one of us is leaving here alive."

"Is killing so easy for you?"

"I know how far I'm willing to go. Even if I don't want to, I'll maul you, I'll tear you to shreds, because you're right, I am an animal. Go head to head with me only if you're willing to kill me."

Suddenly Annie walked out of the room. With long, purposeful strides she whisked past him. Paul tore his wrists against the ropes, fighting to break free. A second later the door banged against the wall as it flew open. She came back in and stood in front of him, a knife in her hand.

"If you don't tell me what you did to her, I swear to God I'll chop you up a piece at a time."

"Go on then. Cut me."

The knife shook in her hand, inching closer.

"Go on, slice my arm. Even up the odds a little. Show me you mean it. GO ON!" he taunted. "If you cut me, I'll tell you about Lena."

With a thrusting movement too fast to register, she slashed his lower left arm. Only when the knife fell from her hands and clinked onto the floor did he realise what she'd done. He knew it was shock that stopped him feeling it, but the pain would arrive soon. He watched his blood drip from the wound, saw the rusty droplets smeared on the blade at his feet.

Annie had collapsed onto all fours beside him, her chest rasping in breathless heaves.

Paul gripped his hands closed, turning his knuckles white. He was energised by the sight of his own blood; his chest swelled, every inch of him tingled.

Annie rolled into a crouch, her chin resting in her hand, her nostrils flaring.

"Don't say I didn't warn you," he panted. "The hardest part of killing someone is having to live with it afterwards."

She flashed a look of hatred up at him. With the aid of the couch arm, she shakily got to her feet. Reaching for a cloth off the radiator, she came towards him and dried off the blood on his lower arm. "I think I'll manage."

She inspected the open wound for a while, then, when she was done, she walked back to her seat in the armchair and crossed her legs. For the first time since she'd taken him hostage, Paul had to admit that the little girl was serious.

CHAPTER THIRTEEN

Ten years ago

It was a busy Thursday night at The Low Road and the bar was crowded, but he still spotted Lena the moment she walked through the heavy wooden door. He watched from behind the bar as she mingled with a crowd he'd seen in there before. They worked at an alternative clothing shop across the road, where he'd been promised a discount if he ever went in. But he'd never seen her with them. He hadn't seen her since that day in the park two years before, the day she'd had her picture taken and had been all set to move in with the dental student.

Lena fitted right in to the picture-perfect clique of urban chic. Her clothes had an effortless appearance that must have taken hours of planning: an artistically faded top, with strategically placed holes, layered over another carefully chosen patterned number. Her straight hair and blunt fringe had been meticulously set, the thick black eyeliner above her lashes drawn on with the steadiest of hands.

Paul waited until she broke away from the group before coming out from behind the bar. He cut her off before she made it to the counter.

"Excuse me, miss, management requires identification."

She prepared to look affronted. Then she looked more closely, realised it was him and tutted in mock annoyance.

He took the provisional driving licence she produced from her bag and laughed. "Little Lena's finally turned eighteen!"

"Six months ago." She pointed triumphantly to the date of birth, as Paul pretended to search the card for flaws.

"Happy belated birthday," he said and pulled her in for a giant hug. He could feel her arms squeezing tightly around his waist. "This calls for a celebration. I'd like to buy you and your friends a drink."

He reached into the fridge with an air of authority and took out a bottle of champagne. He made sure Lena noticed how the other staff danced around him and hoped she would quickly realise how far he'd come since they'd last met. How his clothes set him apart from everyone else in the bar – incongruously clean-cut in his fitted trousers and polished brogues. His voice was different too, more appropriate to the new circles he moved in, his distinctive nasal twang now lost beneath a smooth, assured articulation.

He presented the bottle to her in a bucket of ice and she accepted it graciously.

"How many glasses?"

Lena glanced back at the group she had come in with, some of whom were looking around for her impatiently. "There's five of us, but six if you have time to join us?"

"Course I have." He casually reached down and with one hand picked up some flutes. "I'm the boss."

"Hi everyone, this is Paul, an old friend. He owns this place," Lena announced as they reached the couches in the corner where her group were sitting.

"Actually, I run it for a friend." Paul laughed and placed the flutes on their table.

"Vampires – sucking on the fruits of living labour," a tall, mannish girl with cropped brown hair said. There was a ripple of laughter around the group. "You joined the conversation at an interesting point."

Paul felt his balls shrivel and forced a smile.

Lena found a seat between the two men of the group and Paul tried to figure out which one she was with as he poured the champagne.

"Moët et Chandon, extra brut. Very nice," the handsome lantern-jawed male said as his glass fizzed. "It means extra dry."

"Yes, I know." Paul smiled again as he found a perch on the arm of one of the girls' chairs. The other guy was an older skinhead with leather motorcycle trousers and tribal tattoos. Definitely him, Paul decided.

Lena began introducing each of them with a catalogue of interesting facts. "This is Ali." She gestured to the skinhead. "He used to live on the streets in Paris. Made his living as a graffiti artist. You can still see his tag in some of the tunnels on the Metro. Gabrielle..." The mannish one waved. "She travelled round Patagonia last year photographing volcanoes and some of the indigenous tribes. She won awards. Claudia..." The girl in the chair he was perched on looked round and smiled. "... is from Germany. She's over to improve her English for her PhD studies. And Jared is a model. He's worked for H&M."

They exchanged some nice-to-meet-yous.

"It's really made me think there's a whole big world

out there." Lena continued talking rapidly while the others assumed expressions of magnanimous indulgence. "And I'm missing it hanging around in this dump. I'm going to work in the shop until I have enough money to just go. Travel the world. London first, maybe Rome next."

"You should!" the rest chimed in, and then came a long list of recommendations that covered most of the globe.

"And what about you, Paul?" Ali interjected over them.

"Yeah!" Lena was brimming with enthusiasm. "If you could go anywhere, where would you go?"

"Scotland. I like Scotland."

"Where in Scotland? It's a big country," Gabrielle huffed haughtily.

"Glasgow's pretty alright."

Lena laughed uncertainly, not sure if he was joking, a little deflated. The group threw a few more questions at him, trying to engage him on politics, quoting the names of writers and philosophers and making obscure musical references. He knew nothing about art and cared even less about politics. He knew about making money, but that seemed to be the biggest deal-breaker of all with the group; enigma solved, they moved their attention to something else. When they started discussing female genital mutilation versus the right to religious freedom, he knew it was time to go.

Before he did, he stood up and proposed a toast. "To Lena. All grown up." He hoped he would get the chance to speak to her on her own later. "To your success!" Their eyes locked and she smiled; for a split second they shared a small moment, unnoticed by anyone else.

Until that night, he'd measured the bar's success in the

monthly reports, in the figures in the ledger, the bare fact of numbers. Now he only cared how it measured up in her eyes. From his vantage point in the centre of the room he was able to take in just how many customers were crammed onto the bar's fashionably battered sofas, just how perfect the original artwork was for the walls. He drank it in with a strange mix of guilt and pride. Guilt for those nights when he'd been with Stacy but was thinking about Lena. Pride for how good it had felt to tell Lena he was the boss. Guilt because it was no longer possible to imagine the threadbare old regulars who had once perched there on church-hall chairs, or to pretend that he might turn around and find John or Sheila walking through the door. And pride because for the first time that fact pleased him.

For a week after John's death, Paul didn't leave his bedroom. He had lain there in a fevered state, trying to forget the image of John's broken skull, the bat matted with hair and bone, unable to rid his head of the crunching sound.

The first day, Stacy called in sick for him. She came back into the bedroom and passed on Sheila's annoyance that John hadn't shown up for his shift either. Must have been a late one last night, she'd grumbled. No doubt he'd roll in around noon, eyes bloodshot. Paul pulled the covers over his face. The next day when Stacy phoned in sick for him again she reported that John still hadn't shown up. Sheila was worried he might have fallen down when drunk, banged his head; she was calling round the hospitals. Had Paul spoken to him?

Paul didn't bother to answer. The next day, same thing – did John have a girlfriend? Was he on a bender? Paul fixed his eyes on a spot outside the window, trying not to think about the fact that John wouldn't show up the following day either, or the one after that. Or ever again.

On the sixth day, Manny called. Paul took the phone, anticipating the worst.

"Go back to work," he was told, and that was the end of that.

The next day, when he crossed the road, the familiar doors of the pub in sight, he saw the body of a dead bird lying mangled on the tarmac. His stomach lurched as vomit rose in his throat. Choking it back, he hurried to the pub, pushing his way through the door. He could sense the few morning customers watching him as he walked the endless distance to the bar, his legs weak and heavy. Behind the bar, a red-eyed Sheila offered a brisk hello then busied herself cleaning. He nodded at the customer peering at him over his newspaper and received an angry glare in return; then the man moved to a seat in the corner.

"Any word?" he asked Sheila.

Sheila continued cleaning. "Nothing," she said, without turning to look at him. She didn't ask Paul where he'd been.

He read more than worry for John's wellbeing in the hostility of people around him. He could feel himself coming apart. By lunch the tension was too much to bear; he grabbed his coat and left. His mind swirling, he wandered aimlessly through the streets, bumping into shoppers, parked cars, searching for the nearest route out of the city centre. He found himself crossing down to the banks of the Clyde.

The air was colder near the river. There were fewer people. Resting his arms on the railings, he stared into the water and felt completely hollow. It ran like brown treacle, creasing and dimpling, lapping lazily off the side. He stayed there for an hour, watching the steady stream. The consistency of the rippling bubbles soothed his burning temples until eventually he was able to drag himself back.

When he re-entered The Low Road, Paul was met with a scene that nearly set him running for the door. It took all his discipline to walk towards it, like a boxer turning into a punch.

Sheila was sitting on a chair in the snug, at the front corner of the bar. Her face was crumpled; her hand clasped her mouth, stifling her crying. The bar was unmanned. Standing over her was a figure familiar to Paul because he'd met him once before; except this time he was dressed in a suit, clean-shaven, his grey hair clipped. Paul looked at him wide-eyed, trying not to panic. His heart was beating so fast he felt like he would pass out.

Carmichael's eyes were boring into him. Paul glanced around the bar. There were only four or five customers spread out in booths, but they were all looking over.

"I'm afraid I've got some news about... John."

Hearing the name knocked the wind out of him. Sheila looked up and cried out, saving him from Carmichael's glare. "They found his car parked up near the Erskine Bridge," she yelped. "They think he's jumped, Paul!"

Paul placed a consoling hand on Sheila's back. It felt natural to be comforting his colleague, and it helped him control his anxiety. A whisper of suicide rushed through the bar, rippling the back of his neck like a cold wind of relief. Paul closed his eyes.

"Sheila, it's OK. It's OK." He rubbed her back as she trembled like a tiny sparrow.

She held up her hands, trying to grasp some sense from the air around her. "Why?" she whispered.

Paul couldn't stand to look at her. Needing space, he started to walk to the bar to get himself and Sheila a drink, but Carmichael stepped into his path.

"We're looking into the *possibility* of suicide." Carmichael placed a detaining hand on Paul's chest then pushed him forcefully back. "Let me," he said.

Paul stood still, watching as Carmichael went behind the bar, picked up a glass and filled it with water from the tap. He sensed that a gauntlet had been thrown down and he suddenly wanted Carmichael gone.

He watched as Carmichael brought the glass round and handed it to Sheila. "There you go, dear." She took it weakly.

"Sheila was telling me you've been sick. Anything serious?"

Paul could feel his anger rising. "Food poisoning," he answered sharply. Carmichael's visit wasn't just to bring them the bad news. It was for an interrogation.

Sheila looked up at him.

"When was it you came down with that? Monday, was it?" Carmichael said. "I suppose, now I think of it, that was the day John went missing – the same day? Actually, I was in here that day. Do you remember me?"

"Your face seems familiar." The colour drained from Paul's cheeks. His tongue stumbled over the words. Carmichael was the one in charge of this situation.

"I asked to see John."

"Yeah, I think so. It's a bar. A lot of people come in."

Carmichael flashed his warrant card, his face grim. "Cut the bullshit."

Paul stopped dead.

"Why don't we talk?" Carmichael motioned to the front door.

"What about?"

"In private."

Paul scratched his neck uncomfortably. Sheila was looking back and forth between them in confusion. Carmichael began to walk and Paul saw no other choice but to follow him out onto the street. He knew Sheila was watching them through the window.

Carmichael lit a cigarette and offered one to Paul, who waved it away.

"What do you want, Inspector?"

Carmichael moved his face close to Paul's. "I want to know what happened to John."

Paul clenched his facial muscles, angered now by the filth before him. The familiar pangs helped him regain his composure. "I thought you just told us."

"Drove his car up to the Erskine Bridge? Most likely threw himself into the river?"

Paul shrugged.

"Do you believe that... what's your name again? Paul... Dalziel?"

"That's what it sounds like... Inspector... Carmichael?"

Paul's shoulders tensed under Carmichael's scrutiny. Carmichael flicked away his cigarette. He glanced away casually then quickly spun back towards him. Paul felt a crunch as Carmichael shoved him against the glass front of the pub, smashing his head. Carmichael's elbow was crushing Paul's windpipe.

"Who did you talk to?" Carmichael shouted in his face.

People in the street were stopping to stare at the commotion. Sheila came to the pub door, watching them in confusion. Paul kicked out impotently; Carmichael's arm had fastened him to the glass.

"You little shit. I know who you work for." His spittle flew in Paul's face as he struggled to break free. Paul kicked out again. "Did you tell him? Did you run home and phone Munroe?"

Carmichael pressed hard against his throat and gave one last shove before letting him go. Paul doubled up, gasping for air.

"I'm watching you." Carmichael pointed a finger in his face.

"What... the... fuck? I'll have your... FUCKING... job for that."

"Scum. I'm coming after you."

Carmichael marched off. Paul started after him but stopped himself and instead doubled back, bursting past Sheila back into the pub. From the horror-stuck faces of everyone inside, he knew they had heard. He paced in the middle of the floor, not sure where to go, what to do.

"What are you all looking at!" he shouted.

A strained hush fell on the room, broken by the click of Sheila's feet on the floor as she sidestepped round him like he was some kind of dangerous animal. She picked up her coat and bag, watching his every move with tears in her eyes. When she was safely at the door she spat at him and backed out of the pub. It landed on the floor at his feet. Chairs overturned as others followed her out.

Paul slammed the bar with his fist and knocked over

a stool. Kicking anything else that got in his way, he went behind the counter, grabbed a bottle and poured himself a shot. Whisky splashed over the bar. He watched the tremor of his hand as he held up the glass, then downed it. He banged the empty glass on the bar and poured another. It felt good, the quick sharp flick of his fingers as he upturned the glass, the liquid burning his insides on the way down, leaving behind a hazy numbness.

He drank and poured, drank and poured until he couldn't take any more. His stomach lurched and he vomited into the sink. Wiping the spit from his mouth with the back of his hand, he reached down and turned on the tap. He held his fingers under the flow until they were numb with cold. Then he ran them through his hair and over his sweat-streamed face. He rubbed his eyes with both fists until they smarted and stung. As white dots appeared before him, he placed two steadying hands on the bar and let out a large sob. He knew he had to get out of the upturned bar. In a daze, he began gathering his stuff, switching off lights and machinery.

When he stepped out to switch off the light in the basement, he hovered just inside the door leading downstairs. The quiet drone of the machinery sounded like whispering voices stirring in the chill air. He flicked the light off and banged shut the door, hurriedly leaving the pub, locking in the murmurs and creaks that lingered within its walls.

When Paul told him about Carmichael's visit, Manny laughed. Paul had been expecting a more concerned response.

"But he says he thinks John's death wasn't suicide. Says he's coming after me."

Manny sat back in his chair, amused. "C'mon, you've got to have thicker skin than that. He's messing with you. Rattling your cage. Seeing what you'll give away." He cocked his head to the side as he shrugged away Paul's problems.

Paul tried one more time. "I just don't think it's a good idea for me to be there right now."

"Well you have to. Trust me." Manny leaned his elbows on the desk, his hands in the air.

Paul stiffened. "I don't understand—"

"You don't need to understand." Manny cut him off. One hand went up, suspended in the air, the index finger pointing directly at Paul. The conversation was over. Paul swallowed the bitter taste in his mouth.

Manny winked and stood up behind his desk. Paul followed with his eyes as Manny went to the coat stand and lifted off his coat and scarf. When he turned back round to face Paul his mood seemed jovial.

"Let's go for a walk."

Paul got up from his chair, a tingle running down his spine as he remembered the last time someone had said those words to him.

There was an hour or so of daylight left. The two men walked abreast, their pace fast but not hurried. Paul was several inches taller than Manny, but Manny had a way of making everyone around him feel small. They walked in silence along Clyde Street, down towards the Saltmarket. Manny marched ahead as they neared the entrance to Glasgow Green.

Paul hesitated momentarily at the threshold of the park. He waited a second or two before he stepped over it, following Manny in.

It was late summer and the leaves were beginning to lose their green to emerging speckles of orange and brown. In the delicate twilight the park was beautiful, but in a short while, when darkness fell, it would invite all the dangers of the night. The Green was well known as a place where men could meet discreetly, but not all encounters were consensual. Thieves, murderers and drunks all roamed there after dark. Paul didn't want to be there any longer than he had to. He could see Manny breathing deeply, savouring the crisp August air. Together they continued along the path. The sky was purple; a breeze was rustling the fallen leaves. When they were deep in the park Manny sat down on a bench to rest. He offered Paul a cigarette. Paul accepted and moved closer, settling on the bench beside him. As they lit up, Manny stared off into the middle distance.

"When I think back to the night I found you here, it makes me realise how far you've come."

Paul shuddered. His eyes fell to his shoes and to Manny's booted feet beside them. He waited for Manny to continue.

"There are some legal issues with the ownership. I need to maintain the status quo, avoid any suspicion while I wait for all this to blow over. That's why I need you there."

Manny had never spoken so plainly to him before and never about his business.

"The paperwork's all there. Fortunately John passed on everything to his wife before he decided to go missing. But now is not the time to start harassing the grieving widow. Once she realises all she's been left with is a heap of debts and a worthless flea pit of a pub, she'll be knocking on my door. And I'll be there to give her a generous pension. Take the problem off her hands for a fair price. All women are whores, Paul, never forget that," he said flatly.

Paul found himself nodding. A contemplative silence followed.

"What happened with John was necessary. You proved yourself, and not just to me." Manny turned to him. His quiet timbre forced Paul to listen more intently. "We grew up on the same streets, you and me. In my day it was rougher, more physical; you had to be tougher in a way. Take what you wanted with brute force. But it's a different world now and I see young guys like you... you've got different talents. Hard – I'm not saying you're not – but with other skills too. Skills that I can use. You're smart, Paul. And I need smart guys. I need you in there, running it. Do you think you can keep it together?"

"Yes," Paul said and he meant it.

There was the flicker of some kind of life in the black beads that were Manny's eyes. He put a hand on Paul's knee and shook it, supportively.

Just days ago, Manny had threatened to kill him, but that fact seemed less important than the help and protection he was offering now, and that he'd given him in the past. Paul could never forget that.

He took one last look around the haunting expanse of the park as the two of them got up to leave.

In the weeks that followed his chat with Manny, Paul threw himself into his work. The more he concentrated on improving The Low Road, the less time he had to dwell on other things.

On the first day, he'd faced a mutiny – loyalty to John and

Sheila. It had been expected. Paul followed Manny's advice to scalp the first few troublemakers, and the others then fell into line, albeit grudgingly. He made a point of taking up the slack himself until replacements could be found.

Drinking after hours was next to go; free drinks for staff and friends after that. He made sure that everyone was meticulous in recording spillages and beer wasted in drip trays, and he asked Manny to fit two new computerised tills. When money was still going missing he installed a camera behind the bar. More staff left in protest but somehow Paul kept it going. In time he got new workers who neither knew nor cared about the pub's history. Slowly, the books began to show a small profit, enough for a paint job and the odd piece of furniture.

His first attempts at theme nights failed miserably. There were times he wanted to give up completely. Then he thought about a battle of the bands: he had seen it working in other pubs. Using a former client, he got a good deal at a local recording studio to give as a prize. The old regulars stopped going because of the noise, but bit by bit, through word of mouth, a new crowd started coming. Younger, with more disposable income. The people who played in the bands at the weekend started showing up mid-week; one of them was commissioned to illustrate the walls. Day by day The Low Road took on their character, became their space.

Finally, his decision to let the kitchen staff go was what turned the place around. He used the money to buy in better stock: spirits that didn't taste of turpentine, real brand mixers. One of the staff suggested they invent their own cocktail. Paul came up with the Moonshiner, a lethal combination of all the cheapest spirits, which he sold in jam jars. It proved popular and slowly the crowds grew larger.

But the better life was going in the pub, the worse things went in his personal life. In The Low Road everything was straightforward; everything outside was so complicated by comparison. At night when he went home he wiped all messages. He no longer wanted to see people. Not Stacy, not even Jack. One night she took the baby and left. There had been tears, he'd tried half-heartedly to stop them, but in his heart he knew it was for the best. This time he didn't think they would be back. At night, his only companion was a crushing pain in his chest that never left.

After he'd toasted Lena with champagne in front of her friends, Paul didn't see her again for the rest of the night. He was needed behind the bar and had been occupied until close. By the time he had the chance to look round, their table was cleared. She and her friends had gone.

It took longer than usual to tidy up. When the bar was finally ready and set up for the next day he was grumpy, exhausted and desperate to get home so he could do what he did every night these days: drink heavily while brooding silently. He was due in for the monthly stock-take the next morning He waited, finger poised over the light switch, while Mary, the barmaid whose turn it was to help with the tidy-up, did a final check in the toilets.

He tapped his fingers on it once, twice.

The door of the Ladies opened with a whoosh of air.

"Paul!" Mary hung her head out, her teeth gritted in annoyance. "There's a semi-conscious girl in here."

Paul groaned. Why was it always on his watch?

A pair of knee-high boots were sticking out from under the cubicle door, the worn leather exposing the plastic inside the heel. He stalked over. She was sitting on the floor, her back against the stall wall, her skirt rolled up around her waist. The top of her purple thong reached just about the waistband of her black tights. Her head was bowed and limp, but he could still see it was Lena.

He bent down on his knees beside her. Pushing her black hair, slick with sweat, from her face, he opened her eyelid. "Lena?"

She moaned and pushed his hand away. "Lena, it's me. Paul."

"You know her?" Mary was hovering behind him. "She's pretty wasted. Do you think a taxi would take her?"

"Not in this state."

Mary lifted Lena's purse and went through it while Paul tried to get her conscious. "No address. Should I get the police to pick her up?"

"No." He placed the back of his hand on her fevered forehead. "Lena, have you taken anything?"

He began to put her in the recovery position. She struggled against him, her arms flailing. Breaking free from his grip, she lunged for the bowl and threw up down the toilet. Paul held her hair back. When she was finished she slumped back against the stall wall. He helped pull her top down where it had rolled up and fixed her skirt.

"Where is everyone, where am I?" Black mascara and eyeliner clogged her watering eyes as she blinked, trying to focus.

"They've all left. You're still in the bar. In the toilet."

"They all left?" Her lips quivered and she began to cry.

"C'mon, we need to get you up." He put his hands under her armpits and tried to haul her to her feet. "Lena, did you take anything else?" he asked as he tried to heave her up.

She shook her head.

"Can you stand up?"

She shook her head again but got to her feet after some protesting.

Mary helped take some of the weight. "What're you going to do with her?" she grumbled as she put one of Lena's arms over the back of her shoulders, while Paul took the other.

"It's OK. I know where she lives, I'll drop her home."

Mary looked at him dubiously. "Are you sure that's a good idea? I just mean… Drunk girl…"

"For fuck's sake," he seethed. "You'd rather leave her with a taxi driver? Just help me get her to my car!"

His car was parked on the side street next to The Low Road so they didn't have far to walk. Town was busy, there were people all around, but no one paid any attention to the pair carrying the profoundly drunk girl. Mary helped him get Lena in the front seat. Paul slammed shut the passenger door and marched round to his side.

"OK, goodnight then!" Mary yelled as he jumped in.

"Goodnight." He didn't offer her a lift home or thank her for her help. Out of the rear passenger window he watched her storm off and felt an immediate sting of regret. He could make it up to her tomorrow, let her leave early. As he put the keys in the ignition, his thoughts returned to Lena. He activated the passenger window until it was fully open. Cool air blew into the car, rousing her from her stupor.

Flicking on his headlights, he checked his blind spot and pulled out.

"Lena, I don't let anyone smoke, drink or eat in this car. So I'm not going to let anyone throw up either. OK? That's what the window's for."

She nodded. They drove in silence until they completed the short journey to his flat. He found a space near his front door. As soon as he switched off the engine, she threw the door open and vomited into the street. He left her to it for a few minutes. It seemed to sober her up a little and when she stood up she was able to walk on her own to his front door.

His flat was on the ground floor so they didn't have many steps to climb. He'd been there for about six months, since his split with Stacy, but Lena was his first visitor. He hadn't even got around to emptying all the boxes yet. They were spread out on the hall floor, essential items having been dug out and left beside them in small pools of ordered chaos.

Paul switched on the living-room light and they tripped over to the couch in the corner. A large television and overstuffed beanbag not yet moulded for comfort were the only other pieces of furniture in the room. He sat Lena down while he rummaged through the boxes in the hall, looking for spare sheets. When he came back in, it pained him to see her already asleep, her hair and face stuck to the fresh leather. He pulled off her boots, threw a cover over her and forced a towel beneath her head.

After checking her breathing, which seemed fine, he finally made it to the kitchen and poured himself a four-finger measure of vodka with just enough flat cola to colour it brown. Taking the bottle of vodka with him, he went back into the living room and flopped onto the solid beanbag, which collided with his body like a Mitre football. Eventually, with persistence and hard elbows, he found a comfortable position and lay back, quietly ruminating while drinking his vodka, soothed by the methodical rhythm of her gentle breathing.

A few hours later, when the alarm buzzed him awake, soggy and sore and feeling as if he hadn't slept at all, he found Lena lying in the same position on his couch. She groaned into her cover until he switched off the alarm, but she didn't wake. The towel was lying on the floor.

The hiss of the kettle as Paul made his morning coffee didn't stir her and nor did the clatter of drawers and doors as he showered and dressed. Before he left, he wrote a short note explaining where she was and left it beside the bowl with a half-empty box of paracetamol and a mug of water. He didn't love the idea of leaving her alone in his flat, but what was the worst that could happen? She'd find out how empty his life was? That, or leave a fag lit and burn the house down.

The pub was mercifully quiet and the day passed without incident. The staff sensed his irritability and moved around him warily. At nine o'clock, he handed over to the team leader without ceremony and started for home.

It was dark by the time he pulled into his street. He wasn't expecting her to still be there, but from the end of the path he could see that the lights were on in his flat, the curtains drawn. He approached with apprehension. Slowly, he opened the door.

The first things he noticed were his boxes arranged neatly

in one corner and above them her freshly washed top drying over the hall radiator. He went into the living room and found the clothes horse out, the sheet and towel she had used the night before hanging over it. He felt a stab of annoyance that he couldn't quite explain. In the bathroom the toilet flushed, the snib clicked and the door opened. Lena came into the living room, her hair wet, wearing one of his jumpers.

She jumped when she saw him, then crumpled with breathless laughter, her hand clenched in front of her chest. "Paul! I didn't hear you come in!"

"Hi." His eyes fell on his top.

She looked down, her smile unwavering. "I hope you don't mind," she said breezily. "I'm just waiting for my top to dry. Do you want a cup of tea? Coffee? I don't think there's any milk in. I would have gone to the shops but I didn't have a key to get back in and I wanted to see you, to thank you for last night. I don't usually do that…" She bit her lip, pulling a strand of her hair. "Sorry."

"Don't worry, we've all been there." He looked around dubiously. "Make yourself at home."

She continued with artificial playfulness. "I tidied up a little."

"So I see. You didn't have to do that." He sat on the couch and stretched his legs.

"I like your flat."

He nodded.

She came over and perched on the arm of the couch. "I don't see any toys. Where's the baby?"

Paul exhaled loudly. "He's living with his mum."

"Aw…" She cocked her head to one side in an exaggerated

gesture of sympathy.

"I don't want to talk about it."

She moved onto the couch beside him. "Your bar is great. It's really good to see you doing so well."

He smiled uneasily.

"You seemed annoyed."

"No, I'm just tired. I didn't get much sleep."

"Are you sure? You seem grumpy."

He looked at her and frowned. Her over-familiarity was setting off alarm bells. "What do you expect? I found you in a toilet. I had to take you to my home, lie you on my couch, covered in sick. I was up half the night trying to make sure you didn't choke to death."

She moved closer to him, her hand moving up his arm. "I said sorry. I'll make it up to you."

Her big eyes were staring at him, imploring. He looked at her beautiful face and felt a powerful desire igniting inside him. Part of him had always known it would happen with Lena. When the time was right. She leaned on his knee and pushed her lips onto his. For a moment he savoured her soft mouth. It should have been perfect. She climbed up onto him and kissed him harder. He was still too wound up, felt pressure on his chest. He thought of how she'd been the night before in the bar – urbane and sophisticated, too good for him until she'd smiled and suddenly he'd felt anchored, steady. He didn't feel that now. It should have been perfect, but wasn't. He thought of the time in the park, her filled-to-the-brim bags, of the wreck he'd found in the toilets. He thought of his tidied flat and how much it annoyed him. How comfortable she'd made herself. He could feel his chest deflating. She was kissing him, it was what he wanted. But still he pressed her away. Once again he knew it wasn't right.

"Where are you living these days?" he asked uneasily.

"Here and there." She laughed nervously.

Her dissembling made his heart ache. "Alone?"

"With one of the guys from the shop."

"One of the ones that left you last night?"

She hesitated. "Yes."

"How's that working out?"

She didn't answer and looked away.

With a flare of anger he got up from the couch. "You only had to ask, Lena, if you need somewhere to stay. I didn't need the charade."

"I wasn't doing that."

"C'mon. Don't treat me like I'm one of them. Is it always that easy? A flutter of the eyelashes and you're getting drawer space?"

She was quiet, didn't protest, a sheepish expression on her face. Paul couldn't look at her and stood up, turning away.

"I'm going to turn in, I'm exhausted. You can crash on the couch if you want."

Overwhelmed with tiredness, he went into his bedroom and closed the door, feeling wrecked; alone, adrift at sea, wanting something but no longer sure what, except unconsciousness. Flicking off the light, he crawled onto the temporary mattress he'd been sleeping on for the last six months and climbed into his sleeping bag. He lay staring at the blank walls for a while, despite his tiredness, before finally drifting off into a restless sleep.

The door opening with a creak was what woke him up. At first she was little more than a dark shape. Moonlight shone through the slatted blinds and gradually her full form emerged before him: arms, head, legs, breasts, the light striping across her skin like some exotic cat.

She padded onto his mattress and curled up beside him. "Please, Paul. I want this. I want to do this right. I'm not looking for anything from you."

He ran his fingers through her long, dark hair. "I don't care about that. I care about you." He kissed her. "What if something had happened to you? What if it wasn't me that found you?"

Unzipping the sleeping bag, he brought her under, into the warmth. She leaned her head on his bare chest, her arms tightly around him. The crushing pain in his chest was gone, replaced by a different ache. A good one. Deftly, her fingers slid down his navel, into his shorts. Her skin was soft and silky, almost slick beneath his touch. Brushing up her thigh, he felt her soft-trimmed strip of pubic hair, like velvet beneath his palm. She moaned softly then got on top.

They fitted together; no awkward limbs, no struggle for comfort, the right size, perfect match. She kept her eyes fixed on his. While rolling her hips she never looked away. She was there, in the moment. They both were, enjoying their bodies together. He placed his hands on her hips while she moved faster and deeper. He met her rhythm and they worked towards it together. A shuddering moment of intense pleasure and they collapsed in convulsing contentment beside one another.

Afterwards, in a sated glow, they lay holding each other.

He had never wanted to hold anyone after sex before. Lena's heart beat wildly, next to his.

CHAPTER FOURTEEN

Lena spent the first few days catching up on the sleep she'd missed, on Paul's mattress on the floor. Only afterwards did she realise how exhausted she'd been. A spare set of keys sat on the radiator beside the front door. She'd looked at them, but they remained untouched. Every day she would wake up sometime in the afternoon or early evening, make some tea then go straight back to bed, under the warm blankets. It was usually after midnight when Paul got home, armed with the best take-away dinners Glasgow had to offer. They ate them on the couch together and watched TV until they passed out. After that first night they hadn't had sex. It just hadn't come as naturally as she'd expected.

A week passed. She hadn't gone back into work. She hadn't even phoned to say she was leaving, but doubted any of them would be too upset. She'd left a note for Ali when she collected her things from his flat. A clean break. Each time it became that bit easier to disentangle herself from the ties she'd made.

She didn't see much of Paul, apart from those short periods in the early hours when he came home from work. When she thought back to those first days she'd spent with him, four years ago, stoned on the couch in his tower-block flat, it surprised her to find him now a workaholic. But people changed. She certainly had, although she wasn't sure it had been for the better.

Every day he left money on the kitchen worktop for food and other necessities, which she made use of once she finally started leaving the flat. What she didn't spend, she put in a shoebox she had of old letters and photographs. She didn't think he would mind. He never asked for change.

She knew it couldn't go on like that forever. At some point he would ask her for money and for some kind of contribution to their living arrangement beyond ornamentation. But she just didn't seem to have the impetus to get up and do anything about it. She'd been struck by a bad bout of lethargy, didn't even have the energy to care. She'd mapped out a triangular territory, from couch to bathroom to mattress, and for the moment she was happy for that to be her world. Her two carrier bags sat in transit in the hall, beside his unpacked boxes, waiting for the disaster, natural or manmade, that would send her searching for other shores. With every day that passed, she could feel it drawing nearer.

"How're you settling in?" he asked her one night after work. They were sitting on the couch idling away the night as she'd idled away the day. There was a tightness to his tone that made her ears prick up.

"Fine."

"You've found your way around the place."

She waited while he finished chewing the piece of pakora in his mouth, wondering what he was leading up to.

"I suppose." She prepared herself for disappointment.

He stretched his arm over the back of the couch, close to

but not touching her shoulders. His eyes flickered with the moving images on the TV. "I've taken Saturday off. I thought we could unpack together."

She tried to understand what he meant by that, if she was missing something between the lines.

"And then I thought we could go out for dinner – if you haven't got any other plans."

She shrugged her shoulders noncommittally. It wasn't what she'd been expecting and she breathed a sigh of relief. Out of the corner of her eye she could see him looking at her strangely. She knew her silence hurt him but for some reason that made her feel good in a way that she hadn't done for a long time.

On Saturday morning they went to Ikea to get furniture. Lena followed him through the departments, standing quietly while he chose what they needed, answering his questions about which ones she liked with vague mumbles. Eventually, under pressure, she chose a rug with green and red swirls which she didn't even like, and from his face neither did he, but he threw it in with the other purchases. Now they were both going to have to live with it.

As they passed through the children's section, Paul hovered over a small blue bed shaped like a train.

Lena came up behind him. "You should get that," she said, showing the most interest she had all day.

He nodded. She watched as he made a faint cross on the slip of paper with the small brown pencil. Then he grasped her hand and they moved on.

When they got home Lena put the new utensils and

other bit and bobs in the kitchen while Paul spent the best part of an hour building a chest of drawers with the electric screwdriver he'd bought. The larger pieces – their bed, the wardrobe, the baby's bed – would be delivered later in the week. When Paul was done they began to unpack. Lena's stuff fitted into two drawers. She folded her clothes neatly. They looked nice, not bundled in a bag, the colours mixing like a pretty rainbow. But the sad thing about rainbows, she thought, was that they never lasted long.

"More like a home already," Paul said as she entered the living room. He had just placed down the rug and was pulling the coffee table on to it.

"Oh, I forgot…" He wriggled about in the back pocket of his jeans. "I picked this up for you the other day."

He took out something small and furry on a chain and handed it to her. She looked down at the black cat keyring in her hand.

"For your set of keys. It reminded me of you," he said and smiled.

She looked down. "Thanks."

Her heart swelled, but she wouldn't let herself show it. She put the keyring down on the table and clapped her hands together. "Time to get ready!"

Paul had booked them into Coliseum. It was a restaurant, bar and nightclub rolled into one and had only been launched the week before. Every night queues stretched round the block. You had to know someone to get in. Lena knew he'd gone to some effort to get them a table.

She curled her hair, put in her favourite gold-hoop earrings and dressed in her new salmon-coloured, asymmetrical dress. The day before Paul had handed her a wad of cash and told her to get an outfit. Three hundred pounds. She hadn't wanted to take it. No gift was ever for free. But he'd pushed her hands back.

"Go on. So I know I do all the shit I do for something."

She promised to pay him back but she knew she wouldn't. Her first stop was Princes Square, where she went round all the upper-end high-street stores she wouldn't have gone into before: French Connection, Ted Baker, Moda in Pelle. She bought expensive lace underwear from a shop she'd never heard of, then proudly walked down Buchanan Street displaying her bags.

The skirt was short and bell-shaped and she wore it with nude heels, six inches high. It was summer and the evening was warm enough not to worry about tights. Her legs were long and tanned, freshly waxed.

She looked at her reflection in the bathroom mirror, running her tongue round her teeth, her mouth parted slightly in anticipation. She stole a few under-eye sideways glances, lingering but coy. It was all in the tease. She conducted herself like a dangerously alluring film-noir femme fatale. A little trashy, but there was always room for a little trash.

War paint on, her glad rags donned like armour, she went in to the living room, where Paul was waiting. He stood up and came towards her. Dressed in smart trousers, shiny shoes and a black sweater over his shirt, he looked strikingly good; until that moment she hadn't noticed what a handsome man he was becoming. He was almost muscular, no longer skinny, as if his body were only now catching up with what he knew himself to be already. His features fitted well together.

Before, she'd always put his appeal down to charisma and it surprised her to find this was no longer his sole charm.

Looking away as if he could read her thoughts, she reached for her coat on the arm of the couch. Paul took it and held it open for her, so she could slip into it easily.

"You look beautiful," he whispered and kissed her behind the ear. Her neck hairs tingled. There was no flick of the hair from her, no fuck-me-if-you-think-you-could glance. The best she could manage was a small smile.

Pulling away, she hooked her arm in his. "Shall we?"

Together, they walked out the door.

Paul shook hands with the bouncer on their way into the restaurant. He nodded to the maître d', who showed them to their table. They ordered the taster menu, the courses arriving with a certain fanfare. The longer she sat there with Paul, enjoying the way he looked at her, smiled and fussed over her, the more she began to relax.

"This... this is the kind of place I want to run," Paul was saying. Lena looked around at the elegantly dressed customers and the maple-wood bar where the barman in waistcoat and tie was spinning a cocktail shaker beneath art deco fittings. Walnut panels lined the walls, intricately designed with mermaids and inlaid shells. An artificial white light shone through the milky glass ceiling above them, making her feel like she was on an old-fashioned cruise liner. Their table was in the corner, in a small alcove. All the tables around them were taken. Every element spoke of class.

"But your place is going well," she said, brimming with curiosity. She'd gone down to visit him at The Low Road once or twice, but usually he was too busy to have a drink with her. She got the feeling he didn't want her there. That for whatever reason he wanted to keep her and the bar separate.

He shrugged his shoulders. "Yeah…" He took a sip from his wine glass. "But I do feel it's gone as far as it can. I've noticed the crowd's started changing. Getting younger, a bit more mainstream. And it's good because there's money to be made. I don't care who I'm selling drinks to, but in a few months, when the trendsetters move on, word's gonna filter down and the rest will start moving on too." He sighed in frustration. "It's a shame really, because, with a bit of money…" His face grew animated.

It made her smile despite herself to see how passionate he was about his work. For a second she allowed herself to feed off his energy; his fearlessness made her feel that way too, made her think that she could reach further than she'd ever hoped. But she quickly laid those feelings aside.

"It could be really something," he said, glassy eyed, as if the vision was dancing just before him, just out of reach. "It could be something special. Something that wouldn't go out of fashion. I've got so many ideas for it – to make it the kind of place where I want to work, the kind of place I want to run."

"Do you think the bank would give you the money to do it up?" she asked.

Paul cocked his head to one side then the other as he thought about it, then screwed up his face. "But it wouldn't be the bank I'd need to talk to, it would be the owner."

"Do you think the owner would give you the money to do it up?" Lena watched as Paul took a large swig from his glass.

"Maybe," he replied, uncertainly. "If it was done properly,

presented with all the right numbers, figures. It's possible…" He trailed off and began chewing the inside of his mouth vigorously, full of nervous energy. "If I really thought I could pull it off. It'd be a risk."

In those moments when he was lost in thought, his hand over his mouth, the nails bitten down, she observed him. It wasn't the first time she'd noticed him drifting into a flurry of agitation, his mind clearly turning stuff over, as if there was something darker and not so comically cocksure about him.

"What's he like?" she felt compelled to ask. She'd heard rumours, the name Manny Munroe spoken in hushed tones. For the first time, she wondered what it would be like to work for someone like that. But she doubted Paul had much contact with him. He was just a barman.

He brushed her off with a laugh. "Don't worry, you'll never have to meet him."

She laughed too, although she didn't get the joke. When it faded she found him looking her deep in the eyes, purposefully, as if he had trained himself to do so. He inhaled sharply and dropped his shoulders, trying to force himself to relax. Just as another question was about to form, he interrupted and she lost it.

"And what about you?" he said.

She cringed and began stumbling over her own plans. "I'm gonna start looking on Monday. Get some applications…"

He stretched back in his chair, a look of mild amusement on his face. "You'll work it out. Take your time. Maybe you should give college another go. You can stay at mine as long as you want. I've got money. And I quite like having you around the place."

Paul leaned in and cupped his hands over hers.

"Every man here tonight wishes they were the one sitting opposite you," he said and she blushed. She didn't feel like it was a line. He only had eyes for her and all that he asked in return was that she trust him.

Disentangling her hands from his, she put them on her lap, smoothing her skirt over her legs just as the waiter appeared with the bill. He placed it on the table in front of Paul. Lena tried to peek over but it was too well hidden inside the leather wallet.

Paul paid in cash. "Keep the change," he said to the waiter, who nodded discreetly and walked away. "None of these tight bastards will tip," he said as he stood up.

They went through to the nightclub. Like balls in a pinball machine, they bounced from one person to another as they made their way to the dance floor. A couple of people stopped Paul to say hello. She was surprised how many people knew him. On the dance floor girls were eye-fucking him, some of the guys too. He exuded energy and she did her best to feel it too. The dance floor was one of her favourite places on earth but her body wasn't moving in the right rhythms. She felt rigid, clumsy; self-conscious in a way she never had before.

A slower song came on and Paul pulled her close. She tried to relax into his arms but somehow she couldn't. She put her hands on his chest and pushed him away.

He stopped dancing and stood on the spot, the music blaring, people jostling them on all sides. His shoulders slumped, his face crumpled. "Why'd you push me away?"

She looked at him coldly, feeling a moment of triumph as she realised he cared enough to be upset by her. When he turned to walk away, she panicked and called him back. "Paul…" She reached out her hand and placed it on his arm, but it slipped off.

"Paul!" she shouted over the music. He turned back round and she threw her arms around his neck, kissing him, her tongue catching the side of his cheek. She could feel the saliva sticky against her chin. She kept going in desperation until she felt him gently push her away, wiping his face.

She could feel her cheeks flush. Walk away, she told herself. Do it now because if you stay a second longer you'll never be able to leave. Walk away before the last of your defences come down and you are laid bare. Humiliated worse than you already have been.

She hated herself for not being able to stop herself falling in love with him. She'd never felt so vulnerable; frayed, her head and her heart pulling differently.

In the end her head won. Her body followed. Not caring who she pushed into, she headed at speed for the door. Some angry voices yelled out as drinks spilled, but she kept going. Let them try and stop her. She ran past the bouncers into the street and could feel their eyes on her, laughing. People were still trying to get in, even though the night was almost over. She barged past them in a blind rage, finding comfort in her anger, power in her resistance. Angry at him although she knew she had no reason to be.

She kept going until she reached the tall pillars of GoMA. She threw herself onto the museum's cold stone steps, her head in her hands, doing all she could to hold back the tears. The streets were busy around her, but on the steps she was alone, shaded in the echoing silence, cold in the shadows of the museum's cavernous entrance. She wished she had her coat, which was still hanging in the cloakroom of the club. In front of her loomed the statue of some soldier on his horse, black cast iron, an orange traffic cone on his head like a cheap crown. Crown it all with stupidity, she thought, that's what you do. She hoped it burned, all of it and everyone, to the ground. Her foot shot out in anger, sending her shoe arcing through the air and onto the pavement below. It made a satisfying bang as it hit the ground. A few people stopped to stare.

Paul appeared from nowhere and reached down to pick it up. She hadn't seen him following her out. He walked towards her, shoe in hand, and held it up. "Lose something?"

She took it from him sullenly and awkwardly placed it back on her foot. She could feel herself shaking, but it wasn't from the cold. He hovered a second and then sat on the step beside her. He felt warm beside her but she turned her head away.

"You're hard as nails, Lena," he sighed and rested his elbows on his knees.

She ignored him and stared off into the distance, feeling more and more stupid, knowing she was digging a deeper and deeper hole. Tears welled in her eyes as she waited for him to get up and walk away, unable to bring herself to ask him to stay.

After a long pause he said, "I tried too hard, didn't I?"

Lena looked round at him and heaved a sigh, her anger dissipating.

"The big fancy dinner, the clothes, the furniture today," he went on. "It was all too much. I frightened you off." The expression on his face pained her. His heavy eyes looked downwards. She wanted to stop him talking but she didn't. "I only did it because I care about you." He bumped his shoulder into hers, affectionately. She wanted to tell him to hide some of that emotion, that if he left himself wide open, people would trample on him. "I only did it because I love you."

She stared at him and wanted more than anything to say the words back. Words she had said so many times before but which now failed her. They caught in her throat because for the first time she meant them, for the first time she understood what they meant.

"I—"

He cut her off. His fingers stroked her bare, goose-pimpled arm. "I know you do," he said and moved closer, putting his arm around her.

She didn't pull away but let herself sink into him. Four years of living on and off with Jason, her mum's volatile boyfriend, had taught her how to measure the temperature of a room, how to read others' facial expressions and gauge their emotions without exposing her own. But with Paul that didn't work. The feelings were too strong, they exhausted her. Putting her head on his shoulder, she let him carry the burden for a while because she knew he could.

Their hands knitted together and they sat there for some time, not wanting to break the moment.

In the taxi on their way home they sat in silence but comfortably. They were still holding hands as they walked to their front door. They went into the living room and christened their ugly rug. The fibres felt smooth and silky beneath their skin.

Over the next few weeks she found that when she goaded

him, he walked away. But he was always there waiting, ready to forgive her. He killed the drama. When she was needy, selfish, showed him her worst qualities, he still came back, and loved her a little more each time.

It wasn't easy but over time she began to think that maybe, just maybe, he had her best interests at heart.

CHAPTER FIFTEEN

"Have you got a passport?" he asked her a few weeks later, after he'd come home from work and sat down on his side of the couch.

She had resumed her position on what had now become her patch, where she'd been sitting cross-legged, doodling a picture of the table in front of her on what was supposed to be a job application. She had got up to meet him at the door, which had become a kind of ritual for them: greeting him on the doorstep with an enormous, over-exaggerated hug and a kiss, like he was a soldier returning from war. Maybe too much, but she was always pleased to see him and she did feel happier knowing he was home safe and sound, even if it was just from the other side of Glasgow.

"Why do you ask? Yeah, I do. I got it for a school trip to Disneyland Paris."

She laid the form aside, leaving the tricky referee section for later.

His eyes fell on the defaced application. He reached out and lifted it up. "Did you draw this?"

"Yeah," she said, squinting at the loosely sketched still life in his hand.

"It's good. It's really good. You've got the perspective

and everything."

"But you were saying?" she pressed, wondering why Paul looked like he was about to burst out laughing.

"I booked us a holiday."

"Where?" she asked excitedly, slapping the side of his shoulder. The application dropped to the floor.

"Spain. Next Friday. For a week."

She did an impromptu celebration dance, still cross-legged on the couch, which she knew would make Paul laugh.

"You said you wanted to travel…"

Their flight was from Manchester Airport so the holiday began with a road trip. They started out from Glasgow in the middle of the night, Paul driving and Lena in her sun cap with her bare feet on the dashboard. They sang along to summer songs on the radio as rain obscured the windscreen.

On the plane, Lena sat by the window, Paul in the middle seat. As soon as she stepped on, Lena had an overwhelming urge to get back off again. She had no idea how tightly packed the cabin would be. At take-off she squashed Paul's hand until his knuckles were bruised, her palms slick with sweat. She was petrified by the sensation of being hurled into the atmosphere at two hundred miles an hour and spent the whole flight sipping vodka, watching the sky.

The temperature gauge at Malaga Airport read thirty-seven degrees. It was scorching. They got ever hotter and sweatier as they moved slowly through Spanish Customs and waited ages for the luggage to come through on the carousel. Paul became increasingly tense. When their bags finally turned up, he kissed her on the forehead. "I was worried they'd lost them," he said. He looked like a weight had been lifted.

Their hotel was on the beach in a typical Spanish tourist trap. The place was filled with expats and Scottish, English and German tourists, and the seafront was a maze of tapas bars, pizzerias and Irish theme pubs.

The first thing they did was strip off and jump in the pool. That night they went for dinner and drank caipirinhas, then went back to the room and had first-night sex under the cool white sheets. Next day they went into town and hired a moped. Paul gunned it shakily along the coastal road, the tar soft in the sun, a haze from the heat making it look slick with water. After midnight, the pair met for a secret rendezvous in the hotel swimming pool.

The next day they got up and did it all again.

After lunchtime on the last day, fuelled by alcohol and a general sense of merriment, they went to a tattoo parlour. Paul sat in the chair while the two of them laughed hysterically. The tattoo artist, who spoke no English, inked for hours. First the outline, then the shading of two thorned roses. In a banner underneath, Paul got her name written in elegant lettering. Lena had never seen anything so beautiful and the tears welled in her eyes. Afterwards, they decided to go for a nap in preparation for the big night ahead of them. They drew the curtains, shut the balcony door and pulled the thin white sheets over themselves. Lena drifted off quickly, into a deep, groggy sleep. She was still fuzzy-headed when Paul's phone went off, but he sat up on the bed.

"Hi. Yeah," he said, his voice hoarse. "Good."

She listened to his monosyllabic answers with her eyes closed. He got off the bed and went out onto the balcony. "Yeah, yeah, I know the one," she heard him say before he slid the door shut.

She turned and lay face up in bed, half awake, half asleep, waiting for him to finish and come back and lie beside her, hoping that they would still be able to get back to sleep.

The balcony door soon opened, bringing soft evening light streaming into their bedroom. The blast of cool air was refreshing. Paul left the door open as he went over to his suitcase and began rummaging around.

"What are you doing?"

"I've got to head out for a bit," he said abruptly.

"What?" she asked, sitting up in bed, fully awake now.

"I won't be long." Paul stuffed a plastic bag into his backpack then came over to the bed and kissed her on the head. "Go back to sleep. I'll be back by the time you wake up."

He left in a hurry, before she could say anything else. The last things he lifted from the bedside table were his passport and the keys to the scooter.

She didn't go back to sleep. Instead, she put on her bikini and sarong and went down to the hotel pool. It was always empty at that time of the evening; most people were already out for the night. So she was able to swim back and forth uninterrupted, concentrating on the movement of her limbs, the water on her skin, trying to think of anything but where he was and what he was doing.

The air was nippy when she got out of the pool and she quickly wrapped herself in her towel. Music and laughter were coming from the hotel bar as she headed back to her room, her hair dripping pools of water behind her. She went straight to the bathroom and had a long, hot shower. Afterwards, she took her time brushing her hair, drying and straightening it. She made extra effort with her make-up, taking eye shadows from the bottom of her vanity case, ones she'd forgotten she even had, umming and ahhing over which would be right for that night. Looking in the mirror, she made a point of loosening her jaw, aware of how tight the skin was pulled between nose and lip. She scrunched her mouth around like she was chewing a large piece of food and massaged her cheeks with her fingers. Taking her dress from the wardrobe, she inspected every inch of it before putting it on, admiring the pattern of the material. She didn't usually wear maxis but thought it would be nice for a romantic night-time walk down the beach. She'd been saving it for their last evening.

Then she went out onto the balcony and waited, sipping the wine they'd bought in earlier. She sipped it until the sky grew dark and most of the bottle was gone. Tapping her foot, drumming her nails on the glass. She had no way of contacting him; her phone company wouldn't let her make calls abroad. No way of finding out where he was. She watched the moonlight ripple on the swimming pool and wished she could submerge herself beneath the black and silver water, lie on the bottom observing the bubbles float to the top, feel her body weightless.

She keyed in some texts in the hope that one would get through, but her phone always beeped angrily, "SMS Barred". She huffed in frustration and threw the thing on the table. She waited and waited, until lights from the rooms around her began switching off. Until most of the restaurants had closed their doors for the night.

Then she heard his key card in the door.

She got up to go to the door like she always did. She held her breath, not ready to be convinced it was him until she saw his fair hair come round the door, his sunburned face, half expecting it to be the hotel manager or the police. She didn't give him a hug or a kiss.

"You're back," she said curtly and went to sit on the bed, not wanting her relief at seeing him to cancel out her annoyance.

"Lena, I'm sorry," he said, following her in.

"Where have you been?" She watched him go to the sideboard and waited for an answer. She didn't want to let it drop.

"I had to meet someone and it took a little longer than I thought." He rustled around for the bottle opener and flicked the top off a bottle of warm San Miguel. He took a swig.

"Who?" she pressed, measuring his answer, trying not to let herself be appeased.

"A friend of a friend lives near here, in town," he said, leaning back against the counter. "I was doing my friend a favour. Said I'd drop off some home comforts for him. No big deal."

"What kind of home comforts?"

She thought about the last time he'd got a phone call and had disappeared late into the night, a few days before they'd left. He'd refused to be drawn, just produced two designer bags he'd got off some guy who'd been selling them round the pub.

"A care package. HP Sauce. Potato scones. That kind of thing," he said breezily.

"I don't believe you."

The bottle came down from his lips, the smile gone from his face. He flashed her an accusatory look. A look that said: I thought we had a deal; we both pretend we don't know what's going on and that way we're both happy.

But she'd been worried. Really worried. "Was what you did today dangerous?"

"No," he said sharply, crossing his arms.

"Illegal? What was in the bag?"

"I gave money to someone. It was money."

"Money from crime?" She glanced at her expensive bracelet, pictured her new bikini and summer clothes. He didn't answer. "Are we in danger? Could we get arrested?"

"No. They could have confiscated it if they'd found it at Customs, but they didn't."

She couldn't be sure if he was telling the truth. He uncrossed his arms and swung them by his side, his head cocked impatiently. He wanted the conversation to be over.

"Is that the reason for this holiday?"

Again he said nothing. Avoiding confrontation as he always did. Instead, he lifted the bottle of Grey Goose they'd got in to celebrate the last night and walked out onto the balcony, shaking his head to himself as he went. He disappeared behind the curtain and she heard him pull the door shut, leaving her alone in the room.

She went to bed, throwing her new dress carelessly on the floor, dropping her shoes beside it. She turned off the lights and wrestled with sleep. She must have dozed, because a few hours later she woke up, alone in the bed and with the feeling that time had passed. She reached for her phone and saw that it read 4 a.m. She wrapped the sheets around herself and got up, sliding the balcony door open.

Paul was still out there, sitting on the chair in the corner in the moonlight, the bottle of vodka almost empty on the table in front of him. He smiled at her when she came over, a sad, melancholy smile.

"Paul." She sat on the chair beside him, the sheet trailing along the floor of the balcony, picking up dust. She put her hand on his arm and it was freezing. "Paul, c'mon inside, it's too cold out here."

He looked at her with drunken eyes, then looked away, unable to maintain focus.

"Paul, c'mon to bed." Worried that he might topple over the balcony when he stood up, she took his hands to lead him in, but he didn't budge. Instead, he pulled her hand close, bringing her back onto her chair. His eyes were red and swollen.

"It's all shit for me now, Lena." The words hung in the air, biting. He shook his head drunkenly, then buried it in his hands. "I've done something. Something bad and I can never undo it..." His words trailed off and he squeezed her hand tight.

Her heart felt like lead in her chest. The hotel complex around them was deathly quiet. She listened for movement from close by but there was none. No one to hear what he was saying but her.

"I didn't want to, but I had to," he mumbled into his hands.

There had been times before that night when she'd wanted to ask the question. Times it seemed he'd wanted to unburden. When she'd been curious about the haunted look that sometimes crossed his face. Times he'd been morose like this. Not often but sometimes. He locked himself away and all was dark until he emerged the next day and everything was fine again. But she never did ask. Terrified what the answer might be. Terrified it would change everything.

"I didn't want to but I did. And now it's all shit. I'm shit. You shouldn't be with me. You don't belong in my world." He stopped for a moment and then said, "It was me or him."

That was as far as he went. He looked up at her and she watched the contortions in his face smooth as he regained himself. His eyes flicked like he had just woken up.

"I need to go to bed," he slurred.

With effort, he began to get to his feet, on autopilot. She let him go past her, too numb to speak or even move. She listened to him stumble into the bedroom, crash down on the bed. Part of her wanted to run out of the room. Leave and never come back. Her first instinct was for her own safety. She pictured herself packing her bags in the dark while he slept. Going to the airport. Getting on a flight. Being back in Scotland before he even woke up. Clearing out her stuff and leaving without looking back. She pictured it but somehow couldn't quite do it.

In a daze she got up and drew back the curtain. His light breathing floated through the air. He was lying face up on the bed, his face smooth and peaceful in the silver moonlight. She didn't want to go too close, and watched him from the door. The same Paul she slept beside night after night. The same one she wanted to spend her life with. But in the same breath, totally different. A changeling in his warm, familiar body. She stood there watching until her bare feet grew sore and first light came. Then she got onto the bed and curled into a corner, leaving enough space between them so they wouldn't touch.

In the morning they didn't mention it. They got up as normal, went down to the breakfast bar. Paul downed a few strong coffees, his eyes puffy from lack of sleep.

"My head is splitting," was his only mention of the night before.

They returned to the room, packed, and left their bags with the concierge when they checked out. The driver would be there to take them to the airport in an hour. They went down to enjoy a final drink on the beach. They hugged and kissed and smiled. But they weren't laughing any more. To Lena, as she lifted handfuls of sand and let the fine grains slip through her fingers, the cocktail tasted sour, the air smelled fetid and the beach dragged like rocks underfoot.

They reached the airport without fuss. Right before they boarded their plane home, Paul turned to her and said, "I got the go-ahead for the refurbishment."

CHAPTER SIXTEEN

Annie sat in the armchair, her legs curled up, watching while across the room Paul squirmed in agony. Cold sweats. Hunger pains. Itching. Midnight came and went. He was worried that he might be getting sick. Neither of them had moved for over half an hour, a ceasefire born of fatigue. The subtlest noises in the quiet room – the ticking of the clock, the soft patter of the first drops of rain on the window, the crackle of the fire, now revived in the grate, Annie's breathing – sounded like thunder in his ear.

The knife wound on his arm had clotted: no more than flesh deep. The rust-coloured beads had hardened into a crusty purple. One more scar on a body full of them. Every time he looked up, Annie was staring at it. "Feeling guilty?" he asked.

She looked at him with revulsion. "No. I just don't want you to bleed to death before I find out what I want to know."

He believed her. Her coldness chilled him.

"You and me aren't that different, you know. When it comes down to it, you do what you have to do."

"I'm nothing like you," she snapped, then fell into a sulky silence again. But she no longer looked at his arm.

Wiggling his fingers and toes and rotating the joints as

much as the ties would allow, Paul took a deep breath, held it, then exhaled, attempting to manage the pain, worried about lasting nerve damage.

"When you came into the bar," he suddenly said, trying to take his mind off his aches, "why didn't you approach me? When you left, how did you know I'd follow you out?"

She looked at him with undisguised hatred. "I knew you couldn't resist a vulnerable woman. My first attempt at contact and you took the bait. That was my good luck." Her lip curled. "And then, outside... I was worried you'd know me right away. But you didn't. When I looked up and saw you there, standing beside me at the bus stop, I wanted to run. I recognised you, from the newspaper clippings, but you're different in real life. Uglier. You can see there's a darkness in you. A blackness."

Paul exhaled again, loudly. "You should hear yourself! *A blackness,*" he mimicked. "Know what I think? I think you're bored. I think you're using Lena as an excuse to have some drama in your life. You've filled your life with this incredible fantasy. She's run off somewhere; it wouldn't be the first time. And you want in on the action."

"She'd never leave it this long without getting in touch," Annie whispered, and Paul saw an opportunity.

"I didn't know you two were close."

"We're sisters."

"You say that like it's supposed to mean something. From what I remember, she barely even knew you."

For a second Annie stopped short. She looked injured. But it didn't last long. "I know what you're doing. You're trying to manipulate my emotions. Make me think it's all in my head.

Lie, cheat and manipulate – your grubby little tools. But I'm not my sister, Paul. Your bullshit doesn't work on me."

"I didn't groom her," he said through gritted teeth, finding it easier to keep talking, take his mind off his aching body. "She came into the bar I was working in. I helped her out and we got together. She was eighteen. We were both adults. Nothing dark or sinister there."

Annie shook her head contemptuously. "She wasn't eighteen in the photograph."

"That was from a couple of years before. I met her in the park one afternoon."

"Do you meet a lot of teenage girls in parks?"

They fell into silence.

Annie took out the photograph again and began studying it. Paul watched her eyes flicker over it. Then she put it down, rifled through his wallet once more and found the small passport-sized picture of Jack as a tiny boy again.

"Who's this?"

"My son."

She held it closer, inspecting.

"How old is he?"

"In the picture? Three. Four."

"And what about now?"

"Twelve, thirteen, I guess."

"Don't you see him?"

"No."

"Why not?"

Paul shrugged his shoulders. "He's better off without me."

"Has there ever been anyone in your life that wasn't better off without you?"

Paul smiled. "We talked about having children someday."

Annie baulked. "Because you did such a good job first time round?"

"What do you want me to say?" he snapped. "That I'm a shitty father? That's not a revelation to me."

"Did Lena know about him?"

"Of course. She was good with him – some people just are… good with that sort of thing."

The skin around Annie's eyes softened and turned red.

"I started out with the best of intentions." He lifted his head in defiance. "I never meant for bad things to happen."

Annie erupted. "You work for a man like Manny Munroe and you never meant for bad things to happen? Didn't think you'd wreck lives, leave a path of destruction in your wake?"

"When I was fifteen I lived on a burned-out bus," he retorted. A picture came into his head, of himself washing in public bathrooms, his skin stretched tight over razor-sharp bones. "You try spending night after night in the freezing cold and see if you don't take a helping hand when it's offered. You've never had a difficult day in your life."

"You don't know anything about me," she spat back. "And don't give me that shit about not having a choice. Boo-hoo," she sneered. "All over the world. Every day, people come out of worse. This is Glasgow. The West. We have a welfare state. In other countries people are starving to death. But you bleat about how it's all so sad, how you turned to crime because you didn't have a choice. With a normal job you wouldn't be able to afford Gucci. Is that another of your ploys? To make people feel sorry for you?"

"I don't want your pity. That's all you people have. I'm

trying to explain. But what's the point if you've already made up your mind?"

"Did my sister know she was living with a killer?" Annie shot back at him.

"No."

"So you lied to her?"

"She didn't ask."

Annie gave an exasperated scream. "It's not the kind of thing you ask a partner, is it? *Honey, just out of curiosity, have you murdered anyone?*"

"I was trying to protect her."

"But you couldn't?" Annie perched on the couch, her thin shoulders scrunching forward, her thumb kneading the knuckle of her index finger. "Protect her from who?"

Paul no longer felt like talking. But Annie persisted, burrowing her way in like a worm.

"Did she find out? Is that why she tried to get away from you?" Annie's voice was urgent now. "The first time she came to stay with us, we were told not to let you in, if you came round."

"She wasn't trying to get away from me. She was angry with me."

"Why, what did you do?"

"She saw something," Paul heard himself say, surprised at how the little girl was getting to him.

"What?"

He shifted uncomfortably in his seat, could feel his temperature rise.

"Something with Munroe?"

His eyes stung. Colours and sounds momentarily blurred.

"Tell me!" Annie shouted, rising to her feet. "What did you get her involved in?"

CHAPTER SEVENTEEN

Nine years ago

Even though the bedroom door was closed, Lena could hear Paul in the living room, shouting down the phone.

"I tell you what, I'll buy you some Ibuprofen... I don't care... I've been very patient... No, no... Stop. Just stop." There was silence for a moment before he started up again, building strength for the crescendo. "Do you want me to lose my temper, Dessy, is that it? Want me to come down to Sharkey's Bar? I know that's where you've been when you're supposed to have been fitting my disabled toilet. Want me to lose my temper in front of that tidy barmaid you've been perving over? Because I will, if that's what you want. If you're not at my bar, ready to work today, I swear to fuck I'll come looking for you."

When she was sure the call was over, she came out of the bedroom. Paul had moved into the kitchen. She went in to find him leaning against the counter, a mug of coffee in his hand.

"Fucking morons!" he cursed.

"Everything OK?" she said as she re-boiled the kettle and put a tea bag in a fresh cup.

"Same bullshit, different day," he said into his coffee.

The kettle clicked, she poured in the water, fished out the used bag and threw it in the bin. "Is that the plumber whose mother died?" she asked as she got the milk from the fridge.

"Probably bullshitting about that too. That's the kind of people I'm dealing with." He rolled his eyes and sighed. Beside him, toast popped out of the toaster. He put the two slices on a plate, burning his fingers as he did so, then got the butter and started spreading.

"Apart from that, how's it going?" She leaned against the fridge, mug in hand.

"We'll get there." His head nodded up and down like a plastic dog in the back windscreen of a car. She took in the waxy paleness of his skin, the grey shadows under his eyes. He hadn't come to bed at all the night before. He'd hardly slept since the refurbishment had got underway a few weeks before.

He saw her watching and gulped down his coffee. "Right, I'm off."

"Uh... before you go," she said, tiptoeing over to him. "Have you got any money on you?"

"Again? I just gave you some yesterday."

"I was thinking of getting some extra bits and pieces for tonight – nibbles for the guests. You're still going to make it, right?"

He looked at her, bewildered, and her heart sank.

"The exhibition."

"Right, Lena, of course. I'll be there."

He took out his wallet and handed her some notes, tens and twenties, without counting. "Must be nice having your own personal money dispenser," he said under his breath. She

171

winced a little but took it from him anyway.

"Half seven," she said as she followed him to the door. "Everyone else is coming at eight, but I want to show you around first."

"Right… right," he said as he backed out the door, toast in his mouth. Just before he closed it, he took the toast out, leaned back and kissed her.

She went straight through to the bedroom and opened up her bottom drawer, pulling out her shoebox from beneath some tops. Her stuff occupied all the drawers now, and some of the wardrobe. She carried it over to the bed and sat there with it. When she took off the elastic band, it popped open, spilling notes onto her lap. Ever since the Spain trip, almost twelve months ago now, she'd been making even more effort to save. Insurance; her escape fund, if it came to it. She spread out the money and began counting. She knew there was roughly a thousand pounds there, but she wanted an exact figure. She added in most of the money he'd given her that morning, only keeping back a little to buy some nibbles with, for the guests at the exhibition later.

A moment later she was startled to hear Paul's key turning in the door. She began stuffing the notes back into the box.

"I forgot that list for the supplier," she heard him shout from the hall. "It's beside the bed."

She turned and saw a piece of paper with figures written on it. Quickly, she started to tidy away her shoebox. Heard his footsteps outside the door. But it was too late; he was already in the bedroom before she could get the lid back on it. Stray notes were still scattered across the bed beside her.

As he went over to the bedside table to pick up his list,

his eyes fell on the box stuffed with money. "What's that?" he said, then glanced at his piece of paper, folded it over and put it in his trouser pocket.

"This?" she said, embarrassed, her cheeks red. "It's just some money I've been saving."

"Oh, right," he said and walked back to the door. He stopped in the doorway and turned round. "My money?" His forehead creased, his eyebrows knitted in a frown.

"You gave it to me. I didn't think you'd mind."

"Why would I mind?" he said quietly, his voice low.

"I just wanted to have it put by… you know… for a rainy day."

He began to walk away, then turned back. "You know, you only had to ask if you needed money. You didn't have to hide it behind my back."

She began to explain, feeling aggrieved at his tone. But he wasn't finished. His eyes scrunched into narrow slits, his lip curled. "It's always going to be the same with you, isn't it? One foot out the door, ready to take what you can," he spat.

Lena felt his words like a slap. She could feel a heat rising within her. He'd never spoken to her like that before.

She didn't know what to say.

"Every other cunt's ripping me off and now you are too."

He walked away after that. The front door slammed behind him, shaking the walls.

Lena got the bus to her college in the early evening. As it was the last week of the course, they were having an exhibition of their work. Family and friends had been invited and it was also a chance to say farewell and good luck to the other students. Most of them had applied to art schools, Lena included, but she hadn't heard anything back yet.

A few of the students were already in the classroom, setting up. They had each been given a board, about four feet by six feet, enough to hang five or six pieces. The paint-spotted desks had been moved to the side and covered with a paper sheet on which had been set a row of drinks – Coke and Irn-Bru, boxes of red and white wine – and some plastic cups.

Lena chatted to her friends as she put up her pictures, making sure the edges were all at right angles, the drawing pins secure. One was a pencil drawing of a bird's wing, another a still life in charcoal they had done as a class. The still life sessions had been a real success: their teacher, Mike, had scavenged a selection of objects from round and about – odd-shaped vases and pots, a cat's skull, a hip bone, dried flowers – and the students had drawn them over and over. The results were really good.

It was a nice sunny evening and the doors onto the concrete yard had been left open. When Lena had finished setting up, she went for a walk around the yard on her own, kicking up stones, checking the time.

She came back inside just after seven thirty. The first eager friends and family members had already arrived and were milling around the room. She was introduced to some of them. A few asked her if her boyfriend was coming. She tried to be non-committal, saying that he would if he could get away from work.

She got a glass of wine and wandered around the room, looking at the artwork of her classmates, talking to a few. She went out for some air and came back in, stood by her pictures. By eight o'clock she knew he wasn't coming.

With the party now in full swing, Lena spied Mike, their teacher, moving towards her. He was dressed in a tweed jacket with leather elbow patches, cords and scuffed brown brogues – a young fogey, still only in his early thirties.

"Any word yet from the Glasgow School of Art?" he asked her.

She shook her head. "I heard David M. got an unconditional offer."

"Yeah." Mike nodded. "Great news." He leaned in closer. "He's not as good as you, though," he said and looked around to make sure no one else had heard.

"Bet that's what you say to all your students," she joked, but she knew it wasn't. Of all the people she'd met that year, he had been her favourite. For the first time in her life she was teacher's pet. She'd joined him for a smoke a few lunchtimes. He was a cool guy in an awkward, geeky way. She hadn't told Paul about him. She knew he would only make fun of him.

"What about Dundee?" he asked.

She shook her head. "I didn't go for the interview." She shrugged, knowing he'd be disappointed. "I couldn't move up there anyway, so I didn't see the point."

"Ah, that's right. Your boyfriend – of the painting." He motioned with both hands up to the picture of Paul, then glanced around the room. It was the one she'd worked hardest on, the one she'd spent weeks perfecting. She'd done secret preliminary sketches while he'd been lost in thought, reclining on the couch. She'd experimented with the composition using different media. But the one she'd done with acrylics was her favourite. She'd stopped at just the right point, hadn't overcooked it. That was a big step for her. She'd wanted to show it to him tonight.

"Is he here?"

She winced. More than anyone, she didn't want to tell Mike she'd been stood up. Her eyes dipped and she shook her head, making an excuse for him.

"That's a shame," Mike said in a way that made her feel the full weight of Paul's absence.

The conversation ended and Mike moved on, flitting around the room like a busy moth. Lena stuck out the rest of the evening without enthusiasm, willing it to end quickly so she could go home to the flat and forget about it all.

At the first opportunity, she started to take down her pictures, preparing to leave. Having placed her work carefully in her plastic case, she went round and said her goodbyes. She slipped out as quietly as she could and began to walk to her bus stop, just outside the college grounds, hoping the bus would be along soon. Dusk was falling.

Sitting in the empty shelter, perched on the plastic bench, she swung her legs and became lost in her own thoughts. Ten, fifteen, twenty minutes passed and there was still no sign of the bus. Feeling more and more aggrieved by the way the night had unfolded, she began pacing back and forth.

"Lena!" a voice called out. For a second she thought it was Paul and she spun around excitedly. A sun-bleached old Vauxhall, red with a blue bonnet, pulled up at the bus stop and Mike's head appeared from the driver's window. "Lena, I thought that was you."

Trying not to show her disappointment, she walked over to meet him. "Mike, hi."

"I thought you left ages ago," he said.

She motioned to the bus stop and threw up her hands in exaggerated despair. "No bus."

"Well, I can give you a lift, if you want? Where're you headed?" He scratched his head awkwardly.

"City centre?"

"Sure, no problem."

Lena did one final check for her bus but there was still no sign. It was getting dark now and her folder was heavy. She opened the back door and threw it on the back seat, among a jumble of old water bottles, different magazines and random bits of paper.

"Sorry about the mess," he said as she got in the front and pulled on her seatbelt. He flicked on the cassette player and pulled back out onto the road.

Out of the speakers came the voice of a man squealing about needles and damage and other depressing things. Lena reached for the cassette cover on the dashboard. The song titles were hand-written in blue ink, and little love hearts – now smudged – had been drawn on.

Mike drummed his hands on the steering wheel and hummed along. He turned round and saw her holding the cover. "From my ex," he said. "She made me a compilation, some of my favourite songs."

Lena tried to picture what the women he went out with might be like. She imagined ripped jeans and cigarillos. Someone with a vinyl collection and shelves full of important books.

"Was her taste in music as bad as yours?" Lena joked. Mike gave a sarcastic scoff.

There had been mild flirtation between them all year; mostly her teasing him about his age and him mocking her ignorance of what he considered to be relevant culture. Lena listened to music on her MP3 player and didn't have anything on it that hadn't been in the charts in the last six months.

"I'll have you know, this song is a classic," he said, and quoted some interesting fact about it, which he seemed to be able to do for every song written before the year 2000.

"Do you always listen to old music?" She screwed up her face. Mike tutted. "Sorry it's not *Now 61*."

She laughed and looked out the window as they joined the motorway. As they flew past industrial parks and high-rises, she wondered vaguely about the people that lived inside them. She wondered where Mike lived; probably the West End, she thought. That was where most people who weren't from Glasgow ended up, along with the students and yuppies.

"Do you not have something a bit more upbeat?"

Mike flicked on the radio. A dance song came on. Lena tapped her toe. "Finally. Something from this century!"

Mike just shrugged his shoulders and affected disdain but she could see him bobbing his head.

As they approached her street he accidentally took a wrong turn. It took them a minute or two to get back on track. Lena hummed to herself. When they neared her flat she pointed it out. "There it is," she said, watching it disappear as they passed it.

"You missed it!" she said, louder.

"Oops," he said and drove on to the end of the street, parking a few hundred yards from her front door. He switched off the engine and the music stopped abruptly.

"Well, here you go." He held up his hands. "Your boyfriend in there waiting on you, is he?"

"Yeah," Lena said. She felt uneasy talking to him about Paul. "Thanks again. Hope you enjoy your few weeks off now. Fingers crossed for the weather." Her hand went to the door handle.

"You too," he said.

The handle jammed when she pulled it. She pulled it again but it didn't open.

"Oh, sorry, locked it," he said and went to click it off. He stopped. Drummed his hands on the wheel.

Lena's hand went back to the handle.

"Before you go…" he looked at her sheepishly, drumming some more. "I just want you to know, Lena…" his hands stopped. "That I'm here for you. If you ever need me. I want you to know that."

The words stuttered out of him. There was a moment of awkwardness as it became clear what he was saying. Their eyes met briefly before she looked down. She'd had a feeling something like this would happen but she'd hoped it wouldn't. He placed a hand on her knee.

She yanked her knee away. "I have a boyfriend."

In another life she might have thought about it. He was witty and smart and handsome and fun. But he wasn't Paul and that was what mattered.

"I'm sorry, Mike. You're a really great teacher——" she said, her hand still on the handle.

"Now that you've had your good reference, you don't need me, is that it?" He cut her off. "Forget it! I don't know what I'm saying. You're not my type anyway."

He tapped the switch and the door handle clicked. Lena opened the door. Air rushed in. He nodded towards the street. "And let me know how you get on with the art school," he said and cocked an eyebrow, sounding like a teacher again.

"OK." She got out of the car.

Before she shut the door, she saw his head bow down and heard a sigh. "Cock-tease," he muttered under his breath.

She tutted and opened the back door to get her folder, slamming it when she was done. She stood on the street and watched as his old red Vauxhall pulled off down the road. Hoping she'd never have to see him again.

The flat was dark and empty; she wasn't surprised. Dropping her folder in the hall, she went into the kitchen, poured herself a large glass of wine then took it into the living room and sat there alone in front of the TV.

Paul would have hated it at the exhibition. But it was still shitty that he hadn't been there. Feeling totally deflated, she had to remind herself that it was just one bad day for them. They happened. And a good day would be waiting just around the corner. She had faith in that. It would carry her though. The next day would be better.

Maybe there was a good reason. Maybe he was still annoyed about her box of money. She hoped he'd come home soon so they could talk it through.

Curling up on the couch, she pulled a felt blanket over herself and fell into an unsettled sleep, trying not to think about what she knew in her heart to be true. Whatever was wrong, it was about more than just some money in a box.

The sun was coming up when Lena finally heard Paul's

key turn in the door. It jolted her awake and she sat up on the couch. The room was a dull grey and it took a few seconds for her eyes to adjust.

"Paul?" she shouted. She could hear his feet in the hall. He hadn't turned the light on.

Getting off the couch, she went out to meet him in the hallway.

"Paul? Where have you been?" she asked through the gloom.

He came through the door dishevelled and bleeding from a cut above his eyebrow. It looked like he'd been fighting. Not for the first time.

"What happened?" she said, her voice rising an octave.

"I went to the casino." He brushed past her, into the bedroom.

She followed him in, consumed with worry. "Tell me what's going on."

He looked broken as he flopped down on the bed. "We'll talk about it after. Please, I'm too tired right now."

He put his head on the pillow. She walked round to continue the conversation and get into bed alongside him, but his breathing grew heavy and she realised he was already asleep.

When she woke up a few hours later, the summer sunshine was streaming through the window and he was still in bed beside her. Usually he was up and gone before seven. He was lying motionless, staring at her. She wondered how long he had been like that.

"Don't you have to be at work?" she said, opening her eyes fully.

"I took the morning off." He ran his fingers through her

hair and smiled.

She stared back at him. Looked at the cut above his eyebrow; at the reddish stain on his pillow.

"I'm sorry about the exhibition," he said. "I didn't forget. I just got caught up in something."

She traced her hand down his face, touching the blackened skin around the cut. They lay together for some time, not talking, neither of them knowing what to say.

Eventually she got up and went into the bathroom to take a shower, leaving him alone on the bed.

Bacon and eggs were frying on the cooker by the time she emerged. Paul had laid out cutlery for two on the work surface.

"Breakfast?" he said. It was the first time they'd eaten a meal together in weeks.

She nodded.

Stepping away from the sizzling pans, he came towards her and put his arm around her. She could smell the antiseptic cream he'd applied to his forehead. It rubbed off on her cheek, leaving her smelling of hospitals.

"Did you sort the problem with the plumber?" she asked.

He nodded and kissed her on the head. She watched as he turned off the cooker and began to spoon the food onto their plates. He placed the breakfast on the counter in front of her and began to eat.

She took a forkful.

"You know I love you, don't you? More than anything in the world." He turned towards her.

She nodded uncertainly. "I love you too."

"Once we've had the opening night for the relaunch of the bar, it'll all go back to normal, I promise. I'll make it up to you."

She smiled, uneasily. "Not long now."

He chased his food around the plate. "Do you ever just wish we could run away together?" he asked, then added abruptly, "The two of us, no one else, just getting away... Away from the rain. Away from here."

"Paul..." She sighed. "Is there something you want to tell me?"

He looked at his watch. "Shit, look at the time. I have to get going."

She sighed again. She'd learned not to expect answers.

A few minutes later, he rushed out the door. She barely saw him for the rest of the week.

On the night before the opening he didn't come home at all.

CHAPTER EIGHTEEN

Paul surveyed the newly refurbished bar with satisfaction, enjoying its perfection. He felt a small twinge of sadness as he thought of the waiting customers, knowing the place would never be as flawless again. The old dame had been revamped in style. Embracing her cracks and crags, they had stripped the wall behind the bar down to the bare brick and exposed the steel piping that ran along the roof. Every inch of the stone-tiled floor had been scrubbed. The black, granite-topped bar was unmarked, with not a single streak. Behind it, bottles of every shape and colour sparkled. Each one had been individually polished. Newly fitted low-level lighting gave it a forbidden, illusionary feel, as if nothing were quite real.

There was a queue building up outside.

He took one last look at his beautiful bar. Everyone was at their stations, poised. The door staff, in smart black suits, were ready with glasses of champagne to welcome people as they came in. Waiters in crisp white shirts and black waistcoats prepared to circle with trays of canapés.

The place smelled of lemons and fresh leather. Every detail was perfect.

Apart from one.

Paul looked at the empty space at his side where Lena should have been standing. She hadn't shown up. She was supposed to be there to help with the meet and greet. He nodded at Lauren, the girl he'd put in her place. She wasn't beautiful. She wouldn't charm the customers. Lena wasn't there and he had no idea why.

He did one final check of his phone. No messages. He held his head up. So be it. It was time to open the doors. He adjusted the lapel of his Hugo Boss suit and polished a fingerprint from one final glass.

"OK. Good luck, everyone. Show time."

There was a brief hush before the crowds began to filter in. Paul watched them enter: well dressed; expensive accessories. The celebrated DJ he'd hired for the night started playing. The launch party got under way.

The initial part was a ticket-only affair, due to last from seven thirty till nine. This was his chance to shine. He'd sent invites to all the prominent businesses, and to theatres, television companies and relevant members of the press, but he was overwhelmed to see how many people showed up. It had kept him awake at night, worrying that no one would come. After nine, the doors would open to the general public.

The week before he'd held a training day for all bar staff on how to make cocktails. For the night he'd hired two expert cocktail makers for some extra entertainment – throwing shakers, spinning bottles to wow the customers. He wanted fireworks.

Paul mingled with his guests, fetched menus, prepared drinks, did whatever was needed. He felt like he'd been preparing for this his whole life and his nerves disappeared as soon as things got under way. When a waiter spilled a drink on a woman's new coat, Paul offered to pay the dry cleaning bill. When they ran out of midori, he sent someone to the local Sainsbury's to get an emergency stash. He took everything in his stride. Wherever he looked, customers were being treated like royalty, his staff fighting for each person's approval. He'd invited them all into his handsome abode and was showing them the time of their lives.

When the free drinks were gone, Paul watched as cocktail after cocktail was poured, the pounds piling up behind the bar. Waiting time was kept to a minimum. Everyone was happy.

Before the doors opened to the public, he made a short speech thanking the representatives from the bank who'd given their sponsorship and provided the night's champagne. He thanked the caterers, his staff, the builders and their families. And to finish off, he took a moment to mention John, the previous owner of The Low Road who had tragically passed away. Nobody there knew who he was but Paul thought he would have been proud of it. Finally he thanked John's wife, the current owner, who sadly couldn't be there either. He made her apologies and bid everyone enjoy the rest of the evening.

After the speech Paul spent some time out front with the bouncers, monitoring the members of the public who were now coming in. Getting a feel for the crowd, the numbers. It didn't take long before the bar reached capacity and the bouncers started turning people away. Paul went back inside and mingled some more.

When last orders were finally called, the place was still

rocking. The final drinks were sold, the music cut and the cleaning lights switched on. Only then did Paul get the chance to grab another quick look at his phone. Still nothing. With disappointment he put it back in the inner pocket of his jacket.

A journalist reviewing the bar asked to speak to him and they found a seat in the corner from which Paul could also supervise the clearing up and the customers' evacuation. The journalist wanted to discuss the role Paul had played in the renovation. Paul told him about the initial idea, the challenges of working to a deadline, on budget. But mostly he talked about the effort made by the other people involved. He didn't like talking about himself. He didn't need the accolade. It was enough for him to see all his hard work come to fruition and to know himself that he'd done it. It was him that made this happen.

Mid-way through his prepared spiel, Paul was distracted by a familiar and unwelcome face at the other end of the bar. The white-headed man was dressed in the same shabby cream and grey ensemble of their first encounter, in this very bar. Paul excused himself from the interview and crossed over to confront him.

DCI Carmichael's elbow was propped on the bar; with his free hand, he tapped his cheap watch. "You're past your licensing hour."

Paul looked over at the bar clock. It was a few minutes after half twelve. He glowered at Carmichael. "How did you get in? I hired doormen to keep out the riff-raff. There is a dress code."

Carmichael snorted. "Dress up for this shithole? Why bother? The place stinks."

"Well, why are you here then?" Paul raised his voice and then remembered where he was. Customers were still within earshot.

"I wanted to see what all the fuss was about." Carmichael looked around him in feigned disgust. "Not much. It's like a whore's bedroom." He poked his finger in Paul's shoulder and came close enough so that Paul could smell the drink on his breath. "I just wanted to remind you I've still got my eye on you."

In the background, Paul could see the bouncer looking over. He waved him back, signalling that he had the situation under control. The night had passed without a scene. He didn't want to start one now.

"You've given your message, so you can drink up and get going," he said.

Carmichael held up his half-finished pint and inspected it in the light, scrunching his lips with distaste. "Difficult to swallow." He placed it down on the bar. "Maybe I'll try again when the new lot take over. I take it John's wife was fleeced in the sale?"

Paul was struggling to show restraint. "What sale?"

Carmichael's face lit up. "So you're not in the loop? Munroe and you not as close as I thought. Ah well."

"What are you talking about?"

"Maybe it's time you had a word with your boss. Looks like you'll be out of a job tomorrow," he taunted. "He's got you where he wants you. Bent over a barrel, from what I can see." He noted Paul's shocked expression and smirked. "That wiped the smile off that smug face of yours."

Paul grabbed Carmichael's pint and poured it down the

nearby sink. "Drinking-up time's over."

He walked away to take the tills downstairs and by the time he returned, Carmichael was gone.

Paul dialled Manny's number but it went straight to voicemail. Soldiering on, he made sure that empty glasses were cleared from tables and final customers politely pushed through the doors. When the last one was gone, Paul gathered his staff together and gave them a round of applause. There was no doubt they had pulled it off with style, no denying the night was a runaway success. He handed out free passes for a nightclub in town, with tokens for free drinks, and let them head off; he would finish the cleaning-up himself. A few were disappointed when he told them he'd catch up with them later. One of the barmaids, who'd long been making sheep's eyes at him, used Lena's absence as an excuse to openly flirt. But he couldn't be persuaded. Sending them off on a high note, he decided the news that they might all soon be unemployed could wait till tomorrow.

He remained there alone, mourning his beautiful bar. What should have been a jubilant celebration for him became a funeral wake. He took a bottle of Cristal from the fridge, the one he'd been planning to open with Lena, and popped the cork. The creamy bubbles overflowed into his single flute. He tried phoning Lena again. He tried phoning Manny. Both went straight to voicemail. Feeling utterly deflated, he pulled down the front shutter, locking out the world.

He didn't hear Manny let himself in the back door and only knew he was in the bar when the door from the cellar flew open behind him. He swung round to the sight of

Manny stepping up the last stair, sharply dressed in fitted pin-stripes, no tie, the top button of his shirt undone.

"I didn't hear you come in." Paul sank into his seat and gritted his teeth. The bottle of Cristal was half-finished and his stomach was beginning to churn from the acidity.

Manny dangled his set of keys. "No problems tonight?" He walked across the floor to the bar, like he owned the place.

Paul watched him bitterly. "Usual opening-night hitches. Nothing major."

"So why are you not out celebrating?" Manny went behind the bar and poured himself a malt whisky from one of the most expensive bottles.

Without the restraint of full sobriety, Paul glared at him, unable to hide his anger.

Manny took a swig and then closed his eyes, savouring it. When he opened them and Paul was still staring at him, he stopped and put his glass down on the granite bar-top. "Is something wrong?"

"Is it true you're selling the place?"

Manny smiled. "When I missed your call, I thought—"

"Is it true?"

"Yes," he said slowly. "I've been in negotiations for a week or so now. Sealed the deal tonight." He came out from behind the bar and rested his elbows behind him on the counter.

"So why didn't you tell me?" Paul got up out of his seat and came towards him, stopping a yard or two away. "After all the work I put in—"

"You were well paid for your work."

Paul could see Manny wasn't going to be reasonable, but then he never was. He choked with hatred for the man.

"What?" Manny said. "Just because you put some work into a place, you own it? You don't, Paul. I do. Or I did. Now I have a seven-figure sum in my back pocket."

Paul's temper flared, his body shaking with rage. "You know what? Fuck this! I quit. I don't work for you anymore." He headed for the cellar door.

Manny called him back. "You're going nowhere, son."

Paul pivoted on his heels, energised, the taste of a fight in his mouth. "You can't stop me."

Manny's laughter stoked his temper. "I thought this might happen if I let you get too carried away. Getting big ideas. What're you going to do, run out into the night? And do what, panhandle for a living?"

"I'll go out on my own. Start my own place." Paul couldn't believe how simple it sounded. Why he'd never seriously considered it before.

"Not in this town you won't."

"Somewhere else," Paul said defiantly.

"And how are you going to do that?" Manny stepped towards him. Paul kept the door in sight. "There's a world of difference between owning a bar and managing one, Paul. No running to me for handouts every time you want to do up the place. A schemie with a record. No qualifications, no references, dependents – you think the bank's going to help you? The council? I've heard it's hard to get a licence. You need a bit of influence, some friends in your back pocket, that kind of thing. No, son, not without my contacts, my collateral, my reputation at your back. You're nothing without me."

Paul was backing away. "Then I'll be nothing. I'll go somewhere and I'll serve coffee for a living. I don't need your money."

"I'd find you."

Manny paused to let the full weight of the threat sink in. Paul was locked to the spot. A gust of wind blew up from the cellar, prickling the back of his neck.

"No, I think it's good for you to stay where you are." Manny drew even closer. Paul could feel his resolve dissolving. "I've already got something lined up for you."

"I won't do it."

"Yes you will."

Paul was sweating around the collar, his earlier energy waning. The lights glared too brightly in his eyes. The glass glistened in Manny's hand.

"Because I know of a certain shallow grave, with a certain body, and a certain sealed bag with a pile of bloodstained clothes inside." Manny backed him against the wall. "You look like you want to hit me, Paul."

He did want to. He wanted to floor him. Hit him in the face. Knock his teeth out. Kick him to the ground, have him beg for mercy.

"Do you, Paul? Are you going to fight me?"

Paul raised his fists. Manny moved closer.

"I like it when you fight me."

Manny's lifeless eyes were black, flat like a shark's. Paul's fists slowly unclenched.

Manny sneered. "I didn't think so."

He threw the glass against the wall above Paul's head. The smash rang loudly in Paul's ear, whisky and glass poured down on him. A punch struck Paul square in the stomach and he doubled over, gasping for air, his eyes focusing on

Manny's boots circling beneath him. Manny grasped him with both hands and pulled him over to the nearest table, knocking down chairs on the way. Paul struggled against him but the wind had been knocked out of him. Another blow from Manny, this time to the face, stunned him. Manny forced him over the table, his arms stretched out flat, his cheek pressed against it. As he unbuckled Paul's trousers, Paul, half conscious, felt his body surrender. Sometimes it was easier not to react. He heard Manny undo his own zip. He tried to turn round, but Manny held his head in place.

Manny spat onto his hand and used it as lubricant. Paul looked around the disordered bar. Under the white glare of the cleaning light he could see all the stains and scars as clear as they had always been. He hadn't covered them at all. All the refurbishment in the world couldn't get rid of them.

At the moment of entry Paul winced then forced himself motionless, trying to relax his muscles, his eyes shut tight. Manny's thighs began pounding against him, his cock piercing again, again. He could hear Manny's breath tearing out behind him, Paul holding his, wishing it to be over. The pleasant tingling in his stomach wanting it to last.

Paul felt Manny finish as he did too. Manny patted him on the back, out of breath as if he'd just completed a race, resting momentarily on Paul. When he stepped away, Paul pulled his trousers up, panting. He flopped to the floor, leaning against the booth. Manny sat down beside him. He reached out and put his hand on Paul's face, not roughly, not gently. "What do you do to me?" he said, his jaw locked in a furious smile.

At that moment, out of the corner of his eye, Paul saw

something flutter behind the cellar door. Before he could move, it swung open and Lena stood there, hand over her mouth. Through her fingers, she mumbled, "What's going on, Paul?"

Manny answered. "What's it look like, you silly tart?"

Her eyes searched Paul's face. "Paul?"

He couldn't bring himself to meet her eye. Still dazed and sick with shame, there was nothing he could say. The room was deathly quiet, as if all life in the world had been extinguished with one strong breath. Manny let out a burst of laughter.

Lena fled the room before Paul could make it to his feet. "Lena!" He chased after her. "LENA! Come back. Please!"

But she was already through the door, into the night.

Paul sat sullenly in the car as Manny dropped him home, not openly complaining for fear of what it might stir. He got out quietly, saying nothing, shutting the car door carefully so as not to made a noise. He barely had the strength to make it to his front door. The lights were still on. It gave him hope as he walked in surrender up the path, his body still in pain. Letting himself in, he took tentative steps, listening for some hint of sound in the silence that met him. Straight away it was clear there was something different about the place. He walked from room to room more than once just to make sure she wasn't there.

He checked in drawers and cupboards, the shower shelf in the bathroom. All her stuff was gone. Lena had cleared out. He had no idea where she would go.

Sitting on the bed, in shock, unable to fully grasp what

was happening, he saw the shoebox sitting on the pillow, the one they'd argued about the week before. It was the only thing she appeared to have left behind. Reaching over, he took off the lid. There was no longer money inside; instead there was a smaller box, wrapped neatly in brown paper. Carefully, he slipped his fingers under the Sellotape and lifted up the flaps. The wrapping came off to reveal another box. This one had the word *Rolex* written in gold on the front. Inside lay a beautiful crystal-faced watch on a polished steel band. She must have been planning to surprise him at the after-party. He turned it over. On the back there was an inscription: *To Paul. All my love always, best friend. I love you. Lena*

*

Strapped to Annie's chair, Paul looked down at his left wrist. The watch was just visible beneath the circles of hemp rope around it. The warders had given it back to him when he left prison. He'd thought about selling it – he needed the money – but he couldn't bring himself to go through with it.

It was painful now to look back. Remembering their hopes and dreams. Their lives together, ahead of them. Those small, special moments, growing steadily less tangible, swirling and floating like wisps of cloud. Each one as delicate and short lived as a snowflake.

Afterwards all he was left with was the anger and bitterness of words spoken that could never be taken back, the hurt of insults thrown and selfish acts, betrayals, that would smart and sting for a lifetime. And worst of all, regret. The smothering, consuming regret.

He wore the watch now like a shackle around his wrist.

"She saw me and Manny... together," he said to Annie and waited for her reaction.

"You and Manny together doing what?"

She looked at him with dawning realisation, not sure whether to believe him or spit on him.

"I wouldn't go telling anyone else about it. People have been killed for less." He shook his head as if to rid it of the memory.

"But you told me you loved her." She spoke in accusation.

"I did." His hands clenched and unclenched. "But with me and Manny, it was complicated."

"Complicated how? You loved him too?"

"No." He pondered the absurd duality. "I hated him."

CHAPTER NINETEEN

Seventeen years ago

It was quiet on Glasgow Green, the din of traffic from the nearby street absorbed by the tall, frost-laced trees. Silver moonlight shone through the spindly branches, casting ragged dagger shapes on the dark ground. Paul stood, hat pulled down, hood up, jacket zipped to the neck, trying to stave off the icy wind coming off the River Clyde. One hand was buried deep in his pocket while the other, numb and red, held a shaking cigarette, the glowing ember a ruby speck in the gloom. He'd hoarded the cigarette all day, not wanting to smoke it too early and leave himself disappointed. He had to wait for the perfect moment, for when he needed it most, when he needed his mind and body to be in freefall, to calm his nerves for what he was about to do.

Three minutes and it was gone, the warm rush fading with the slow intrusion of hunger, anticipation and the damp smell of foliage. He was sixteen and all he wanted was a bed, a decent meal and something to ease the pain.

His eyes turned to the pathway, the darkness looming like a cold breath on his shoulder. Endless days waiting for night, endless nights waiting for day.

A figure appeared from the shadows, moonlit. Showtime, thought Paul. He watched the man walk towards him: head bowed beneath a cap, collar turned up, middle-aged, medium height, casual clothes, neither expensive nor cheap. For a brief second it seemed that he might walk past but at the last moment he looked up, a coy smile on his face, just visible in the gloom. Paul prepared himself for action. Flashing a quick glance over the man's shoulder to the bushes where his friend Paddy was crouched, he raked the ground with his foot.

"You got a light?" the man asked.

"You got a cigarette?"

The man reached for his packet and offered Paul one. Paul lit the cigarettes and for a short time they smoked in silence.

Up close, Paul was able to measure him more closely. The man was shorter than him but his posture was upright, commanding more space than was necessary. Paul was tall for his age, but slight. The man's stocky build made him more imposing than he first appeared.

"Looking for someone?"

"I'm not here for the fresh air, son."

"Hundred quid. Money up front." Paul closed in on him, reeling him in but ready to run if things turned ugly.

"Fifty." The man's eyes looked Paul up and down. Paul clocked the wedding band as the man reached out his hand and placed it on the nape of Paul's neck. "And you swallow."

He tried to focus on the man's face but couldn't help shooting another quick glance beyond him to the shifting shadow coming towards them. That, and the slightest tremble in the air as the weapon was wielded was all it took to alert the man. He flinched, cigarette dropped, and the pipe that was supposed to crash into his skull instead smashed into his shoulder.

Like a bear, the man lunged at Paddy, knocking him to the ground, the pipe bouncing into the bushes. Paul leaped on the man's back, trying to bring him down, but the man was strong and threw him to the ground with a sharp thud. Prone on the damp grass, Paul watched as the man stomped full force on Paddy's groin. Then, with blood on his lips, he turned to Paul, bounding towards him, his grey hair wild.

Paul tried to get up, to run. But there was no chance of escape. Grabbing him by both arms, the man smashed his head into the bridge of Paul's nose. Paul heard a crunch and his neck jerked back. There was shouting and then running, fading footsteps pounding on the concrete. Through a film of blood, Paul saw his friend disappearing down the path and into the night. The rabid snarls of the man intensified as his face slowly appeared above Paul, nostrils flared, side teeth bared. A boot connected with Paul's face again and again. It took some time before everything fell into darkness.

He woke up to the smell of disinfectant, a flickering strip light above him, the machine beside him beeping. He tried to speak but couldn't; his jaw had been wired shut. His tongue felt too big for his mouth, his teeth ragged. All movement was restricted by the tight white sheets that hemmed him in. His right leg hovered above him, in traction. There was so much pain it was impossible to tell where it was coming from. He managed a low moan. A nurse's feet padded towards him; her fingers checked his pulse and the clear liquid she injected into the drip slowly dissolved the pain.

His first few days in intensive care passed in a drug-addled blur. His body functioned with the aid of machines. At night he woke up screaming. The doctor said it was to be expected. An attack of that nature.

There was a shadow of the man's boot on his brain.

Images came back to him in shuddering flashes: the man's snarling face, Paddy running into the night. Abandoned and alone. Trapped with a monster. Given the chance, would he have done the same? Probably. Hot tears formed behind his eyes.

They moved him to a general ward after a week, among frail old men clinging to their last breaths of life, their grey skin marbled with blue veins. His morphine dosage was reduced and he wondered how the others survived in so much pain. He couldn't eat. He couldn't sleep. Pissing and shitting mostly blood into a bag. Locked inside himself. Mute. Immobile. He felt like he was eighty years old. He was broken. Broken into tiny pieces that could no longer fit back together.

"You need to try and get better," the doctor told him. "If you go on like this you're going to make yourself ill. Really ill. The bones will mend," she reassured him. Paul could see in her eyes, in her lapses into silence, that she wasn't speaking of the other things that wouldn't mend. The sunlight reflected off the pretty gold cross around her neck, sending gold dots around the room. He barely heard her when she spoke.

He closed his eyes, tears running down his cheeks. There was nothing left in him. He was empty, just a receptacle for pain and fear. He didn't want to survive. At times he wondered if he was already dead and was actually living in hell. The police came to see him but he told them nothing. He was well versed in the Glasgow code. The doctor nodded and they left him alone.

No one else came to visit until the third week. By that time he'd begun to eat without assistance, through a straw. At first he could manage only liquids the consistency of water, but slowly he was able to take things that were more substantial: milkshakes, yoghurts, working up to pureed vegetables. The bruising and swelling had gone down. The wiring in his jaw remained and his leg was still in a cast, but with each day that passed, another tube was removed. He was beginning to appreciate the bed – its warmth and the fact he couldn't smell himself. His undernourished body was being replenished with the nutrients it had been missing. He always knew where the next meal was coming from.

Sometimes the doctor stopped and talked with him, told him about her brothers and sisters, some of whom were his age. He noticed that she was very pretty when she smiled. He tried not to look at her in case it made her hate him. She told him she had contacted some charities that could help find him a flat; on account of his age, she thought he would be seen as a priority case. It sounded like a fairytale for nice people like her to believe in. He sank beneath the warm covers and prepared himself for nights on cardboard.

On the day his visitor arrived, the doctor came to see him with a furrowed brow. "You've got a visitor, Paul. Your uncle?"

Paul pushed himself up in bed. He didn't protest that he had no uncle, and nodded.

She left and returned a few minutes later with a man. Paul watched him approach.

"I only just got word you were here, son," the man said, beaming. "Glad to see you looking so well."

His clothes were different. Smarter, the kind of clothes you wanted people to notice. Not like the last time. Paul stared in horror at his face; not one he would forget easily. It had kept him awake ever since that night in the park. The doctor gave Paul a curious look, but he didn't raise the alarm. She walked away and the man scraped a chair across the floor, pulling it close to the bed.

"Didn't expect to see me again," the man said under his breath.

Paul looked at him, lost for words even if the wire hadn't been holding his mouth shut.

"I'm just here to check it out in the flesh. That it's true. You're still alive."

He said it in a way that made Paul want to apologise for the fact. Paul searched the faces of the other people in the ward, sitting with family members. But they were smiling, laughing. They didn't notice him sitting mere feet away, weak with fear. He felt like he was in a dream, one where something bad was chasing him but his screams were silent, his limbs were rubber.

"Thought we might celebrate together," the man continued, his tone menacing.

Paul nodded and mumbled through the wire.

"Ssh, ssh. Don't try to talk." The man held up his hand to quiet him.

Paul sank into his pillow, paled by the effort; saliva dribbled from the corner of his mouth.

The man leaned forward in his chair, a hand on one knee,

elbow on the other. It was how Paul's grandfather used to sit. He found it strangely comforting – he'd liked his grandfather. He was a decent enough old bloke.

The man looked Paul up and down, shaking his head slowly from side to side. "You've been left in a right mess. That's a shame. That is a shame."

Paul watched every move closely.

The man laced his fingers together and snapped them backwards, crunching the knuckles. "Still, I don't have to worry about the polis knocking down my door to arrest me for beating a rent boy to death in the park." He barked the last words as if they were the punch line to a joke. "That would have placed me in a very awkward situation. You and your friend… Paddy… nearly placed me in a very awkward situation."

Paul flinched at the mention of his friend's name. He had a sudden image of his friend strung out in the street, trusting anyone who offered to give him a tenner. He wondered how long it had taken before Paddy had given up his name.

The man clasped his hands together in front of him. "He's not going to be talking to anyone soon. Fucking coward. What kind of lowlife runs off and leaves a friend to take a beating?"

Who was this man? There weren't many could walk into a ward full of people and casually talk life and death. There weren't many who could so brazenly threaten someone mere inches away. He was someone, this man.

Paul suddenly started to see, in the light of day, what he hadn't seen under the cover of darkness. The man's dead-fish eyes stared at him. Somewhere a spark of recognition ignited and he realised he'd seen them even before the night in the park. Staring out from black-and-white pictures in tabloid newspapers, staring out from underneath headlines. *Gangland. Murder. Torture.* The dawning realisation registered on his face.

"You know who I am?" the man asked.

Paul nodded his head, slowly.

Manny Munroe smiled and nodded. "You fucked up."

Paul gripped the sides of his bed.

Munroe's face became deadpan. "So that leaves me with one problem."

Paul choked back bile. Munroe continued, calmly; he was a man used to speaking to people in mortal fear. "So you understand what I have to do?" His voice was almost regretful.

Paul shuffled up the bed, trying to put as much distance between himself and Munroe as he could, but his leg kept that distance tight. A cold sweat laced his brow. His breath came out in bursts, his jaws fought to part, but the wires held them closed. He could taste blood in his mouth. Some heads in the ward turned towards them.

Munroe stood up and Paul shrank back. With unblinking eyes he watched Munroe root around for a glass and pour some water from the jug. Paul didn't want it, but he took the glass, hands shaking so much he could hardly hold it. Munroe helped place the straw in his mouth and Paul choked it back. To anyone watching, it was the kind gesture of an uncle to his favourite nephew. Munroe smiled at the people around them and sat back in his chair. Deep creases in the skin around his eyes made them appear like black hollows. He waited for Paul to compose himself before he went on.

"I already know you didn't talk to the polis," he said evenly. "Or they'd've already been picking pieces of you from the rubbish heap."

Paul shook his head and let the empty glass roll onto the covers beside him.

"It's who else you might go blabbing to that's a problem for me."

With his head now resting on the pillow, he closed his eyes. There didn't seem any point in trying to protest. What would it matter to a man like Munroe? Even if he offered the world, Munroe had probably heard it all before, and more. Such promises would be meaningless to men like him.

"The doctor said I'm the first to visit you."

Paul opened his eyes and nodded. It was true. No one to miss him if he were to suddenly disappear.

Manny watched him, measuring him. "No people?"

Paul shook his head.

"Do you have some place to go to when you get out of here?"

He shook his head again.

"Not had much luck, son, have you?"

Paul shook his head and almost laughed. To be pitied by the man who wanted to kill you. It was one way to twist the knife.

Manny's face was dark and ugly. He stared fixedly at Paul. "It's a shame you being so young..."

Paul did his best to meet his gaze. If Munroe was going to kill him, at least Paul could look him in the eye. One last fuck you, in the series of them that had made up his short life.

"It wasn't a bad gig – one acting as bait, the other springing from behind. In the middle of nowhere, no witnesses, it would probably go unreported." Munroe held up his hands matter-of-factly. "But you picked the wrong guy."

Paul cursed his own bad, fucking luck.

There was a pause. Paul could look no more. His eyes fell to the floor, to the scuffed toes of Munroe's boots. He ran his tongue over his tattered teeth. Munroe put a reassuring hand on the covers, over Paul's knee, and shook. Then he stood up and pulled the curtain round them, the hooks clicking rhythmically against the rail. Paul's spine tingled. He felt like he'd been left alone in the dark with a venomous spider bristling just inches away. *This is it,* he thought, it's going to happen right here and now. He'd always imagined his death being something bigger. Some kind of fight to it, maybe some tragedy. Even if it was just defending his corner in a turf war. He didn't want it like this. Anonymously. Silently.

Manny walked over and placed a strong hand on Paul's injured shoulder. He pressed. Paul squirmed under his grip. Manny reached into the inside pocket of his jacket. Paul held his breath. He watched the hand come out. In it Manny was holding a folded-over sheet of A5 glossy paper. It floated down onto the bed and Paul read the name of a pool hall on the front.

"When you get out of here, I want you to come see me." Still squeezing, Munroe leaned in and spoke very quietly. "You know who I am. But you don't know what I'm capable of. Speak to anyone about what happened and you'll be finding out."

Munroe gave one final squeeze. Paul had to stop himself crying out.

"Don't make me come looking for you," Manny said, before disappearing behind the curtain.

Paul drew his hand along his sweat-streaked brow.

Three weeks later Paul was released. His wires were removed and he was able to walk out the front door on crutches. The doctor was true to her word and he was given a flat in the Anderston high-rises. A meeting was set up with the Job Centre. She told him to ask about taking a college course.

The first night he sat alone in his empty flat, a torn poster of *Scarface* the only thing left behind by the previous owner. He held the flier Munroe had given him in his hand and stayed up for hours, thinking. The next day he went down to the pool hall. Bucky and Dunsmore were waiting outside in the winter sunshine. Terry was just inside the door.

Would Manny really have come to find him if he hadn't gone? At the time, it hadn't felt like a choice. If he'd known then how things would turn out, would he have left, started a new life on his own? At what point did it become too late? If he'd never been born, would the people he killed still be alive?

*

Paul kept his eyes on Annie. "There were things between me and Manny. I tried to keep it from Lena."

Annie's face was impassive; her eyes flat, revealing nothing.

"After she found us together, it was a few months before I saw her again. I think you know what happened then."

He watched for some kind of sign from her. He was bound and weary, his muscles sore, his chest tight. Her mouth was shut in a hard line.

"I remember," she eventually said, though it seemed to pain her to do so.

Paul watched her reclining onto the couch, sitting in

judgement, her face a blank slate, neither smiling nor frowning.

CHAPTER TWENTY

Nine years ago

Within a week of the relaunch party at The Low Road, Manny had moved Paul to another of his businesses, a nightclub called Limbo. Defeated and detached, Paul had relocated without protest. Soon after, he moved house as well.

Lena was gone – he hadn't seen her for weeks, since the night she ran off, leaving behind only the watch. He'd searched for her, called her but got no answer, gone to her mother's house to see if she knew anything. Nothing. It was like she'd disappeared off the face of the earth.

On his way home from his shifts at Limbo, it became his nightly habit to detour via the casino. He would pass away the small hours listening to the shuffle of razor-sharp cards, the snap as they were placed on green felt. Like a reliable friend, the casino was always there for him when he needed a lift. Sitting among like-minded people, he could make sense of the chaos. At daybreak, when the sun threatened, he'd roll out the door and walk home through the dewy dawn, his only brush with a day that he wouldn't be a part of. Sometimes he had company, sometimes he didn't. It didn't matter. Women, like the drugs and the money, came easily to him since he'd started at Limbo. He'd sleep until evening, when he would get up and prepare for another night. It suited him, this hazy existence among light shows and artificial smoke, living only in the night, freed from continuity.

Manny had brought him in to Limbo on the understanding that it was for supervisory purposes. On paper it was his nephew Dario who owned and managed it. Son of Manny's only sister, Dario had been Manny's big hope since childhood. Manny had paid to put Dario through a number of private schools – from which he was repeatedly expelled. Also through a business degree at university, though after three years he was still on the first round of exams. Dario was now twenty-eight, with no experience or qualifications, but Manny still hadn't given up on him. In the meantime, Paul had been brought in to babysit.

Dario's management style included showing up when he felt like it, often drunk, to distribute free drinks to his ever growing entourage. It was Paul's job to actually run the place while keeping checks on Dario, to make sure he didn't pimp out all the profits on orgies with underage girls. For Dario, the chances kept coming. Some guys had rich and powerful uncles, some were born into families of lowlifes. But those were the breaks. Paul knew there'd be an opportunity to outmanoeuvre him – with people like Dario there always was – but he was going to have to be smart about it. Paul may have been the nephew Manny wished he'd had, but blood was blood.

The casino was quiet for a Friday night/Saturday morning. Some people crowded round the bar, a fair number at the roulette tables, but Paul had no problem finding a seat at one of the card tables and had managed to gather a few stacks of high-value chips not long after. Enough to get himself a nice suit. Straight to the jack. He watched the croupier slide across some more to add to the pile. Flush in hearts. With a little more luck, some nice cufflinks.

The overweight, middle-aged woman sitting beside him leaned over and clucked, "I know where Lady Luck's residing tonight, and it's not with me."

Paul managed a thin smile. From the moment she'd sat down, Paul had identified her as a talker.

Full house! The croupier doubled his stack. Paul's hands closed around the mound of black chips that appeared before him. He enjoyed the satisfying click as he rippled them up and down.

"Tell her to shift down one!" the woman squealed.

He just managed to stop himself from telling her to fuck off. Casino or not, a degree of respect was still called for towards women of a certain age.

"Walk away while you can, son, or you'll regret it. The house always wins," she cackled in his ear.

How many times had he heard that? He looked at her roll of twenty-pounds, meant to last her the night, and then to the roll of fat around her midriff. At least playing cards might one day make him rich, he thought; chronic overeating was never going to make her thin. She was gambling every day with her health; he wondered why she couldn't see that.

"I'm telling you, son, it's a sickness."

He nodded at the irony.

And that was the turning point. For the remaining

hands, Paul played like he was hell-bent on throwing away all his money. There was a certain determination to his losing. Silently, he lost chip after chip until eventually he had only one left. He watched as the croupier beat his pair with a flush.

The woman flashed him a smug, satisfied smile. "Should have walked away."

As he left the card table Paul had his head held high. True, he'd lost, but you've got to take the rough with the smooth, he thought; the yin and the yang. One day Paul knew he would hit the jackpot. Not that day, but some day. People like her never would. He gave her a cheeky wink as he walked away.

On the way to the exit he veered towards the spin of the roulette table. There was something drawing him there, he could feel it. The large table was just a few steps from the front door. A row of slot machines flashed and beeped beside it. Obnoxious tunes exploded intermittently, only one or two diehards feeding coins into the greedy mouths. More people were gathered round the roulette table. Cutting his way through the circle, he slid across the last of his notes to the croupier, who quickly replaced them with a stack of red chips. Paul began placing them down, letting his intuition guide him. When last bets were called he was satisfied with the spread he had on the table.

Trying to concentrate on the croupier's spin, he found himself distracted. He knew she was there before he saw her. While everyone else focused on the spinning ball, Lena and Paul's eyes met across the roulette table. A faint flush appeared on her cheeks. Her long hair was tied up in a tight, high bun; kohl-lined eyes smouldered beneath them. Her slim curves were fitted into an elegant black cocktail dress.

The croupier called, "No more bets." Beside them the ball clicked into a space. They both looked towards it. She'd won. He hadn't. With perfectly manicured hands she cashed in her chips and collected her winnings before leaving the table. Paul watched her climb the broad staircase, drawing her hand along the polished brass rail. He noticed how she wore her dress as comfortably as her own skin. There was no fussing and tugging as there was with other women. She looked back for a moment, found him, then turned and continued up the stairs.

Paul waited a few moments before following her up. He climbed the flight of red-carpeted steps to the landing where the stairs diverged; he took the ones to the right, just as she had. The upstairs lounge was empty apart from a small group sitting round a table nursing drinks, and a bored-looking waiter slouched behind the bar. Through a set of glass doors at the far side of the lounge a poker game was going on. Paul looked around for Lena. It took him a while to spot her outside on the balcony, leaning against the railing.

As he opened the door to go outside a gush of cold air blew into the warm casino. The night was chilly, his jacket little comfort. Lena didn't look round as he came out but he could tell she knew it was him. There was no one else on the balcony. Moving in beside her, he rested his elbows on the railing next to hers, close enough to feel the warmth of her body. Lena's bare shoulders quivered in the icy breeze that was coming off the river. She stared off into the distance.

"Glasgow city skyline – none finer." Paul's voice broke the silence. "And what's on the menu tonight? If we look down to the right we have one of Glasgow's specials: a tramp peeing. Just slightly off to the left we have couple number one throwing punches; a rare delicacy, these unique fighting creatures are specially bred and cultivated for that extra zing. Up to our far left we have a First Bus delight – Irn-Bru bottle through the window; and from the frozen selection we can offer you tits-and-arse tart for the finer palate. Don't you just love it?"

The hint of a smile flitted across her face. He took off his jacket and offered it to her. She didn't take it so he placed it around her shoulders. Together they looked out over the black water studded with amber crystals that twinkled in the moonlight; no hint of the dangerous currents that raged underneath.

"I searched everywhere for you." He looked sideways at her, finding it easier to stare at the dark seduction of the water; her eyes two scorching embers beside him.

"My mum said you'd been round," she finally answered.

His eyes fell on the diamond necklace delicately clasped round her slender neck and he wondered vaguely if it was real. "That Jason's a fucking prick." A spray of spittle came out and he awkwardly licked his lips dry as he looked up at her, her cheeks a sanguine blush against her coffee-coloured skin.

"Yeah, he is," she said tiredly.

Paul tried to take her hand but she pulled it away, suppressing a shudder.

"Not now, Paul. Not here."

He watched as the hurt in her face was quickly replaced by something else, something he couldn't quite place but that made him squirm, at first with shame and then with anger.

"Well, when?" Wisps of white cloud formed when he spoke, the sound carrying thinly in the night air. "Are you just going to disappear again?"

She took his jacket from her shoulders and pushed it into his hands.

"Lena?"

He stared as she turned on her heel, opened the door and went back inside. Through the glass he could see her almost gliding across the upstairs lounge. He hesitated a moment then sprang from the railing and went after her, swishing through the door. He reached her at the stairs.

"Lena, don't walk away from me, please." He placed a conciliatory hand on her shoulder, her skin like velvet.

The heads of the small group nursing drinks turned towards them.

She shrugged him off and began to descend the staircase, only making it a few steps before she stopped, hovered and turned back to him, her face an accusation staring up at him.

"It's too late, Paul. It's just too late."

He began fishing for his pen in the inside pocket of his jacket. Alongside it his fingers edged a rectangular card. Hastily he pulled it out and, meeting her on the step, leaned on the brass banister and started to write. "My new address. Phone number. Any day, any night. Please. I need to talk to you."

He finished the semi-legible scrawl and handed it to her.

Lena took the card, turning it over in her hand. Paul watched her thumb etch the embossed gold lettering: *The Pink Pussy Cat.* She inspected the curvaceous blonde scantily clad in pink lingerie. Manny had given him a bundle of free passes to hand out at Limbo and one had made its way into his own pocket. He was a single man now.

She turned the card around in her hand, his address facing up.

"Please call. Even if it's just to let me know you're alright."

She looked back at the card. "Don't you know…" Paul watched her slip the card into her bag. "I always land on my feet."

"There you are! I've been looking all over for you," a voice called from the half landing. They both looked towards it. Paul saw that it came from a man in his late thirties or early forties; tall, dressed in a smart dinner suit, his thinning hair neatly trimmed. He had a strong, educated Scottish accent – the clear, over-enunciated voice of someone who spent time out of the country and had to make himself understood by foreigners. The voice of a man with soft, clean hands and clipped nasal hair.

Lena began walking towards him and Paul watched from over the banister as they embraced. "I just needed some fresh air," she said, still within earshot of Paul. Her hand massaged the man's arm.

He looked over at Paul, unsure of what he had interrupted. "Is everything OK?"

Lena wiped away a tear from her eye. "The cold made my eyes water."

Paul remained motionless as in front of him Lena's demeanour changed. She was suddenly all cool elegance and practised charm, her words accentless, very much a mature woman rather than the girl she really was.

"Well, I've got a taxi booked. We'd better get a move

on." Coolly, he looked up at Paul once more, then ushered Lena down the stairs.

As Paul watched them disappear, the sight of the man's tanned hand stroking her bare arms, a white circle on the left-hand ring finger where a wedding band had been recently removed, brought on a bout of almost overwhelming nausea.

He retreated to the bar and ordered a neat vodka from the slouching barman. He downed it in one and ordered another. He chased that one with a beer then ordered another. The night was no longer young but he was just getting started. He continued for another hour until finally he tipped the barman what was left of his chips, grateful that he'd poured the drinks and asked no questions.

It was still dark out as Paul set off for home, the wind biting as he staggered along the Broomielaw. He kept the river to his left, occasionally glancing up at the wall of futuristic titanium-coloured office blocks on his right, now emptied for the weekend. The road was well lit until it passed under the motorway bridge, but then it became steadily darker. The Clyde was still just visible alongside him, but across the way, grey buildings awaiting demolition loomed out of weed-strewn wastelands.

The road was empty of traffic so he walked down the centre of it, not always in a straight line, but heading in the direction of home. Dressed in his suit, with his expensive watch, he was a perfect target for muggers. He walked with a certain swagger, almost hoping someone would try something, relishing the thought. He primed himself, not letting his guard down for a moment, a solitary figure on the dark road. His steps loud in the quiet night.

Eventually the road curved round and in the distance he saw the reassuring black lines of the old Finnieston Crane. He was close to home. The new development of riverside condos that housed his apartment stood a few hundred yards ahead of him. There was a tense moment as he passed a line of brown-leaved trees, their branches leaving dark shadows, but he reached his front door undisturbed. Drunkenly reaching for his keys, he fobbed himself in through the security entrance.

The foyer was still freshly painted, the air rich with the smell of pomegranate. Bowls of potpourri rested beside vases of luscious green shoots that reached to just below the ceiling, secured in pebbles. A CCTV camera pointed at the lift. Paul stared into it while he waited. It seemed that everywhere you turned in Glasgow there was a cheeky purple lens winking at you. Another one met him inside the lift and followed him to his stop on the seventh floor. He walked along the quiet corridor: no sign of life. He wasn't sure he had neighbours; at least, he'd never seen any. A lot of flats in the development had yet to be sold. He liked the emptiness and hoped it would stay that way.

Opening his front door, he went in without switching on the lights. The large open-plan space felt vast, the generous square footage giving it an airy feel. The flat still smelled new. Kicking the door shut with his heel, he tripped over to the kitchen area, barely out of its plastic wrapping, and extracted a bottle of vodka from the fridge. A dark mood descended.

With difficulty, putting the bottle under his armpit, a glass in his hand, he pulled down the handles of the French doors, one at a time, and opened them wide. He hovered for a few moments, breathing in the night air, gazing at his waterfront view, little more than a blur to his eyes. But the couch beckoned. He stumbled back towards it, hitting his shin on the coffee table, banging the bottle dangerously onto its glass top. His heart weighed heavily in his chest. After searching for so long, he had finally found her, only to lose her all over again.

The glass was drained. Hot tears ran down his cheek. Fear and anger flushed through his system like rancid bile. He'd let her slip through his fingers. She'd cringed from his touch. Paul reached for the bottle, desperate to finish, terrified he would run out. He filled his glass until it was almost overflowing, drank it and poured again. His kidneys ached. Vomit rose in his throat but he choked it back. He put the filled glass to his lips but nausea rose again. He knew he couldn't get it down and thumped it onto the table. Taking the half-empty bottle, he rolled it back and forth in his hand for a second before getting to his feet. With force, he hurled it against the wall. He heard the crunch as it smashed. Heard the crunch of John's skull again as the bat smashed into it. Saw Manny's smile as he swung. The heavy sole of his boot as he lay on the ground. Fragmented images of what she must have seen came and went: him and Manny together on the ground.

Razor-sharp shards littered the room, glistening in the moonlight, the alcohol forming streaks across the polished hardwood flooring. Paul tried to cry but it came out in strangled heaves. He felt the darkness take hold inside, rotting him from the inside out. He had to stop it. Had to let it out. Falling to his knees, he half slid, half crawled towards the broken glass. Reaching for the nearest piece, he grabbed it up and slowly drew it along his forearm. The sudden and sharp pain was sweet relief. Blood drained from his arm along with his energy and he dropped on to his back. Shadows danced around the tall walls and high ceiling, dark shapes transforming before his eyes.

The room was almost light when he was roused from his fitful sleep by the sound of knocking. His heart was beating furiously in his chest, his head swirling. He was lying on the same spot, blood smeared on his arm and the floor. Glass strewn in all directions. The room was cold, the balcony doors still wide open.

The knocking continued and he realised it was coming from his front door.

"Fuck off!" His slurred words rang out into the pre-dawn.

There was a momentary pause, then the knocking started again.

Paul groaned. With an effort to coordinate body and limbs, he struggled to his feet, nursing his sore arm. He took a few moments to right himself before cursing his way to the front door.

Through the dome-shaped spy hole he saw the distorted figure of Lena. "Shit." His head made a dense thud as he banged it against the wood with more force than he'd intended. With his good arm he reached down and unlocked the door.

She was dressed in the same floor-length cocktail dress she'd been wearing earlier, each strand of hair still perfectly placed. She had her clutch bag in one hand, a folded-up suit carrier in the other. He noticed with a stab of annoyance that her eyes were puffy from crying.

"What do you want?" His voice was hoarse from sleep,

his tongue soggy with alcohol; the bitter taste and smell emanating from his pores was making him nauseous. A piercing pain had settled at the front of his head and the light from the hallway was burning his eyes.

"Can I come in?"

"What're you doing here?"

"You asked me to come."

Paul, disorientated, took a step back. She walked past him into the entranceway. He shuffled behind her to lock the door, putting on the chain.

"Did I wake you? Paul, it's cold in here."

Stumbling back to the couch, leaving her where she stood, he could see her taking in the chaotic state of the room. Next she took in his own dishevelled appearance. Without saying anything, he sat brooding in the silence, listening to the sound of her breath.

Her eyes reflected the grey half-light like two marbles. It took her a few moments to notice the wound. She gasped. "Paul, what happened here? You've cut yourself."

He watched her scramble back to the front door to the light switch. The explosion of light when she flipped it on left him momentarily blinded. He shaded his eyes. Slowly the blurred figure in front of him came into focus.

She rushed to the kitchen, picked up a fresh towel and ran it under the tap.

"Just leave it, it's nothing," he growled scratchily. The blood had stopped flowing, the wound a crispy purple line on his arm. He spied the glass of vodka on the table in front of him. Taking it in his hand, he dripped some onto his arm, the sting long and deep. The rest he poured down his throat.

Lena stood in front of him aghast, the damp towel in her hands. He snatched it from her and started to rub the blood from the surrounding area as she watched in silence.

The broken bottle of vodka lay between them.

"Where's your necklace?" Her hand moved to her neck and Paul sneered.

"How did you…?" She didn't finish the sentence.

"A present for his wife?" He wondered how she'd got through the security entrance. But then Lena never did need a key. Doors just opened for her.

She shrugged. "I got to wear it first."

His head nodded, his jaw set bitterly. As he tried to stay focused on her, Manny's words rang through his mind. *All women are whores.*

"Do you want me to go, Paul?"

"I don't know. Can I afford for you to stay?"

He watched her face contort; hurt, sad. She did it well. But he didn't believe it for a second. Not this time.

"Paul?"

"Did you at least shower tonight after you fucked your old man?"

She gave a small gasp, her voice raised. "I came because I needed a friend."

Paul watched her with loathing. "What is it this time? Some boyfriend need battering?" The words bubbled out of him in varying degrees of coherence. "Sugar daddy's not leaving his wife for you?"

The anger was building inside him, fuelled by an overwhelming hatred towards her, for the expression on her face. The same one as before, the one that made him feel worthless.

Earlier he hadn't been able to place it. But now he recognised it. Disgust. It was disgust she felt towards him.

"Whores. All women are whores," he spat, his voice breaking.

"You're drunk, Paul. I'm leaving."

She walked towards the door, her high heels clicking on the floor.

He started to get off the couch. "Friend? Is that what I am to you now?" He was up on his feet and swaying. "Friend cos I'm a bender? Is that all I am, a bender friend?"

He steadied himself against the arm of the couch. "Seriously, you think I'm a poof or something? Some fucking rent boy that can be fucked and used?"

Lena picked up her pace and moved at speed towards the door.

Paul stumbled after her, drunken slurs escaping his mouth. "Want me to show you I'm not a fucking gay boy? Want me to show you?"

He banged into the kitchen counter, knocking over a vase. It crashed to the floor.

Lena screamed and lunged for the door, desperately trying to unlock it. "Stay away from me, Paul!" she yelled, her voice shrill with terror. "Stay away!"

Paul watched as she curled, shrinking, against the door, her brown eyes dilated with fear. It stopped him in his tracks. Even in his drunken stupor he was able to see what he was doing to her. He stood back in shame. "I'm sorry. I'm sorry. Please, Lena. I'm sorry."

She cowered even closer to the door. He knelt down beside her and tried to hug her, but she fought him, hissing and scratching, wriggling in his arms.

"Lena, I'm not going to hurt you!"

223

She kicked and screamed until all the energy was out of her. Her body slowly became limp. He felt her heaving, sobbing against his chest. Her arms squeezed around his body.

When he awoke later in the morning, she was lying beside him in bed, staring at him. His good arm was around her. His head was aching. He had only a vague recollection of the night before; the last remnants of anger evaporated in the light of day. Her fingers traced the shape of his face. As he came to consciousness, she moved his arm and got up. She closed the door of the en-suite behind her.

A few minutes later Paul heard the sound of water rushing in the shower. He lay in bed, still drowsy and half drunk, willing the room to stop spinning.

He listened as the shower switched off and she moved about in the bathroom. When she came back into the bedroom she was dressed in a neat black suit, with polished heels and a crisp white shirt. Her hair was damp, her make-up was perfect.

Her eyebrows trembled in quiet discomfort. "It's my mum's funeral today."

CHAPTER TWENTY-ONE

She sat on the edge of the bed and told him what had happened. There had been a fire the previous weekend and her mum had been unable to escape. The blaze tore right through the house.

"Were you there?"

"No," she whispered quietly. "I hadn't been round in weeks."

Paul cast off the blanket and pulled himself out of bed to sit beside her. He realised he'd seen the headline as he'd passed the newspaper stand at Central Station a few days before but had thought nothing of it.

"Was anyone else hurt?"

Lena shook her head. "They dragged Jason out. He'd tried to rescue her, according to him, but they were both shit-faced. It was a cigarette. The materials they use in houses nowadays, they just burn right up in minutes. There's toxins…" She mimicked the tone of an official reporter.

He hugged her, the immediate focus of the funeral taking his mind off what had happened earlier. "Do you want me to go with you?"

She nodded. "I can't do it alone," she said fearfully.

Lena sat quietly in the car as they drove to the crematorium. Paul concentrated on the road, a piercing pain in his temples. After his shower he'd thrown up a couple of times, giving him temporary relief, but now the throbbing was back. Adding to that was the repeating flashbacks from the night before. The horrible image of Lena huddled in the corner of the hall, crying. The terrified look on her face. The insults he'd hurled. In a way he was thankful for the hangover, dreading the moment his head cleared and he would have to face in total sobriety what he had said and done. But he kept it to himself as they headed up the drive to the bleak, grey building; his morose apologies and excuses weren't going to make her feel any better.

Lena held his hand tightly as they entered. The room was small, which gave the appearance that the service was well attended. Paul wanted to sit further back but Lena held him close as she moved down the aisle to the front row beside a man, a woman and a chubby red-headed child of about ten years old. They hugged Lena and sombrely shook Paul's hand, but there were no introductions. He smelled of alcohol, his eyes were bloodshot. He didn't blame them for the suspicious looks they threw at him, an intruder in their intimate moment of grief.

On the other side of the aisle, Paul recognised Jason. He was with two women, about his age, their faces hard and stern. Paul later found out they were his sisters. There was no denying he looked distraught. Even before the ceremony began he was openly weeping. His arm was bandaged where it had been burned; his face was pale and drawn. Scumbag, Paul thought. As the funeral started, Jason stared ahead. So did Lena.

The service was short. The humanist minister read a brief eulogy, concluding it with some quotes celebrating life. She read a poem about how dead people are still around in the snow and the wind and the stars. Paul shivered and took his mind somewhere else. It closed with Lena's mum's favourite song, a Tracy Chapman number. Lena kept her composure throughout. As the coffin with her mum's remains rolled into the committal chamber she gave a small sob, but that was as much emotion as she showed. Outside, the next group of mourners was waiting to come in. The minister announced a gathering at their local pub, inviting people for a drink and a sandwich after the service.

Having slowly made their way out of the crematorium, Paul stood by Lena's side while she received awkward condolences from the others. It amazed him, her strength. How she managed to keep it all in. Saying all the right things, remembering to invite people to the small wake. There was a lot of pawing and tugging from every direction, but she handled it with the grace of a politician. From Paul's vantage point, though, it wasn't hard to see the strain it was putting her under. There was an eerie emptiness in her eyes. He worried that a meltdown was due sooner rather than later. At least he would be there when it happened. Their hands gripped tighter.

Leaves had fallen from the trees and been mashed to the ground in a squelching mush. The sky was pearly silver, promising rain. Once most of the mourners had disappeared, Lena introduced him to her friend from school, Gillian. When he shook her hand there was a degree of hostility from her which he couldn't explain. As far as he was aware, they'd never met before. He briefly wondered if he'd jilted her in some previous life, but the muffin-shaped rolls of fat bulging over her trousers and mannish clothes and shoes made him suspect not. Still, she wasn't too proud to take a lift from him when it was offered, whatever the insult. She squashed into the back of his car while he and Lena sat in the front.

He started up the engine, hoping he wouldn't be pulled over during the short drive, worried he was still over the limit. The pub they were going to was a few streets away from Lena's old home. As he drove, Lena and Gillian chatted about nothing in particular – people from school, the jewellery shop Lena was working in, Gillian's love life or lack of it. Paul was glad she was taking Lena's mind off things for a while. He continued to drive, concentrating on the road. A few minutes later he was shaken from his daydream when he noticed a sudden silence had fallen in the car. It took him a moment to realise he'd taken the wrong road – in that area they all looked alike – and had accidentally driven past the derelict remains of Lena's house. There was police tape around the garden. Quickly speeding off in the right direction, he looked apologetically at Lena, who smiled and put her hand on his. In the back seat Gillian sighed and huffed.

A few minutes later they pulled up at the pub. Paul found a space in the staff car park. A small crowd was gathering at the entrance and Gillian fussed over Lena as they walked towards them, in a way she hadn't done without the audience. When they joined the group, Gillian and Lena were warmly received, while he was given a cool reception – a pattern that was beginning to become obvious. It wasn't just Gillian that was giving him the cold shoulder. He brushed it off. It was Lena he was there for. Her grip was still tight around him and he wasn't letting go, whether he was welcome there or not.

Inside, most people congregated round the bar. Various sandwiches and finger food had been provided. In a booth to one side, Jason and his sisters sat together. Their free drinks were finished and they already had a kitty going. Paul glowered over in resentment. It was going to be a long day. What with the snide comments from Lena's family and friends, and the monumental hangover that was almost making his nose bleed, he was going to suffer. Still, Lena was bearing up well, putting on a brave face in between the small looks of quiet desperation she gave him when she thought no one else was watching. When Lena went to the toilet, a group of females in attendance, he took the opportunity to slip outside and call Dario, passing over the reins at Limbo for the night, just hoping the place wouldn't be burned down in his absence. Lena was coming home with him tonight.

When the phone call was over, Dario now on board, Paul took a moment in the fresh air. He sat on the steps overlooking the car park with his glass of Coke and cigarette, the buzz of traffic and life outside a welcome break from the funeral chatter. He was enjoying the brief respite when a small foot in his back caused him to jump and nearly choke on his drink. The chubby red-haired child from the funeral was giggling behind him.

"Are you Lena's boyfriend?" she asked coyly, knowing in some way, for some reason, her behaviour wouldn't be approved of. She continued to giggle.

"I'm just a good friend."

The answer seemed to disappoint her. Her brow concertinaed as she thought of a more testing question. She sat beside him and shrugged. "What's a half caste?"

Paul's eyes narrowed. "That's not a very nice word for little girls to be using."

"But my mum said it."

"It means when someone's mum and dad have different-coloured skin."

The girl seemed satisfied with the response. "I have two mums," she said. "One of them died in the fire. She's the one who gave birth to me." She offered up the information with a child's awareness of the strange curiosity adults had for knowing other people's family background. "My other one is the one I live with. It's OK for me. But my sister only had one mum. She's not even got a dad either. She's an orphan. I like your car."

"How do you know which car's my car?"

"It's a BMW but it looks funny."

"It's called a convertible."

"My dad says it's a drug dealer's car."

"Yeah?" Paul took a long draw on his cigarette. "Your parents have a lot to say."

The girl laughed, pleased with herself. "I can name all the makes of cars. Ford. Citroën. Golf. Polo. Pea-u-got."

Paul laughed out loud. "'Pea-u-got'? It's pronounced 'Peugeot'. It's French." The little girl was miffed she'd come off looking stupid. Paul shook his head in amusement and suddenly thought of his own son. In a few years Jack would be her age. It was going to be fun. That was the age when they really started to entertain you. He suddenly couldn't wait for the day to pass. Sunday was his day with Jack and all he wanted to do was see him and hug him.

A shriek from inside interrupted their conversation. Both Paul's head and the child's flicked automatically towards the burst of sound. A second later Paul was on his feet, telling her to stay put, while he raced through the doors.

Inside, Lena was standing in the centre of the pub shouting at Jason. He had risen from his seat and was pointing a finger at her. Between ranting sobs she cursed him as he began to shout back.

"It's always about you. The love of my life dies in my arms and I'm treated like a leper. I've not been given my place today. It's disrespectful!"

"It was your fault! Your fault!" Lena shouted at him while others held her back.

Jason's temper ignited. Paul heard the word "bitch", which was enough to make him wade in. "Call her that again, you fucking prick…" He stood toe to toe with Jason, their chins nearly touching.

Jason stood like a breezeblock in front of him. "Fuck off! I'd kill you, you fucking little bastard!" His finger wagged in Paul's face.

"Yeah? Real man…" Paul demonstrated with an accompanying backhanded gesture. "I thought you only knocked about women and children. Go on then – go for it!"

The two of them stood like bulls, locking horns, sizing each other up. Paul could hear Lena sobbing in the background but didn't dare take his eyes from Jason for a moment.

"Go on, big man."

Jason lunged, grabbing Paul by the throat with his

bandaged, fire-injured arm, backing him against a pillar. His massive hand was like a vice constricting Paul's airway. Paul grabbed the dressing and pressed hard. Jason roared, beads of sweat forming on his brow, but he continued to hold Paul's throat, squeezing with both hands.

"Let me go," Paul rasped. Jason's grip wavered, Paul's didn't. "Won't just be a broken jaw this time. If you don't let go, it'll be the last thing you ever do."

Paul let the threat of violent repercussions sink in while he prepared to crack Jason's jaw, knowing it to be soft from the previous injury. He watched as Jason relived the last beating; Lena had told him Jason had received counselling after that.

"You know I'm connected." Paul pictured Manny and assumed the same wide-eyed, hole-boring stare he knew made grown men quake.

He felt Jason's grasp loosen. A rush of excitement cascaded through him as he realised he'd tamed him. He continued to squeeze Jason's arm, forcing him onto bent knees. Jason's sisters moved to his aid, their shrill voices screeching like nails down a blackboard, but he waved them back.

"Apologise to her." Paul's voice was still hoarse.

"No." Jason held his sore arm, which Paul was still squeezing as tightly as he could. "My arm! Let go."

"Apologise."

Paul dug his fingers in. Jason's eyes rolled in agony.

"Sorry!" he gasped. "Sorry!"

Paul let go.

Jason seemed to diminish in front of him. A tear formed in his eye, the comedy mask of a scolded child resting on his steroid-pumped face. "I loved that woman."

Paul stared him down, disgust building for the superman before him, his fake tanned muscles and hard-man disguise stripped down to reveal the serial victim that hid beneath. Exposed and humiliated in front of everyone he knew – it was what people like Jason deserved. Paul had been itching to do it for a long time. He watched him wallowing in self-pity.

Behind him, Lena was being gently ushered out the door. Paul went up to the group, feeling a few inches taller. "Lena, are you OK?"

Lena cried into her hands, too upset to speak, propped up by some of the other women. The little girl's mum was leading the group; although she couldn't have been more than forty, she dressed like she was in her sixties. She gave him a look of reprehension.

"She will be if she keeps away from the likes of you. You should be ashamed of yourself. Have you no respect?" Her voice had the acerbic tone of his old primary school head teacher, sadistic in the soft, slow way the barbed words rolled off her tongue.

"I wasn't talking to you." He blocked their path, prodding Lena gently. "Lena, do you want to come home with me?"

"My husband and I are taking her home." The little girl's mum brushed him off, her head held imperiously high.

"Lena." He shook her gently, but she broke down, crying inconsolably. "Lena."

The group continued to move outside. Paul tried to intervene again. The little girl's mum put a detaining hand out to stop him.

"Nothing but a petty thug." She looked at him like he was a piece of dirt. "Can't you see the poor girl's been through enough? She needs people around her who care for her. Not an animal like you. Annabelle!" she shouted over her shoulder.

From under the table, the little girl emerged, running past him, scuttling after her mum.

CHAPTER TWENTY-TWO

"You caused mayhem at my mother's funeral," Annie said. "I watched from under a table. I'd never seen grown men fight before."

Paul remembered the satisfaction he'd felt at seeing the asshole down on his knees. "Jason deserved it."

"You should hear what he has to say about you," Annie retorted.

"Stories from people that didn't know me. That didn't know her," he volleyed back.

He could feel her watching him, her senses alert to every tick, every stammer, to the moments when he held his breath, when his breathing grew heavy – waiting for him to unwittingly reveal some significant truth.

"You know?" She sighed wearily. "You're right." His ears pricked up. "I don't have much to go on. I have the accounts of a handful of people. I have my own memories. And I have what you know. But you're refusing to tell me. I can think of only one reason why."

He shook his head. And laughed.

Annie's face remained stony. "You think this is funny?"

"You have me tied to a chair and you wonder why you're not getting my full cooperation. I'm in pain. I'm dehydrated.

You need to contact someone. Ask them for help."

"There is no one, Paul," she said, sitting on the edge of the armchair, her elbows resting on her knees. "No one cares. That's why this happened. Because no one cares. Lena was vulnerable. She was on her own in the world. She had no mother. No father. That's why this happened to her. Because you thought no one cared. But I did. I do. I fucking care. Wherever she is, I want her to know that someone cared!"

He clenched his teeth together.

Annie got up and went over to the mantelpiece. She rested her elbow on it. She had a sickly pallor to her, as much a captive as he was. But he knew now not to underestimate the steeliness inside her.

"The day of the funeral..." She twisted her fingers together. "Nine years ago. I was just a child. I remember the itchy grey dress I had to wear, how it scratched all the way through the service. Everyone was sad but I didn't understand why and it made me want to laugh but I knew I wasn't allowed to. I remember being told that my mum was dead but it didn't make sense because my mum was sitting beside me, telling me to sit up straight, say my prayers.

"I remember the fight. The loud voices. Lena screaming. Me watching from beneath a table. I remember the words I heard after the funeral, hushed words I wasn't meant to hear. Thug. Gangster.

"If I had the power to go back in time and find out what happened, I would. But I can't do that. All I can do is warm up stale memories, looking for something, some answer, some key. But the answers aren't there. Because you have them. You're the only one that can give them to me."

Paul fidgeted uncomfortably. He turned his head away. He didn't want to listen any more.

Annie continued, determined, her voice thin and delicate. She left the fireplace and returned to the familiar terrain of the armchair. "You said Lena and I weren't close. And in a way you're right. But I want you to know about us."

She perched on the arm, her hands clasped together between her knees, her shoulders curled. "We didn't get to spend that much time together growing up," she said apologetically.

Paul closed his eyes, reminded himself it was a game she was playing. From the Dummy's Guide to Interrogation.

"Lena was eight when my dad – Frank – and her mum got together. A year later I was born. For a time we were a regular little family. But my dad left when I was two or three, taking me with him. Later, a long time later, I found out it was because of our mum's drinking – you only find these things out when you're older. He tried to take Lena with us, but she wouldn't leave our mum. After that I didn't see her very often: birthdays, Christmases, some weekends."

Annie took a deep breath before she went on, her voice quivering. "But I remember how much fun it was when she was there. She wasn't like other big sisters; she was never mean and always had time for me. There's a nine-year age gap between us, but she never treated me like a nuisance. She was kind to me, talked to me like I was a friend, not an annoying little sister."

As Annie spoke about Lena, she began to glow. Paul remembered how Lena often had that effect on people.

"My dad remarried and my new mum was everything

237

a mother is supposed to be. She made dinner every night, school lunches, always went to parents' nights, made sure my uniform was clean. She raised me as if I was her own." Annie paused briefly. "It's funny how, when you look back on things as an adult, you see things differently. It's hard sometimes to admit people you love have flaws."

Paul tried to distract himself, looking round the room for something, anything, to draw his attention away, help him escape from it. There was something there, in the look. The faintest resemblance he'd not noticed before. It dizzied him, weakened him. They didn't look alike, but in the facial expressions there was something.

"Gloria, my step-mum, she was never fond of Lena. I see that now. She would say things about her: that Lena was a bad influence on me, her behaviour around men was provocative, she didn't like the tone of her conversation, that Lena forgot sometimes that I was only a child. Gloria is one of these people that doesn't put value on material things. She thinks if you wear nice clothes and take an interest in your appearance it's a sign of vanity and shallowness. She looked down on Lena because of her beauty. She used it as a sign of her bad character. When you're young, you believe your parents, they have a big influence on you, so in some ways I probably believed her. I saw Lena even less.

"She stayed with us after the funeral, as you know. I remember you kept calling, but Gloria told you Lena didn't want to see you. Truthfully, Lena wasn't able to see anyone. She cried all day and wouldn't get out of bed. She needed to be looked after, fed. She couldn't talk to anyone. I understand now she was having some kind of breakdown, but people don't talk about these things, especially not to a child. Gloria nursed her back to health. She loved a charity case; any excuse to feel superior. Lena gradually recovered.

"That's when the problems started. She and Gloria began arguing. Gloria tried to remodel Lena's whole life – change the way she dressed, the times she came in and went out, the people she mixed with. Gloria had a particular grievance against you. The way she spoke about you… In our house, you were a monster. I know Gloria meant well, but she drove Lena away. One day Lena just packed her bags and left. When I came back from school I found out she was gone. I was heartbroken. I think Gloria felt betrayed because I was so sad. It's not easy raising a child that's not your own and Gloria seemed to worry sometimes that the bond wasn't there between us…" Annie trailed off. "I just want you to know how important it is to me that I help Lena now. I wasn't old enough to then. I can't abandon her now."

The tears were flowing from Annie's eyes. She took the photograph out of Paul's wallet again and walked towards him, holding it close to his face.

"I need to know why she was taken away from me," she sobbed. "Please. She was twenty years old. She was beautiful and smart and kind and funny. Those earrings. Our mum bought her those for her sixteenth birthday. They were expensive. She'd had to save. She was wearing Versace Blue Jeans perfume because that was her favourite. The rose-shaped ring on her finger she got from a Christmas cracker. She was full of life. Special. She was my sister."

Paul looked at Annie with her grey face, her eyes puffy from tears, and realised she wasn't acting. It was her pure, raw grief he was seeing. He looked at his own trembling hands, aching for Lena. For her touch on his skin. Annie's words brought her back so clearly.

Slowly Annie fell back onto the couch, pressing her fingers to her cheeks to stem the tears.

And then she was there, sitting with Annie on the couch, her arms around her. Dressed like she was the last time he saw her. Black hair trussed up under a black fedora, wearing a beige trench coat and knee-high boots. She was singing sweetly in Annie's ear and, through her tears, Annie was smiling.

He looked away. When he looked back she was gone, the image disappeared. Annie was sitting alone.

"Why? Why can't you tell me?" Annie cried into her hands. "I just want you to tell me what you know. If you loved her, you'd tell me what you know." She looked round slowly, her tear-stained eyes slits of pain. "You've been asking me to understand. That's why you told me about Manny, because you're laying the groundwork. You want me to listen without judging. You want me to know how hard it was for you. That what happened wasn't your fault. I get that now. I'm willing to listen. Tell me about you and her. What happened after the funeral? That winter after she left our house?"

"I loved her," he said quietly, more to himself than to Annie.

"I loved her too," Annie said softly. "We both did. So tell me about her. Anything. Everything. I want to know."

Paul wasn't even sure he could trust his own voice when he began to speak. Not sure if once he started he'd ever be able to stop. Not sure how far he'd be able to go.

"After the funeral, I didn't see Lena for some time," Paul

said, his face turning grey. He breathed a sigh of resignation as all the air seemed to rush out of him, his upper body slumped like an empty sack. "Not for over three months. I tried to get in touch with her, but your mum and dad made it very difficult. The next time I saw her, she was in trouble – as usual."

CHAPTER TWENTY-THREE

Nine years ago

It was afternoon, but in the back room of Limbo it always felt like night-time. Stale sweat and old beer from the bar permeated the office, where Paul sat sifting through paperwork and listening to the gentle patter of the cleaner's footsteps and the slop of her mop as she made her way through the empty club.

The phone interrupted him: an internal call from the new girl he'd hired to deal with the nuisance of lost wallets and jackets. "There's a Detective Chief Inspector Carmichael here to see you, Paul." The concern in her voice caused a flare of irritation in him.

He sighed. "Send him up. He knows the way."

Paul kept working, to let Carmichael know he didn't have time for this today. Since Paul's promotion to manager at the club, Carmichael had started to appear more often. His growing interest was just one more worry for Paul to deal with.

Laboured footsteps echoed through the quiet club. Pantomiming his impatience, Paul only looked up when Carmichael stopped in front of him. He didn't get up but cordially held out his hand.

"Carmichael."

The sturdy inspector ignored his offer of a handshake and stood squarely at the desk. At one time Paul had thought him imposing, but with the passing years, each one bringing Carmichael a little closer to the final salary pension, his posture slackened, his white hair thinned, his muscles softened, his skin became chalkier. War wounds of weariness.

"Mr Dalziel."

"To what do I owe the pleasure? Is there a reason you're here? Or just general *police* harassment?"

"Same reason I'm always here. The bad guys." Carmichael drifted around the office, lifting various objects and putting them down again.

Paul frowned. "Do you think there's a bad guy hiding under that plant pot?"

"No. But I think there's one hiding behind a jumped-up thug in a suit."

Carmichael stopped lifting things and instead leaned back on the filing cabinet, making himself comfortable. Pinching the bridge of his nose, Paul put down his pen. He didn't have time for this today. It had been a long week. Things with Dario were coming to a head and tensions were high. Paul was losing patience.

"I heard there was an incident here the other night. You got a bit lippy with some of my men." Carmichael smiled smugly, knowing the annoyance he was causing.

"I'm trying to run a business here," Paul said in frustration.

A nimbus of satisfaction beamed around Carmichael.

The incident he was talking about had started when Dario had burst into Paul's office a few nights earlier. It was late, an hour or so from closing. Dario's eyes were glassy and speckles of white powder stuck to the rim of his nostrils. Paul had been winding down for the night, cashing up the tills.

"One of the young team is ripping us off." Dario stopped in front of Paul's desk and hopped from foot to foot.

Paul groaned and kept his eyes on the calculator. Bucky and Dunsmore had also been let loose in the club that night and the combination of all three of them was a preordained headache for Paul. "What?"

"I was in the toilet," Dario rattled on, "and a good mate of mine complained he'd just snorted lactose. His fucking guts were killing him. Another said he'd been sold aspirin. I'm telling you, those young guys are taking the piss out of us."

Paul began the ritual of placating Dario. "Did you hear who it was that was selling?"

Even before Dario explained who it was, Paul was picturing the kid – barely eighteen, if he even was that yet, good-looking, a bit smarter than the rest. Cocky, too – reminded Paul of himself at that age.

"Small. Brown hair. Connor or something."

Paul nodded. Of course it was.

"Thievin' little cunt." Dario was wound tight like a spring about to break loose.

Paul sighed. "OK, let me talk to him. I'll deal with it. Just go… enjoy the rest of your night."

"Bucky went through his pockets and pulled out a packet of aspirin."

"Bucky? What do you mean? Where are they?"

Dario retreated a little. "Outside, in the back car park."

Paul slowly counted to ten to calm himself. If Bucky and

Dunsmore were already outside, raring to go, there was little Paul could do to stop them. He closed his eyes and rubbed his temples. "Fuck sake, Dario."

He got up from his seat and started making his way down to the car park, Dario in pursuit. By the time he got there an ambulance had arrived. A police siren screamed in the background. Connor was being stretchered into the back, barely conscious, his face plastered with blood. Paul watched the doors being closed.

Dario shrugged his shoulders. "He needed to be taught a lesson."

"Get in there and wipe the fucking CCTV," Paul growled.

At least Dario had managed to do that.

The ambulance charged off and the police arrived. The night that followed was long and painful.

Paul found out later from one of the other youngsters that Dunsmore had grabbed the kid's arm in both hands and snapped it. The kid fell to the ground screaming. Not satisfied, Bucky pulled out a knife and tore it across his face from temple to cheek. Then they took his stash and dealt it out among themselves before running off. A passerby called the police and ambulance.

After the lengthy interrogation with the police was over, Paul consoled himself with the thought that maybe he had been too soft. Maybe they had started to take the piss. He tolerated a little margin; he'd done the same when he was their age. But it would do no harm to make an example when one of them overstepped the mark. I've been kicked, he thought. We've all been kicked. It's just that this time I'm doing the fuckin' kickin'. And sometimes that was how it had to be.

But when the kid had shown up two days later, stitches stretching like a train track across the length of his once handsome face, wanting to know how much he owed for the missing stash, Paul couldn't bring himself to look at him. He told him to write it off. Gave him a bonus for keeping his mouth shut with the police. But the damage was done. The kid looked at Paul in a way that chilled him. He was going to have to watch out for that one from now on. He'd turned bad overnight.

"Haven't you got better things to do than harass me about a bar brawl?" Paul stood up behind his desk. "Those guys weren't even from my club. Just passing by. Like I said in my statement."

Carmichael's face became serious. "I heard the kid that got his face all cut up works for you."

"Well, you heard wrong."

Carmichael moved over to Paul's desk and rested his knuckles on it, hard and calcified like a boxer's. His gravelly voice grew sincere. "Son, you might think you're smart, mucking us about, but you're getting in deeper, aren't you? Manny's taken a real shine to you."

Paul stiffened.

Straightening up to his full height, fully aware of his intimidating bulk, Carmichael went on. "One day very soon, it's going to be too late for you. Because I'm going to have something on you. You've done time before, Paul. Are you ready to do it again, for him?"

Paul's face went blank. He was tired and he'd heard it all before. It was always going to be the case that Paul stood on one side, Carmichael on the other.

Paul had come a long way from back-street muggings and peddling his wares on the rainy streets of Glasgow – sleeping on cardboard, hell-bent on self-destruction, not caring who he brought down, no way out of the hole he was in. It was Manny who'd given him a chance. Where they came from it was the smart ones that became junkies. Unemployable, unintelligible, undesirable – who wouldn't want to numb themselves to that? People like Paul didn't get breaks. No one else had ever done as much for him. There was a part of him that had been forged by Manny; that needed, worshipped and feared him in equal measure. Some days he wished for enough strength to stab him in the guts, crack him in the skull with a paperweight or kick him under a bus, but because of loyalty he never would. Carmichael could never understand that.

Paul owed his life to him.

"What do you know about a container? A special cargo being delivered to Ayr harbour this weekend." Carmichael's question caught him off guard.

"I don't know what you're talking about," Paul answered suspiciously.

Carmichael banged the desk in frustration. "I came here to warn you! It's coming. This is your last chance."

Paul exhaled and began to shuffle the papers on his desk. "Like I said, I've got work to do, Inspector. Please, if you don't mind."

Carmichael looked at him sideways and nodded his head. "I'm wasting my time." He hovered over the desk while Paul looked stubbornly down at his work. "OK. I'll leave you to it. See myself out."

"Have a good afternoon cracking skulls or whatever it is you do for fun," Paul hissed after him.

Carmichael spun round. Suddenly he was a police officer and nothing more. "Speak to me like that again and you'll be spending the night in lock-up." He marched out.

Paul tried not to think about what happened the last time someone let their guard down around Carmichael.

That night, Dario was celebrating his birthday at The Pink Pussy Cat. Paul's attendance was expected. He was held up by some business at the club, so by the time he got there, in the early hours, the party had started without him.

Climbing the familiar stairs to the entrance, Paul swaggered across the terrace. He was met outside by a meaty bouncer who filled the doorway.

"Can I help you, sir?"

"You must be new here," Paul said, trying to place the bouncer's accent as he started to move past him into the club. "I'm Paul. A friend of Johnny's. I work for the owner."

The huge bulk in front of him didn't budge and Paul was forced to take a step back. Without saying anything else, the bouncer pulled out his radio. "Johnny, there's someone here called Paul, says he's a friend of yours."

His eyes measured Paul up and down with military precision. "I don't know. He looks shifty."

South African, maybe? Paul would usually have made a scene but instinct told him to take another step back. The bouncer stood with the confidence of a professional soldier, not the usual specimen.

"So where you from, South Africa or something?"

"Ya. Rhodesia."

The bouncer remained motionless, filling the doorframe, and for a second it was as if Paul could read his thoughts. *If I have to, I will rip your throat out. If it comes down to it. I wouldn't want to, but if you force me…*

Paul started to shuffle, keen to get indoors. A few seconds of agonising silence followed before Johnny the manager appeared at the door.

"Paul!" He held out his arms in a welcoming gesture. "Let me take you straight through. The party's already started."

The bouncer stepped aside. "See you later, bru."

Once inside, Johnny turned round. "We've been having a bit of trouble lately. He's very thorough."

Paul said nothing, just nodded as an icy shiver ran down his spine.

The club was smoky. The velvet-lined horseshoe-shaped booths were all full and the circular tables scattered around the room were packed with groups of rowdy men. Underwear-clad waitresses weaved back and forth from the bar with trays of drinks; others rested on customers' knees or led them off for private dances. On stage a guy was on all fours, trousers down; a girl stood behind him with a riding crop dangerously poised while his friends cheered her on.

"Busy night tonight."

Johnny nodded and grinned as he led Paul through to the private VIP room at the back. Before they disappeared behind the curtain, Paul caught a glimpse of the dancer as she emerged on stage. In an elegant arachnid contortion, she wrapped her arms and legs around the golden pole glistening in the centre. Her supple limbs extended and stretched in arousing poses. The murmur of excitement from the floor became muffled as the thick velvet curtains sealed behind him.

The private room was packed with a crowd of Dario's closest friends. Bucky and Dunsmore were in the corner with girls. On the velvet couch in the centre, Manny sat beside a pretty brunette in her late thirties, stripped down to her underwear.

Paul walked over and joined them. "Enjoying yourself?" He sat down on the seat beside Manny's couch.

"Best girls. Best champagne. Best blow!" Manny held up his glass. "Tina, get the man a drink. Make him comfortable."

The woman on Manny's knee disentangled herself and left to get some champagne.

With the two of them now alone, Paul took the chance to speak to Manny about the afternoon's events. "DCI Carmichael was round again today."

"Probing?"

"Usual bullshit. He was asking about the fight outside the club the other night."

Manny sighed. "Dario knows how it is. He's had his knuckles rapped. The others too. You don't shit on your own doorstep. Anything else?"

"He mentioned something about a cargo delivery. Ayr harbour."

A smile slowly spread across Manny's face, his golden incisor glistening as he winked. "Whoever his sources are, they're feeding him crap." He shrugged.

Paul sighed with relief. "Nothing to worry about then?"

Manny rubbed the top of Paul's head. "You're a good lad, Paul." His hand lingered longer than it should have.

Tina came back with a bottle of champagne and he dropped it away. They both watched as Tina began to pour the champagne into flutes.

Manny put his hand on her ass. "Tina, you like your job, don't you?" he said jovially.

"Yes, Mr Munroe. Very much," she said with a broad smile as she handed out the drinks.

"That's what I'm saying." Manny laughed and gave her a playful slap. She squealed and sat at his side, putting her arm around the back of his neck. They all laughed.

"See, Paul. All I'm doing is providing a service, employment, helping the economy function." Manny was enjoying having an audience. "If I didn't, someone else would. Whether it's drugs, or women or whatever – if there was no demand for it, would there be any point in me supplying it? What's the problem with that?"

"Hear, hear." Paul held up his glass.

They clinked glasses and Manny proposed a toast. "To the birthday boy."

"To the birthday boy," Paul repeated and clinked again. "Speaking of which, where is he?"

Manny motioned to the back room. He patted Paul on the knee. "It's a party. Relax. Sit back. Unwind. These girls don't disappoint." Rolling up a twenty, he reached over and snorted a line of coke from the spread on the table. "Have a good time!" He passed it to Paul, who helped himself, feeling an instant rush, the irritations of the day suddenly behind him.

As if on cue, Dario re-entered the room. As was usually the case, Paul heard him before he saw him. The grin was coming towards him from the back of the room. Dressed in well-cut jeans, fitted shirt and a designer blazer anyone else would have looked a fool in, Dario strolled over. With his suave brown hair that curled below his ears and year-round sun-kissed tan, he was able to carry off the look with style. His hands rested on the back of the seat Paul was sitting on.

"Paul, my man – you made it!"

"Many happy returns." Paul reached up and shook his hand, then moved onto the same couch as Manny so he could face him, uncomfortable at having Dario looming behind him, looking down.

"Let me introduce you to my ladies." Dario smiled expansively. "Top-drawer cocktail – I call them my White Russian. The perfect blend of coffee and cream. Ivona, Milena, meet Paul and Uncle Manny."

Under the heavy make-up and mounds of hair extensions, Paul barely recognised her. There was something sharper about her appearance. She stood in front of him in a baby-pink thong and six-inch heels, her body muscular and toned. Paul looked at Dario's hand, placed strategically on her upper thigh, and for a moment it all went quiet.

Ivona's perfectly spherical breasts and washboard belly rubbed against Paul's cheek as she climbed onto the couch beside him. She ran her hand through her long, plutonium-dyed hair, placed his hands on her firm behind.

Across the table, Dario sat down. Lena was giving him similar treatment. Paul could feel Manny's eyes on him as he watched Lena slink coquettishly over to Dario, her body waving provocatively in his face.

"Sorry about the other night," Dario shouted over to Paul while Lena climbed over him with sleek feline prowess and an air of haughty seduction. Dario's hands slid up and down her body, caressing the small of her back. She moaned a little and looked over at Paul with wild, blazing eyes.

On his knee, Ivona battled for his attention, but to no avail. Paul manoeuvred her aside.

"What are you doing here, Lena?" Paul called over to her.

Lena's eyes narrowed. "I'm working."

"So, do you two know each other?" Dario beamed.

The muscles were oddly strained on Manny's usually expressionless face.

"Since when?" Paul started to get up.

"Since now." She turned her head to ignore him and ruffled her fingers through Dario's coiffed hair.

"I'm telling you, Paul, she is one dirty little minx." Dario laughed and motorboated her tits. A second later, Lena leaped away like a scalded cat. Her hand went to her breast, where Paul saw a small bite mark. Dario was grinning broadly.

Paul felt Manny grip the back of his shirt but it didn't hold him back. Breaking free from it, he crashed over the table.

"Fucking animal!"

He punched Dario in the face. Blood spurted from his nose. Paul sat on top of him and got one more punch in before he was dragged off by Bucky and Dunsmore, one on either side of him. He punched out and continued swinging, caught one of them, but a sudden, sharp jab in his windpipe sent him to the floor gasping for air. It was followed by a boot to the ribs.

He could hear a voice, it sounded like Manny's, shouting, "Stand back. Let him handle it!"

Two huge hands grabbed the back of Paul's shirt and

the skin underneath at the same time. His face was pressed against the red carpet, which was strewn with broken glass and dusted with white powder. The two hands lifted, the carpet became distant and he was flung through the air towards the fire escape. He caught a blurred glimpse of the Zimbabwean bouncer as he smashed through the doors and rolled out into the alley.

The bouncer slammed the door shut behind him so it was just the two of them alone in the alley.

"Yarpie fuck!" Paul moaned from the ground.

With a fist like a wrecking ball, the bouncer swung towards him. Paul's hands moved to cover his throat. It was the last thing he did before everything turned dark.

CHAPTER TWENTY-FOUR

The taxi driver shook Paul awake. "Right, pal, that's you at the hospital. You need to get out now."

Paul opened his eyes. Through the rain-streaked taxi window he could see the blurred lights of A&E.

"C'mon, pal, you're bleeding all over my seat."

Paul began to feel about for his wallet, but the driver stopped him.

"The fare's been taken care of. Hope you get the chance to thank the pretty lady. I wasn't for taking you, but… I'm a sucker for a pretty face. Shame about yours," he added sympathetically, and waited while Paul, dizzy and disorientated, dragged himself off the seat and out onto the street.

Sucker for a pretty face, Paul thought. He wasn't the only one.

A&E was packed with people. Paul staggered in and propped himself against the front desk. Through clenched teeth he rasped out some noises to the receptionist, who, miraculously, managed to understand them. She sent him over to join the crowd of walking wounded and a nurse brought over forms, a glass of water and gauze for his forehead, which was still seeping blood. He prepared himself for a long night ahead.

In the sobering yellow glow of the hospital, he began to understand just how seriously he'd fucked up. Putting his fingers to his aching, swollen jaw, the taste of blood in his mouth, he recalled Manny's hand trying to hold him back. His fist smashing into Dario's nose. If his own face wasn't messed up already, it would be by the time Manny finished with him. Trying not to think about it, he willed his turn with the doctor to arrive soon, hoping that when it did he would prescribe something strong.

An hour passed, then two. Teams of bedraggled girls in miniskirts blurred in and out of focus, wailing. Drunks shouted. Slashes, gashes, burns, vomit and blood. A wash of colours and voices in a surreal circus show. The pain in his head had intensified and all he could think about was curling up in a dark room. The halogen light glared down as once again the waiting area was in uproar. Two stretchers were wheeled in at breakneck speed, a murmur of a stab wound rippling from person to person. Beside him, a young mother hugged her injured toddler even closer, her thin arms like roped steel around him, whispering words, singing songs. Paul tried to doze but found it impossible.

Finally, unable to bear the freak show any longer, he got up and left the hospital.

Outside, the sun was coming up, the cool air fresh against his skin. At the taxi rank, the drivers were surprisingly kind and without fuss one drove him straight home. When he got inside, he took a slack handful of painkillers and some heavy-duty sleeping pills and flopped down on the bed. The sleep that followed was shallow and fragmented. Voices whispered around him. He could feel the presence of other people in the room with him. His room, but different, like the reflection in a funhouse mirror. Aware he was dreaming, but not completely convinced, he tried to move, but his body was paralysed. He couldn't even summon the strength to wiggle a finger. Drifting in and out of consciousness, it could have been seconds, it could have been hours later when the phone rang and he blinked awake, the last remnants of his fevered dreams causing him to look around and make sure he was definitely alone.

When he answered, his voice was hoarse and heavy with sleep. "Hello."

"Drive down and pick me up at the pool hall. Wait out back. And bring five grand."

"Manny?" he asked but was met with the dialling tone. The earpiece felt cold and soothing against his sore face. Patches of dried blood dotted his pillow.

The bedside clock read 9 a.m. He'd slept for just over two hours. Dragging his aching bones out of bed, he made the short walk to the bathroom and switched on the shower, waiting until steam filled the cubicle before getting in. As he washed his sweat-grimed body, he was careful to keep the water away from his head, face and forehead.

When he got out of the shower he was seized by sudden light-headedness; feeling his way to the bathroom door, he opened it to let in the cold air. The hazy splodge of pink, purple and black looking back at him from the bathroom mirror came into focus. He dried away the excess condensation to examine the damage. One side of his jaw was thick and rounded, the purple skin stretched taut like a drum. One shiny eye was half closed, crusty with blood. As carefully as he could, he dabbed the blood from his face, avoiding the congealed gash on his head. Then he pulled on fresh clothes and started on a delirious journey to Manny's pool hall.

He waited out the back, just as Manny had told him, his head on the steering wheel, willing himself lucid but barely able to keep awake.

A few minutes later, Manny emerged onto the fire escape, slowly descended the metal staircase and approached the car. Paul leaned across the passenger seat and opened the door. A pain tore across his middle. Withdrawing back into his seat, he did his most convincing impression of someone in the peak of health.

Manny took a quick look around and got in, shutting the door firmly. Without speaking, he inspected every inch of Paul's face with exaggerated disgust. Paul pulled a pained smile and did his best to appear alert, but Manny's face was stony. Paul was fooling nobody. Half expecting another blow to his already wounded face, he turned the ignition, his throat dry.

"Turn the car off."

The humming engine died.

Together they sat in agonising silence while Manny continued to stare at him.

"Are we going somewhere?" Paul asked groggily.

"Did you bring the money?"

Paul reached into his inside pocket, sweat streaming from his brow, and slipped a brown envelope filled with the notes across to Manny.

"We can put this towards reparations."

Paul watched his money disappear into Manny's jacket. He followed the movement of Manny's hands. To his surprise they moved to the door. It clicked open and Manny started to get out of the car.

"Is that it?" Paul slurred in stoned confusion.

Manny put his head back inside the car, his face a furious inferno. "Is that it? Is that it!" Paul flinched as Manny's voice dropped an octave as he strained to regain control. "What do you want me to say?"

Paul could see him shaking, his face steak-coloured and pulsing.

"You come here looking like that! Bleeding. Off your tits. A fucking disgrace. I'm not getting in a car with you. Go to the fucking hospital, get yourself fixed up!" he roared and slammed the door shut behind him, nearly taking it off its hinges. The car bounced on its axle.

Back at the hospital, Paul finally saw a doctor. He wanted Paul to stay in for observation on account of the head injury and because drink was involved, but Paul convinced him he was OK to go. The doctor wasn't happy and at least wanted to contact someone to pick him up, but finally he relented. More than anything, Paul needed his own bed. That, and he had no one to call.

When he got back to the flat he was able to sleep, this time uninterrupted. It was late afternoon the following day when he woke up. Once again he set out for Manny's pool hall, but now with his forehead stitched and his pain properly medicated. On the way he detoured via The Pink Pussy Cat in the hope of finding Lena.

He slipped in, keeping a low profile, and selected a booth in the corner. It was quiet: just a few punters and a handful of girls at the bar. One jailbait girl broke off from the group and walked towards him, her spindly legs faltering like a fawn learning to walk in a pair of six-inch heels.

"Can I get you something, honey?"

Up close he could see she was older than she looked from a distance. She had undernourished hair the colour and consistency of straw, which reached down to her waist and smelled of mould; her sickly, translucent skin was stretched tight over her protruding bones.

"Yeah, I'm looking for Lena. Is she working today?"

The girl sat down beside him, stroking his arm, pressing her oversized fake breasts into him, pushing the hard sell; ones like her had to. "There's no Lena here. Just little old me. Don't you want a dance from me?"

He looked at her limp hair and skinny, knobbly knees. Her holdups had a run from thigh to shin. "Not today, sweetheart."

She didn't bother trying to persuade him. Just got up and walked off, throwing a cutting remark as she left, which he didn't catch. She crossed the room and began whispering to another girl at the bar. Both girls stole an angry look at him. It was only when the other girl began to approach him that Paul recognised her from the other night. She was dressed in a different underwear combo and her plutonium hair was scraped into a high ponytail. He cringed a little.

"Ivona?"

She rested her hands on the table.

"I heard you're looking for Lena." Her accent was

thick and guttural, her mouth downturned in a smirk. She appraised his broken face.

"Is she around?"

"She doesn't work here anymore." Ivona's cherubic face puckered in a derisive scowl. "Thanks to you."

"Shit." He felt a small sting of guilt, tempered by a wave of relief. "Do you know how I can get in touch with her?"

"Sorry." She shrugged.

"Sorry you don't know, or sorry you won't tell me?"

Not amused, she gave him a cool look, turned and strutted away.

The sky had already turned grey by the time Paul reached the pool hall. Terry buzzed him in. It was late afternoon and most of the tables were in use. Manny was in the corner playing with Marv, the laidback, lanky, motorcycle-booted kitchen manager. Marv's handlebar moustache was as well maintained as his vintage hog outside, the deep, distant look in his eyes a legacy of his experiments with mind-altering drugs.

Manny and Marv both glanced at Paul as he approached. Manny's top button was undone, his trousers hitched up. The game continued, the two players spurred on by the presence of an audience and by their lifelong rivalry on the baize. The tension rose as both men raced round the table to finish on black. Even Manny was laughing when Marv finally whacked it in.

"Best out of five?"

"I don't know, Manny, can you take another beating?"

"That sounds like fighting talk." Manny mock-hit Marv with the pool cue. Marv laughed at the gag.

"Play the boy here, he looks eager to have a shot." Marv passed his cue to Paul. "I've got kitchen duties. Can't spend my day shooting pool, drinking beer."

Paul predicted humiliation over the course of the night for Marv, as usually happened when Manny didn't come out on top. But something in Marv's infinity stare told Paul it wouldn't shake his world. Paul wondered what past sins had led Marv to coming under Manny's fiery charge.

"I thought that's what I paid you for," Manny joked, but Marv had already turned his back, making a show of laughing all the way into the kitchen. When he was out of sight, Manny mumbled under his breath; something about a "useless cunt".

Paul moved in closer in case he had been meant to hear it. "What was that, Manny?"

"What are you waiting for? Rack them up," he growled.

Placing down his pint on the baulk end of the table, Paul set up a new game and rubbed the tip of his cue with chalk. "You want to break?"

"On you go."

Paul leaned over the table, expertly lined up the cue and smashed the white ball into the neat triangle of reds, knocking them explosively across the table.

Manny nodded approval at his shot. "How's the face?"

A shard of light shone through the window, catching the tiny specks of dead skin that swirled and glistened around Manny.

"Bit better."

"You look like ten pounds of mince squashed in a five-pound bag," Manny sneered, his mood seemingly upbeat – which wasn't to say a burst of extreme violence wasn't waiting round the corner. He bent down to take his shot.

Paul watched him closely. He was well used to reading the warning signs indicating that restraint was about to slip. His concern was rising. Manny's fingers were clamped to the handle of his cue, his knuckles turning white.

"Listen, Manny, about the other night…" Paul began. "I don't know what happened."

Slowly Manny's fingers unfurled. He eased the cue gently to the base of the white ball, hit it to make a perfect pot.

"*You* don't know what happened?" Manny straightened, stretched and rested on his cue. "Neither do *I*."

"It's just, me and Dario, we've been having some problems at the club—"

"You broke his nose." Manny cut him off. "At his birthday party, paid for by me. In front of a lot of people. His people."

Paul took his turn, knocked a few balls in, but his mind wasn't on it. He was hitting too hard. Smashed the white into the corner pocket. Manny took it out and placed it carefully on the semi-circle.

"I'll apologise to him," Paul offered, but Manny put up a silencing hand.

"It's not fucking him you should be apologising to."

"I'm sorry, Manny."

Manny leaned over the table, lining his cue with precision, easing it back and forth between his splayed fingers, gauging the right moment to make the shot. He took it. The white rebounded off a cushion, the red he'd been aiming for knocking the rest of the balls into mayhem. Dropping the cue on the felt with finality, he held his hands up to Paul.

"I'm heading off for a meeting. We can talk on the way."

Paul nodded and reached for his coat.

The two of them left the pool hall and began a brisk walk along Glassford Street. The pavements were still busy with shoppers, but there was no weaving in and out: when Manny walked, no one got in his way. They turned onto Ingram Street and started in the direction of GoMA. Paul skipped to avoid a woman wheeling her oversized pram. Gridlocked traffic thrummed beside them. Manny marched on in silence. Entering Royal Exchange Square, they passed the European-style cafes with outdoor seating where customers, coffees in hand, were braving the strong winds and light drizzle with dogged determination. When they reached the upmarket cocktail bar nestled in the corner of the square, Manny stopped and pulled out a packet of cigarettes. He offered one to Paul and lit them both.

"I'll take care of Dario." Manny glanced over his shoulder and lowered his voice. "As far as I'm concerned, the incident is over. You two still have to work together, and I don't want to hear any more whining from either of you." He took a long draw of his cigarette and trained his eyes on Paul. "But you need to know the score. No more fuck-ups."

Paul nodded his head in acquiescence.

"Those other guys," Manny continued, "they're morons. But they do what they're told. Don't think too much. Know what I'm saying? Dario, I love him, but there's no substance there. I need to know I can depend on you, Paul. If some bird flashes her knickers, I need to know you're not a liability. Remember what you're good at. Thinking with this..." Manny tapped Paul's head. "And not with this." He pointed to his crotch.

Paul flinched at the mention of Lena. He'd been hoping

to keep that part out of it.

Flicking away his cigarette butt, Manny opened the door of the cocktail bar, a twisted glint in his eye. "After you."

Paul stubbed his fag out and entered the dark bar with a creeping fear that an ambush was imminent. Inside, his eyes darted to every corner of the room. Something wasn't right. He could tell.

He followed cautiously behind Manny as they walked past the square bar in the centre, to the booths lining the wall at the back. From across the floor, Paul could see a woman waiting in one of the booths. At first all he could see was the long, black hair and he hoped desperately it wasn't her. But of course it was. She was dressed in jeans and a T-shirt.

"Paul, I wanted you to be here to welcome the newest member of our team."

Lena smiled up at him. Manny shuffled into the booth beside her. Reluctantly, Paul lowered himself onto the edge of the bench.

"What's this about?" Paul felt the blood rush to his face, his lips pale.

Lena cut in. "Mr Munroe has offered me a job. To help with recruitment and the promotion of the club. Escort a few important clients to dinner. It means I don't have to dance anymore and I'll be doing something I'm actually interested in. It's a really good career opportunity for me."

"See, that's why I like her. She's smart. Like you, Paul. I know talent when I see it. There's always a role for a beautiful, intelligent woman in business." Manny winked at Paul. "Makes all kinds of men lose their heads. Not you though, Paul. You think with yours. Isn't that right?"

265

Manny's message was crystal clear. She was his investment now. And it was hands off.

"Isn't that right, Paul?"

"Right, Manny."

"Good. So we're all happy to work together. I'm glad. I see great things."

Manny reached into his inside jacket pocket, pulled out an envelope and turned to Lena. "OK, so your first job's tomorrow. Details are in here. He'll meet you in the bar of the Central Hotel at seven thirty. Dinner reservations have been made for half eight at 78 St Vincent under the name Rose. He's from out of town, so just show him the city, give him a good time. There's money in here to get yourself a nice dress, get your hair done. Make sure you look the part."

Lena took the envelope from his hand and put it into her handbag. "OK, wish me luck." She smiled at him.

"You'll be great," Manny assured her and stood up to leave. "Any problems, you know how to contact me." He tipped his hat. Paul stood up to let him out of the booth. "Now, if you'll excuse me, I've got somewhere I need to be." He gave Paul one final challenging look, then patted him on the shoulder. "Thinking with this." He pointed to his head and walked away.

As soon as Manny was out the door, Paul leaned over the table and grabbed Lena's arm. "What are you doing?"

She yanked it away with a yelp. "You just said you didn't have a problem." She looked tired, burned out, possibly medicated.

"You're going to get us both killed!"

She looked at him incredulously.

Paul could feel his chest constrict. His vision blurred. "Lena, I can't protect you from him."

"Protect? What are you talking about?"

"You have no idea how dangerous he is." His hands went to his head in exasperation. "It's my fault for putting you in his way."

She gave a sharp snort. "This has nothing to do with you, Paul. I put myself in his way. It was me who did this. I'm not your responsibility. I can take care of myself."

"Like you did the other night?"

She shook her head, unravelling before him. "No one asked you to do that." Her voice was sullen, petulant.

"What if I hadn't been there?"

"You weren't. It wasn't then that I needed you." She gave him a strange, haunted look. In the sad empty shell before him he barely recognised the girl he once knew.

He took her hands across the table. They were small and cold. He'd always remembered them being warm. "Come away with me. Tonight. Just the two of us. We can start again, some place else."

She disentangled her hands from his. He could tell he was losing her.

"And miss all the fun?"

Paul could hardly bring himself to look at her. Tears were forming in his eyes. "You leave me no choice, Lena. I have to walk away. For your sake as well as mine. This time I can't help you."

"So walk," she said listlessly. "There's nothing here for you to stick around for."

He looked into her hardened eyes. No hint of emotion

in them. He wasn't even sure if she was there any more. So beautiful. So damaged. Manny would use her. Give her the helping hand she barely needed. And she would bring Paul down with her.

The only way out was to never turn back, the only way out was to never turn back.

Though it broke his heart to do so, he stood up from the table and started walking towards the beckoning glare of the distant doorway.

CHAPTER TWENTY-FIVE

The following night, Paul was looking out over the heaving dance floor at Limbo, his arms resting on the balcony. The rotating mirror ball cast flecks of white onto the hazy mass of dancers and merging kaleidoscopic colours waltzed round the walls. Security melted into the background, allowing people the peace and freedom to enjoy the music and spend at the bar. It was an existence he'd grown to love. It was his livelihood, the source of his self-respect. He'd built his life around it. Without it, he didn't know what would be left. But as Paul turned away from his balcony vantage point and weaved his way through the chaotic bordello-style corridors, via the plethora of red and purple velvet swags, fleur-de-lis flock wallpaper and threadbare baroque carpets, he knew it would be for the last time. The next day he was leaving it all behind, on a train bound for London. And Lena was going with him.

Because he couldn't turn away. He'd tried. The night before, after he'd left her in the cocktail bar, he'd taken the long route home. He made it as far as his front door before sighing deeply and finally accepting he wasn't capable of walking away. He couldn't watch her destroy herself, let Manny use her up and pretend not to care.

At seven fifteen the following night he walked into the bar of the Central Hotel because none of it mattered. It was worthless without her.

Her back was to him as he came through the doors. The leather soles of his Italian brogues clicked as he walked across the smooth marble tiles.

"Lena?"

She turned, twisting round on her high stool at the bar. A halo of light was shining on her from the domed glass roof, small twinkles from the chandelier falling like diamonds on her waist-length black hair. She wore a slim-fitting sleeveless red dress that stopped above the knee.

The rose she'd been holding in her hand dropped beside her barely sipped glass of champagne. Her face registered surprise; she'd been expecting someone else.

"Paul, what're you doing here?"

"I came to ask you not to do this."

Lena's surprise turned to annoyance. Her brows closed together. "Why can't you leave me alone?" she sighed.

There were only a few other people in the bar: two waistcoated barmen behind the bar, a couple at one of the high-chaired tables against the wall, and one or two others around the table beneath the large curved window overlooking the concourse of Glasgow Central Station. Paul could sense their ears pricking up as they tuned in to the conversation.

One of the barmen made tentative steps towards Lena. "Is there a problem, miss?"

"There's no problem," Paul answered.

"No, he's leaving," Lena answered simultaneously.

"Not without you, I'm not." Paul stood resolutely, a

finger up to silence the barman.

"Go away, Paul!" She turned her back to him, heaving an even louder sigh.

"I'm on my knees, Lena. I'm begging you."

"Miss, do you want security called?" The barman avoided eye contact with Paul, his hand resting on the wooden bar separating them.

Lena lifted her head, drummed her red nails on the bar. "No, there's no need. Sorry… I can handle this. Can you watch my drink, please?"

The bewildered barman nodded as she dismounted her stool onto kitten heels, took Paul by the arm and pulled him through the doors and into the quiet corridor of the hotel. The closed doors of function suites and meeting rooms ran the length of it, interspersed with photos of famous former guests. Lena stopped in front of a black-and-white portrait of Gene Kelly in the 1950s; in thick woollen coat, his collar pulled up to his ears and a cheeky smile spread across his face, he was walking on cobblestones, the familiar station clock behind him.

"My client's going to be here any minute. You have to go," Lena whispered.

"No!" Paul said loudly. "Fuck that guy, Lena!"

"Stop making a scene," she hissed under her breath.

"I'm not making a scene. I'm asking you to come away with me!" he said, the volume rising.

"I already told you no!"

A head popped out angrily from behind one of the closed doors. A balding middle-aged man. "Can you keep the noise down!" he snapped, and quickly disappeared again with a slam of the door.

They paused for a second before starting up again.

"Why, Paul? Why would I go with you?" she shouted, getting irate now.

"Because I need you. And because you're not safe here."

The back-and-forth continued for some time until the door at the far end of the corridor swished open and a uniformed security man marched towards them. They both stopped talking and watched him approach.

"I've had a noise complaint."

"Sorry – we're having a discussion," Paul said calmly. "We'll keep it down."

"Are either of you guests at the hotel?" the security man said and stopped beside them.

"I am. He isn't," Lena said.

Paul flashed her an angry look.

The security man turned his attention to Paul. "Then I'm going to have to ask you to leave, sir."

"I'm not leaving unless you promise to go with me," Paul continued, ignoring him.

"Sir, can you leave, please." The man stood squarely beside Paul, his weight resting on the balls of his feet.

"Lena, I'll tell you everything. No more secrets. I'll do anything to make it up to you. Tell me what I have to do!"

"If you don't leave I'll have to call the police."

"Call them," Paul said irritably, brushing him off.

The doorman pulled out his radio.

Lena shook her head.

"Don't do this, Lena. Don't throw it all away."

The radio crackled. The doorman mumbled into it. "We

have a customer refusing to leave…"

Paul looked from the doorman to Lena. He held up his hands to her. "Please, Lena."

"… causing a disturbance, showing aggressive behaviour." The radio crackled again.

"Wait." Lena put her hand on the security man's arm.

A few minutes later, a grey-haired, middle-aged businessman in a neat-fitting tailored suit strode along the empty corridor and with a waft of expensive cologne entered the hotel bar. He circled twice, looked at his watch, then stopped at the bar in confusion. His eyes fell on a glass of champagne, a single red rose. His mouth pulled in an ugly grimace. Expecting the beautiful female he'd been promised, it seemed instead that all he would be met with that night was disappointment and an empty chair.

It took a while, but Lena managed to convince the security man to cancel his call. She assured him that the argument was over, that they would adjourn peaceably to her room and cause no more trouble. He let them off with a warning. After he left, they went up the wide, carpeted staircase to her room.

When they'd closed the door behind them, she turned to him and said, "Where would we go?"

He decided to tell her straight. "I don't know. Somewhere far."

She walked to the window and peered through the net curtain onto the street. Paul rested on the corner of the bed. Now there was the slimmest of chances, he didn't want to push too much and scare her off.

"For how long?"

"Just until we know it's safe to come back. I don't know how long, Lena."

"What will we do? How will we live?"

Paul shifted along the bed. "I have fifty grand in my flat, under my bed. Money I haven't stashed in the bank. Half of that we can take with us, the other half I need to leave for Jack. It should be enough to help us get set up. It's not much, but it's a start. I can get to the bank tomorrow, get a little more."

"And what about Manny? Would he look for us?" Her eyes flickered with fear.

Paul slowly got off the bed and leaned against the window beside her. "I think he would."

"Our lives would be in danger?"

"If we stay here, we have no life. I won't let anything bad happen to you, I promise."

He ran his hand absently up and down her arm. She looked back out the window, a lost expression on her face, the sweet scent of her hair filling the air. He watched her shoulders sink, the last of her resistance draining.

"A quiet life away from Glasgow, Lena," he entreated. "Away from Manny, away from all the madness. I don't know what life I can offer. But we'll survive as long as we're together. We have to believe it will work out. We have to believe in this chance of happiness."

Lena didn't answer him, just continued staring through the net curtain. They stayed there, not talking, and for a second he thought all was lost. Then he saw her brow furrow and realised she was looking for something, or someone, in the street. He wasn't even sure she'd been listening.

"What's wrong, Lena?"

She drew her eyes away from the window and breathed deeply. "It's probably nothing," she said. "I've just had this strange feeling all day that someone is watching me."

"What makes you say that?" Paul's heart thumped in his chest. He instinctively took a step back to behind the floral curtain, out of sight of the street.

"When I left the bar yesterday after talking to you and Manny, I noticed a man on my way out. I noticed him because his face… it looked like he'd been in some kind of explosion. I saw him again later. Near my flat. And again today, passing the station. Maybe it's a coincidence. Glasgow's a small place."

Paul pulled her out of view of the window and couldn't hide the growing concern in his face. "It's not a coincidence." He wondered if Terry had seen him entering earlier.

Lena's face flushed and her eyes watered.

"I'm not trying to scare you, Lena. But you're mixed up in this now. Can you see that?"

She nodded and suddenly the question of her leaving was answered. "What should I do?"

Paul nodded to her travel case on the bed. "Terry will be looking for a woman in a red dress. Have you got a change of clothes?"

She nodded and with little fuss followed his instructions.

She swapped her dress for trousers and a top, and hid them beneath a beige raincoat, collar up. She trussed her hair up under a black fedora. Paul took her new phone number and told her to go outside directly, keep her head down and get in a taxi straight to his flat. If Terry knew where she lived, it wasn't safe for her to go back there. He told her to make a list of all the things she needed and he would pick them up from her flat later. Passport, clothes, whatever else she could think of. They exchanged keys. London first, then who knew? Paul would try to sort things with Stacy early the next day and they could be travelling by the afternoon. The rest they could think about later. Once they were at a safe distance, they could go their separate ways. He hoped she wouldn't.

When it was time to go, Lena followed him to the door like a shadow. He opened it to send her on her way but she hovered and pressed her hands into the muscles in his arm.

"Thank you, Paul."

"When you get to mine you should try to get some sleep. I don't know when we'll have the chance to rest next."

She suddenly hugged him close, burying her head in his chest.

He watched from the window as she appeared in the street below, crossed it and got straight into a taxi. There was no sign of Terry. A few minutes later Paul crept out too and made his way to Limbo for his last night of work.

As he strode towards the front door to let his bouncers know it was last entry, there was a heaviness to Paul's step. He contemplated his and Lena's imminent escape.

The entrance to Limbo was in an alley. Its blinking lights enticed people up the dark pathway but at this time of night it was all but deserted. The blaring music from the club echoed down the cobbles as he opened the door to go outside.

The bouncers stepped inside to enjoy some heat before the end of the night, when they would be back monitoring the throng of people pouring out. Paul stood just outside the door, making the most of his brief break. The cold air was biting; it was forecast to snow that night. There was a strange amber glow to the sky that made him think it was close.

Leaning back against the alley wall, Paul took a long draw on his cigarette. As he exhaled the final puff, the bleached poster on the opposite wall caught his eye. It was advertising a classical concert which had passed two years ago. The font was superimposed over the image of an angel. The ink had faded so you could no longer tell he had once been surrounded by a beautiful blue sky, the brilliant golden wings now an insipid yellow.

A faint grunt made Paul jump. The silhouette of a man emerged slowly from the end of the alley. His sturdy steps were meandering yet purposeful, his head draped in shadow. Paul watched as he teetered along, supported on buckling legs – two steps forward, one step back – and wondered if there was some device built into drunks that set them in the direction of home. Paul dipped to see the face but it was too dark. The figure hovered a few feet from him, his radar telling him the thoroughfare was not clear. Paul flipped his cigarette off the poster and turned to go back into the club.

He heard the steps rush towards him but didn't see the figure lunge at him. He was knocked into the wall, his face grazing the damp bricks. Two strong arms turned him round and he was hit by the smell of whisky. Carmichael. The inspector's face was pressed up against Paul's, his drunken eyes rolling. He began beating Paul over the head with a folded newspaper, making crazy, indistinct noises like the hee-haws of a donkey.

"Scumbag! Fucking…" Spittle flew from the corners of his mouth. "I thought it was drugs."

Paul was surprised the old man had so much speed. He pushed Carmichael forcefully in the chest, hard enough to send him stumbling. The paper fell to the ground and Carmichael tripped over his own feet and landed hard beside it. He rolled onto his back like a beetle, unable to right himself. Hysterical laughter blasted out of Paul as he kicked Carmichael in the gut, knocking the wind out of him. He stuck the boot in again. Carmichael rolled about, clutching his swollen belly.

Behind Paul the door to the club flew open. Two bouncers ran towards him.

"What happened? What's going on?"

Paul spun round. "This pathetic piece of shit fuckin' ran'n jumped me." With his temper up, his accent came through thick and guttural. He savoured the aggressive growl of the words.

The bouncers lifted Carmichael to his feet. His head lolled from side to side between his shoulder blades, which poked up like two lumps. His white hair was dishevelled, feathered around his ears. Paul experienced a small attack of nausea and turned away.

"Throw him at the end of the alley. And be gentle. When he's not a drunken retard, he's polis."

"No problem, boss," one of the bouncers said as the two of them vigorously ushered Carmichael back into the darkness. Paul heard a couple of kicks followed by groans but left them to it, his attention now focused on the crumpled tabloid lying at his feet. He bent down and read the headline.

Lifting the paper to inspect it further, he read and reread the story until he could make some sense of it.

When he closed his eyes, a terrifying image settled behind the lids. Ayr beach. Naked grey bloated skin piled on naked grey bloated skin. Limbs intertwined, caked in froth and loam. Dank hair dripping like limp, dead weeds.

A sickening dread rose inside him. Clutching the paper in his left hand, he charged off into the shadows of the alley, heading for Manny's pool hall. With his other hand, he felt for the flick-knife resting in the hidden pocket sewn into the tails of his suit jacket.

The light in Manny's office was still on, as it often was at that hour on a Saturday night. The only time Paul could count on him being alone. Paul pressed the buzzer. Shuffling from foot to foot, he stared into the camera and imagined Manny watching the grainy, grey image. His heart was racing. Waiting in the cold, dark street, the acrid smell of fish from the nearby mongers still potent from trade earlier in the day, Paul listened closely. Finally he heard footsteps thudding down the stairs, a hand fumbling the lock, the bolts clicking out of place. He took a step back as the door swung open.

Manny appeared, his face sculpted by shadows, his gold incisor sparkling.

"Paul. Wasn't expecting you."

"I need to talk to you." Paul tried to control the tremor in his voice. He moved closer to the door, but Manny was blocking the entrance, looking him up and down. The waning moon shone down on them.

"I said, we need to talk." Paul rested his hand on the wall

279

and held his gaze.

Silently, Manny stepped aside, allowing him to brush past. Paul climbed the stairs to the pool room. The lights were off, the empty bar stools and lonely rows of green tables just visible in the shard of light from Manny's office. The plastic-coated benches that encircled the room were bare, but still Paul felt like someone was lurking there, in some dark corner.

Manny's steps sounded behind him. The office door creaked as Manny opened it; in the wash of orange light his massive shadow engulfed Paul. Turning his back on the cold draughts of the empty pool room, Paul followed him into the office.

Inside, it was stifling. The heater in the corner shed a fiery glow around the room. Condensation misted the grilled window. Paul could feel his palms starting to sweat.

"So what is it that's so important?"

Manny leaned against his desk, facing Paul, his hand resting near a half-drunk mug of coffee. Paul's eyes fell briefly on the framed photograph of Manny's wife. It captured her well – attractive, confident – and would have been convincing if Paul hadn't recognised the same forced loyalty that he himself displayed. Beside Manny's wife sat their two daughters. Paul had never met them; to him they were almost mythical creatures, ephemeral abstracts in a photograph, with their pearly white smiles and perfectly groomed hair. Manny had once told Paul that if his daughters ever brought home a scruff like him, he'd break his legs. Paul was only good enough for Manny to toy with. Manny's daughters wouldn't dance in one of his clubs, wouldn't lie doped on a bed in one of his brothels, getting fucked by strangers.

Or wash up on a beach somewhere.

Paul threw the newspaper onto the desk, the front page facing upwards.

Manny glanced at it, not even a hint of acknowledgement. "What's this?"

"It's the cargo. The one I told you about the other day."

Manny looked at him blankly. "Don't know what you're talking about."

"You dumped them – so you wouldn't get caught."

Manny's dead black eyes stared at him.

Paul pointed a finger in Manny's chest. "You knew when I said in the club the other night—"

Manny slapped his finger away, bunched the front of Paul's shirt with his fist and pulled him in close. Paul could feel the heat of Manny's breath. With his free hand Manny patted Paul's chest. Paul realised he was searching for a wire. Satisfied there wasn't one, Manny pushed him away. Paul stumbled but caught his balance.

"So what if I did?" Manny began to pace back and forth. "Do you think it's easy what I do – being the boss? You stand there and judge me? You! The runt from the streets!" He ran his hand through his silver-flecked dark hair, leaving it standing up in two points behind his ears. His customary measured whisper had become a roar that reverberated around the room. "I make the difficult decisions no one else will. I do what it takes. It wasn't me that made this happen. I didn't want it this way."

"They are dead, Manny. Eight women are dead." Paul's thumping heart felt like it was about to crack through his ribs.

"A lot more than that, my son." Manny stopped pacing. "There's always a price; it's always at the expense of others."

Paul tried to picture himself and Lena together – blue skies, the rush of the sea – but the image distorted into bulging alabaster eyes, glazed and cracked like antique ceramic, threads of blood pumping through them, squeezing out. The sputtering cries of the drowned women rang in his head.

"Just because I understand, that doesn't make me the bad one." Manny's words were slow and considered again now. "Just because I don't sit around in my tidy house, choosing to see just enough so that I can live with myself, letting someone else get their hands dirty. I bear the responsibility for all of you. But there's blood on all of our hands. All of our choices count."

"I can't do it anymore," Paul pleaded. "You know you can trust me. I won't say anything to anyone. But I'm finished. I have to go."

Manny stood squarely in front of the door. Under his dark gaze, Paul found himself rooted to the spot. He wondered why he'd never noticed how ugly Manny was before. How spittle gathered at the corner of his lips when he spoke; that his teeth were brown and rotting and his eyes were empty. Hideous. He'd never considered what it must be like to wake up in the morning and have those eyes staring back from the mirror. The thought made him nauseous.

"Get away from the door, Manny," Paul said weakly.

Manny's mouth turned down in a mean smirk. "No."

Paul could suddenly feel the weight of the knife buried in the back of his jacket. "I'm trying to be reasonable, Manny."

"Reasonable?" Manny laughed. "How about a couple of

quid for the slut to fuck Dario. Call it a belated birthday present. Does that sound reasonable?"

Manny took a step closer. Paul backed away, not taking his eyes off him.

"I thought you were a fighter," Manny sneered, his hands bunching into fists. "A player. Never took you for a pussy, Paul."

The light flickered and Paul became aware of the incessant buzzing from above. "Get back, Manny."

Manny shoved his shoulder with the heel of his hand. Paul stopped backing away and stood his ground.

"That's what happens to pussies, Paul. Is that what you are? A pussy? Is that what you want? A lifetime of rolling over? Think you can protect your family, being a pussy?"

Manny shoved him again, more forcefully. Paul pressed the butt of his head against Manny's.

"You stay away from them," Paul growled.

"That son of yours?" Manny whispered, so close Paul could smell his canine breath. "Think he'll grow up to be as big a pussy as his father? Do you think when I check on him in a few years he'll be as big a disappointment to me as you are? Do you think he'll be looking for a real man to show him the ways of the world? Or maybe some cock-munching like his old man?"

Paul threw a swift right hook. It connected with the side of Manny's head, but he barely flinched. Teeth bared, Manny's hands went up and coiled tightly around Paul's throat. He squeezed, pressing his thumb into Paul's windpipe.

"I'll break your neck before I let you leave."

Paul struggled against him but Manny's grip was too strong.

"I'll break your son's neck."

Manny pressed harder. Blood pumped into Paul's face, his temples bulged.

Manny's eyes stared steadily into his. "I found you. I own you. I'll never let you go."

White lights began to flash and Paul could feel the life slipping out of him, could feel his pulse grow weaker and weaker.

There was no alternative. Manny wouldn't allow it. Manny, who had taken him off the streets, given him a chance when nobody else would.

"Understand?"

Paul nodded.

Manny shook him by the neck. "Understand!"

Paul's eyes rolled in his head and slowly closed.

Manny let go and Paul fell to his knees, gasping for air, the bitter taste of blood and defeat in his mouth. Manny paced around him, his boot soles thudding. He was talking, but Paul couldn't hear the words over his own hacking and wheezing.

The boots stopped and Manny stood in silence above him. The coughing slowly subsided and Paul began to breathe again.

"OK?" Manny said, looking down at him.

Paul massaged his throat with his hand.

"I said, are you OK?"

Paul took a deep, steadying breath. "Yes," he rasped.

Manny reached down and with two hands hauled Paul to his feet. Paul propped himself unsteadily against the wall. He turned his head away.

"I hate having to hurt you." Manny placed a hand on Paul's face and turned it back towards him. "But all this talk of you leaving… It's over. I don't want to hear it again."

Paul nodded, cautiously reaching back inside his jacket, Manny's hand still locked on his chin.

"I need to know you understand how it works."

Paul's jaw set stiffly, his brow knitted in a frown. He nodded again. Manny moved his hand up through Paul's hair, put his arm around him, pulled his head down into his chest.

Paul's hand clasped around the handle of the knife. A second later he plunged it into Manny's stomach, up to the hilt. Paul yanked it out and stabbed it in again, this time into Manny's lower ribs. He packed power behind it. Heard a crunch of bone. Blood spurted over his hand, onto the floor.

Manny looked at him in wide-eyed surprise. Then he fell against Paul, his eyes closing. Paul spat on his body before running down the stairs and out into the street.

CHAPTER TWENTY-SIX

Light snow started to fall as Paul left the pool hall. The streets were quiet. Without meeting a single soul, Paul weaved through darkness and shadows and found his way down to the riverside. Adrenaline had kicked in and he struggled to control the violent shaking. He threw the knife into the Clyde, then wiped what he could of the crusted blood off his hands and threw the jacket in too, also covered in Manny's blood. Only a thin shirt now protected him against the numbing cold. His breath hung in the air in front of him.

From there he started for home, a brisk twenty-minute walk away. He could make it in less if he ran, but running attracted attention and that was the last thing he wanted. The clock on his phone read 2 a.m. It would be dark for another five or six hours, which was to his advantage.

As he walked, he scrolled down his contacts with his bloodstained thumb. Stacy. He pressed the call button. It seemed to ring forever. But on the tenth ring she picked up, her voice slurred from sleep.

"Paul?"

"Yeah, it's me. Where are you?"

"At home. Why? It's late. You'll wake Jack."

"Just the two of you?"

"Fuck off! What's it to do with you?"

He took a deep breath and stammered out, "Something happened tonight. I need you to pack a bag and take Jack round to your mum's." His teeth were rattling and he couldn't stop them.

"Paul, what're you talking about?" she shrieked at him.

"Stacy," he said, sharply, "I don't have time for the histrionics. You're not in any danger. It's just a precaution. I don't have time to explain. Take Jack around to your mum's and lock the doors. I'm going to try and send someone round to look after you. He's polis. Ask to see his warrant card before you let him in."

"Paul?"

"Just do it!"

He hung up.

Not even Manny and his men would go after a kid. Even in Glasgow, where anything went, no hard man would survive that. But Paul wasn't taking any chances. Reaching into his inside pocket, he fished out his wallet. Still walking, he pulled out a card and dialled the number.

A gruff voice answered. "DCI Carmichael."

"Carmichael? It's Paul. Paul Dalziel."

He could hear Carmichael clearing his throat on the other end. When the inspector spoke again, his voice was quiet, as if he was leaving a room and didn't want to disturb someone. "What do you want?" he asked angrily. There was still a slight slur to his voice but he sounded reasonably sober.

"I need your help."

Carmichael was silent, so Paul continued, the phone shaking in his hand. "I need you to make sure my son and his mother are safe." His mouth dried. "They could be in danger."

"Dial 999." Carmichael was fully awake now.

"You're the only one I trust," Paul said.

Carmichael hesitated. "Why, what's happened?"

"I can't get into that right now, Carmichael. Will you do it or not?"

There was a long pause. Paul's body felt numb. The snow was getting heavier as he neared his flat. The rumble of an occasional car on the nearby motorway was the only sign of life. The street was deserted. His building came into sight. The building where Lena was waiting for him.

"What's in it for me?" Carmichael retorted.

"What do you want?" Paul said grimly. He stopped and took a moment to survey the scene. The road to his front door was clear.

"Information."

"About what?" Paul said breathlessly, the pressing urgency making him sick. He thought of Jack. Maybe one day there'd be the chance to make it up to him. Some way further down the line to reach out to him.

Carmichael huffed impatiently. "Give me something. Anything!"

Paul knew that time was running out. His body was throbbing with the cold. He had to keep moving. And Lena was waiting.

"I can give you information. About John's murder," he said, with resignation. "Me, Manny, Bucky, Dunsmore, Terry, we were all there. You were right: he didn't jump into the sea. His head was crushed by a baseball bat. His body is buried in a shallow grave at an abandoned farm.

288

There's evidence there. If you guarantee the safety of my son and his mother, I'll tell you where. Just promise me you'll look after them."

Carmichael exhaled loudly down the phone. "OK, I promise. But, Paul," he warned, "when the time comes, I'll be looking for you to help me get them off the street. You know what I mean."

"I'll be there," Paul sighed. It was a promise he hoped he could keep. "Now, do you have a pen and paper?"

"Go," Carmichael said.

Paul carefully recited Stacy's address, checked and rechecked that Carmichael had taken it down correctly. Before hanging up, he hurriedly gave Carmichael the location of John's body.

The next call he made was to Lena, to tell her he was coming. He was getting closer and closer to his front door. After ten beeps it went to voicemail. He cancelled and redialled, listening as it rang out. He tried a third time, but once again, it clicked to voicemail.

Lena wasn't answering.

CHAPTER TWENTY-SEVEN

Paul continued to stare at an invisible spot on the floor. Annie's eyes bored holes in him. She tried not to notice how sickly-looking he had become, his grey skin lacquered with sweat, his body wan, starved of nutrients and sunlight.

"She left," he finally said.

"What do you mean? Where?" The words fired from her mouth like bullets. In his chair, Paul fidgeted and squirmed.

"When I got back to the flat, she was gone. Taken off. She got herself out of there. I don't know where she went, but when they came for me, she'd got away."

"You're lying!" Annie shouted.

Paul's voice had taken on a pleading tone. "You know everything now. So it's time to let me go. Let me go and I'll walk away. I'll do that for your sister. Because I loved her. And because I want you to know that I loved her."

"Why are you lying to me, Paul?"

Paul started to twist his arms, trying vainly to free them from the ropes. "I'm not lying," he moaned.

Annie was on her feet. "I know she didn't leave without you, Paul. Because after she left you at the hotel, she didn't go straight to your flat. She came to see me. She came to say goodbye. Said she was leaving with you and that she loved you. She told me she'd be in touch!"

Paul shook his head.

"She said you were going on an adventure. But that she'd be safe because she was going with you. Dressed just like you described her."

Paul's eyes filled with tears. He closed them, tried to empty his mind.

Annie began rattling him, desperate to shake the truth from him. "What happened?" She shook him some more.

"She's gone!" Paul shouted and jerked free of her, unable to listen anymore. "Can't you just leave it at that? She didn't suffer."

Annie stood in stunned silence, visibly deflating, like a withered balloon. She hovered there limply, trying to process his words. Her body smarted as if it had been freshly skinned and rubbed in salt. It was what she had known all along, but it didn't stop the hurt.

Paul didn't speak, didn't look at her. His nostrils began to flare as if he was offended by his own stench.

"You knew all this time. But you let me go on hoping."

"Stop it!" he shouted and tried to bury his head in his shoulder. Strangled grunts escaped him as if he was trying to cry. His shoulders curled, his muscles flexed. He strained against the ropes. The whites of his eyes grew red and pulsed, ready to burst; the veins in his temples throbbed purple. Annie watched as he fought to pull free. Tearing the skin off his hands. Yanking and ripping.

One hand broke loose. Annie spied the knife across by the window and ran over, grabbing the cold black handle. By the time she'd spun round, his other hand was free.

He was bent over, untying his leg. She bolted for the door, grabbing desperately for the knob. Behind her, Paul's chair thudded to the floor.

She ran through into the hall, racing to the front door. His feet pounded on the carpet as he chased her. She tried to open the door and escape, fumbled with the chain, but he lunged from behind and pinned her against it, his arm arching over either side of her. Close up, she could feel his strength; even in his weakened state, he was far stronger than she was.

Turning so her back was against the door, she pointed the knife at him, her shaking hands slippery with sweat. Paul leaned closer, the knife puncturing the threads of his T-shirt.

"You shouldn't threaten someone with a weapon unless you're prepared to use it!" he panted, his eyes bright and hungry.

"Don't think I won't!"

"Because they can just…" Her eyes briefly went to the knife. He grabbed her wrist and twisted. She felt it slip from her fingers. "… take it off you, and use it against you."

With a steady hand, he pressed the knife close to her face. She felt the blade cold against her cheek and didn't say a word as she waited for him to use it. Closing her eyes, she waited and waited.

The knife made a loud clink as it landed at the other end of the hall. It happened so fast, her eyes flashed open just as Paul grabbed her by the upper arms and banged her forcefully into the door. Her head cracked off the wooden panelling and her last sensation before she lost consciousness was confusion.

When she came to, she was sitting on the couch. Her hands

were tied behind her back and her mouth was gagged. The rope had been tied tightly, digging into her skin; he hadn't left any space, and the gag was already wet with saliva.

Paul came into focus, moving around the living room. He looked different. Alive, energetic. Manic.

He picked up her handbag and turned it upside down, spilling the contents onto the floor. She watched him rummage on his haunches through loose change, crumpled receipts, a broken lipstick, until he found her keys and lifted them out. Isolating the car key, he bounced to his feet with satisfaction and came towards her.

"Is it parked outside?"

She nodded.

His wrists were red where the ropes had been, deep grazes where he'd torn them free. He rubbed them absently. "OK, we're going for a drive. If you scream or try to get away, I'll break your neck."

She nodded again. Her eyes stung and her nose tingled. She fought to hold back the tears.

He dug his fingers into her arm and pulled her to her feet. There was nothing to do but go with him. He dragged her first into the hall and then into the kitchen, slamming through drawers and cupboards to find a torch. On the way out, he lifted her red coat off the stand and put it over her shoulders, pulling her hood up so it hung over her face.

"Don't try anything stupid," he threatened. Together they stepped out into the gloom. Closing the door carefully behind him, he put his arm around her shoulders, drawing her in tight. Her face pressed against his chest, the stale sweat from his underarms making her gag. They progressed downstairs like two bodies in a three-legged race; to anyone watching, they would have looked like two inebriated lovers holding on to each other for support.

It was dark outside. The wind was blowing. There was no one around. Paul held up the keys and pressed the central-locking button. Her car beeped and they made their unsteady way towards it.

"Get in." He opened the passenger door and when she hesitated he shoved her in, slamming the door after her. She followed him with her eyes as he walked casually to his side. Her hands throbbed behind her back. He got in and reached over her to pull her seatbelt across, clicking it into place. The sound made her heart sink, her movements now restricted to the few inches of space around the seat. She had to lift her head up just to see out from under her hood. Only her knees were free. She wondered if she would be able to knock the gearstick once he started driving. When she looked up, she found him staring at her, steadily and with loathing, as if he had just read her mind.

"Try it and see what happens."

Her knees clenched and she knew he meant it. It chilled her to think how close she'd come to believing him, that she'd almost pitied him. She had no idea where he was taking her but knew it was nowhere good. When the moment came, she would fight him with every fibre of her being.

He drove carefully, calmly, aware of the speed cameras. As they reached the motorway, familiar landmarks disappeared. They rolled past bridges and buildings she'd never seen before. Once or twice she tried to catch the eye of a passing driver, but none of them looked her way. Even if they had, most of her face was covered by her hood.

Eventually he pulled off the motorway into an area she didn't recognise. Paul flicked the headlights off and the car crept along the dark, deserted streets. There would be no one to help her here, in this post-apocalyptic wilderness. Most of the tenement buildings were abandoned: metal sheets soldered over the windows, refuse piled in the gardens, plastic bags sprouting like mutating weeds across the landscape. The skeleton of a burned-out car lay in the middle of the road, its charred doors open as if, like the rest of the place, it had been abandoned in a hurry.

They reached a dead end and the car rolled slowly to a stop. Silently, Paul got out. A chain-link fence barred the way forward and a sign proclaiming *Demolition Site: Keep Out* filled the windscreen. A mountainous pile of rubble was heaped behind it, with metal beams poking out from beneath tons of crumbling concrete, like the last remnants of a sinking ship.

Annie's door flew open and a wash of cold air blew in. She watched from under her hood as Paul reached in and leaned across to undo her seatbelt. As soon as the lock clicked open, she mustered all her strength and struck out, hitting him with her head, knees, every body part she could charge into motion. A few good blows connected and she continued kicking, his arms flailing in the enclosed space, trying to restrain her. Her legs kicked furiously. Her shoe flew off and she felt her stockinged foot sink sharply into something soft and warm. Paul gasped in pain and doubled over, holding his groin. Seizing the opportunity, Annie leaped from the car and made a run for it. But a hand grabbed her foot and she lost her balance and landed hard on the cold ground.

Despite the shooting pain in her shoulder, she scrambled quickly to her feet. But Paul was already on top of her. His hand closed tightly around her shoulder. His breath was tearing out of him, the other hand still clutching his aching groin.

"Fucking bitch." He hobbled to his feet, pulling her up with him. Together, they started towards a break in the fence. When she stopped walking, he dragged her, scraping her legs along the pavement. He held back the stray piece of fence and pulled her through.

In the centre of the demolition site was a derelict block of flats. The thirty-odd floors loomed ahead of them. She looked back to where its twin had once stood, now reduced to the rubbly mound by the fence. Curtains still hung in some of the broken windows, but no lights were on. Still, she had the feeling of eyes on them, watching in silent anonymity. She could only imagine what manner of life inhabited its dark corridors and abandoned rooms, what nocturnal activities went on behind its grey concrete walls. They crossed the wasteland until they were directly underneath. She thought it was their destination but he pulled her past and onto a dark, overgrown track.

Long grass and nettles stung her lower legs, snagging her tights. Stray roots played beneath her feet, tripping her, and the sprigs of bushes pulled her hair and scratched her face, but their brisk pace never slowed. They carried on, the ground becoming softer underfoot, and soon she heard the rush of water. The sound grew louder. Finally, they reached a tall concrete wall. He tugged her towards an opening and hauled her through and onto a tarmac pathway that followed the water's edge. The black water of the River Clyde raged under the silver glare of the stars.

Looking back desperately, she saw how far they'd come. The dark shadow of the high-rise stood in the distance, its blacked-out eyes purposefully closed to the world. The faint light of the motorway glowed behind it.

On the other side of the river was a steep embankment and beyond that a scattering of houses, too far away for anyone to spot their two solitary figures. Up ahead, stretching over the river, was a large iron railway bridge. Annie wasn't sure if it was still in use, but there would be no trains at this time of night anyway. The river rushed noisily beside them, too loud for anyone to hear.

Paul dragged her on, towards the bridge. The entrance to the tunnel beneath it was covered in graffiti, the grass around it littered with weather-bleached cans and drugs paraphernalia; a damp couch sat beside the remnants of a campfire scorched into the gravel. The air stank of putrid ash mixed with the damp spray of the river.

Inside the tunnel the shadows swelled and shrank.

Paul flicked on the torch. "Go in."

Annie shook her head, her eyes wide and desperate.

He shone the torch under the bridge, the thin trickle of light flying over syringes and along the oozing, crumbling bricks. The river rushed dangerously close.

"Go in."

He nudged her forward, inch by resistant inch. With every step, she could feel the temperature dropping. The arched brickwork of the roof reflected the water in a kaleidoscope of shapes. It was quieter underneath. Their breathing echoed above the din of the river beside them.

Paul put the torch under his armpit to free up his hands. The beam lit his face, like a monster. Sobbing with fear, she searched around for somewhere to run to, but there was only the river and darkness. Suddenly the light flashed into her eyes, momentarily dazzling her. Instinctively she tried to shield them, but with her hands tied behind her back, the force of her movement knocked her off balance. She stumbled to the ground and rolled.

The ground was wet and muddy. She could feel his hand on her. His fingers tugging on the rope around her wrists as she sprawled there, helpless. The torch, lying beside her, shone into the river, which was closer than she'd realised. Another inch or two and she would have been in it. Paul must have pulled her back. Her protests were muffled by the gag. She could feel the rope squeezing tighter. She yelped in pain, then exhaled in sudden relief as the binds loosened. She rotated her wrists, the rush of blood sending a flood of agonising tingles to the tip of each finger.

Breathing hard, she pulled down her gag and scrambled to her feet. Paul was standing at the edge of the water, leaning over, looking into the river's depths. He'd lost all interest in her. Annie backed away to a safe distance, but she didn't run.

"Why have you brought me here?" she said, her voice trembling.

"Because this is where it all ended."

His words rang starkly around the cold brick walls.

CHAPTER TWENTY-EIGHT

Nine years ago

Standing outside his apartment block, the snow obscuring nearly everything by now, he tried phoning Lena a third time. This time the call connected. A voice came on the line.

"Hello, Paul."

The cracked, mid-Ulster tones of Terry stopped him in his tracks. Snow was still falling silently, absorbing the sounds of the street, of the river. His own voice and Terry's breathing on the end of the line were magnified in his ear.

"Terry?"

"We have her, Paul. We have your girlfriend."

Paul let the words slowly sink in. He swallowed back the large lump in his throat. "You have Lena?"

"Unless that was someone else we took kicking and screaming from your flat tonight," Terry said, impatiently. He didn't like having to explain himself twice.

Paul looked up at the sky, at the steadily falling snow, and had a sudden feeling of vertigo, as if gravity had abandoned him and he was hurtling into oblivion.

The river. Darkness. Hot tears welled up inside him. They had her.

He spoke again but his voice didn't sound like his own. "Where?"

"Somewhere safe. For now."

Paul's breath burst out of him in punctured gasps, which he struggled to hold in. Heavy, teeth-chattering gasps. The more he tried to hold them in, the more intense they became. He took the phone away from his ear, put his hand over his mouth to try and muffle them, terrified as a surge of complete helplessness overtook him.

He could hear Terry's voice, tiny, in his hand. "You still there, Paul? Paul?"

Slowly he lifted the phone back to his ear. "I'm here…" he stammered.

"It's not her we want, Paul. Surrender yourself and we'll let her go." Terry's breathing rasped in Paul's ear before his voice crackled again. "Should have finished the job, Paul. Should have checked he was dead, Paul. A soldier would have checked."

They knew. Manny was alive. Or at least, he'd stayed alive long enough to tell Terry and the mob who it was that had carved two large holes in him. Manny, who knew no limits. Manny, who would get revenge any way possible. How could that be? Paul had stabbed him, not once but twice, twisting the knife. Watched the blood pour out of him. His eyes closed.

Terry's voice started again. "Remember John? That was child's play, Paul. That was a mercy killing compared to what we're going to do to you."

Paul fought back the vomit rising in his stomach. "Just don't hurt her," he whispered.

"Do as you're told and we'll see about letting the little lady go."

"I'm listening," Paul said, the phone shaking in his hand.

"On the empty plot of land beside your flat, there's a car. It's waiting for you. The boys will get you there, understood?"

"I understand."

Terry had stopped talking. Down the line, Paul could hear the sound of footsteps, then someone shouting, screaming. The screams got steadily louder. Suddenly Lena's voice came on the phone, shrill with fear.

"Paul? PAUL? Paul, help me! Why are they doing this? PAUL!"

The phone was grabbed away and her voice faded, although he could still hear her shrieks.

"Hurry, Paul," Terry said before the phone went dead.

"LENA?" He shouted into the mouthpiece, but he knew they were no longer connected. "Lena." He cried quietly, this time to himself, dropping his arm with the phone at his side.

In the distance, Paul could make out the dark outline of the Finnieston Crane. There was no one else around. Shivering in the night chill, he headed straight towards the empty plot Terry had directed him to. He reached it in a matter of moments. His eyes focused on the small speck in the centre, where amber car lights shone through the blurry haze of the snow. He watched two figures get out of the car. Their shadows loomed over him as he walked, without faltering, towards the beams.

"Stop there. Put your hands on your head. Cunt," Bucky said, a knife flashing in his hand.

Paul stopped a yard from him and placed his palms flat

against the back of his head. Bucky took a step closer and held the knife to Paul's throat. Dunsmore opened the boot and stood waiting beside it.

"Get in!" Bucky hissed through yellow teeth and walked slowly around Paul, pointing the knife at his back. Paul could feel it poking him in the shoulder blade, pushing him forward. His instinct was to struggle, but he stopped himself. He approached the boot evenly, glancing inside at the dark space, which was empty apart from a scattering of pine needles – someone had transported a Christmas tree. There was nothing that could be used as a weapon.

Everyone had predicted a white Christmas and now it looked like they might just be right. That was the thought going through Paul's head as he slowly turned around and eased himself backwards into the boot. He'd given Stacy the best part of a grand to get Jack whatever he wanted. He was four now, needed all sorts of things. She had taken the money but asked him not to come round on Christmas Day. It would be better if Jack could see him on Boxing Day. Paul hadn't been happy about it but he'd agreed. He'd hoped he would get the chance to take Jack out, build his first snowman with him.

A few snowflakes fell on him and he watched them melt onto his black trousers as he lay on his side and curled his legs up to his chest. Bucky and Dunsmore stood over him. "After all he did for you?" Dunsmore said, and spat in his face. Then the boot door slammed shut and he was in darkness.

Ten minutes of twists and turns, starts and stops, then fifteen of steady motorway driving. The twists and turns started again, but only for a short time, before the car pulled to a slow stop. From inside the boot, Paul listened to doors opening and voices talking, loud but indistinct.

He lay very still.

Without the road to concentrate on, the boot seemed to shrink as his thoughts expanded. Fear filled every pocket of air in the cramped space as he tried not to picture all the horrific ways they could kill him. Roll him in the river; the water would fill his lungs. Set the car alight; his clothes would burn, the plastic melting into his blistering skin, toxic smoke choking him to death, burning his eyes. Or maybe they'd do it slow. He thought of John's head collapsing beneath the baseball bat. The cramp in his lower belly seized.

Suddenly the boot flipped open and he gasped a huge lungful of air. A torch shone in his face.

"Right, time to go," Bucky sneered as he and Dunsmore reached in and grabbed Paul by a shoulder each, hauling him out of the boot and onto his feet. A strong fist hit him in the side of the head, starting a ringing in his ear. It took him a moment to find his bearings.

They were in a car park. A thin layer of snow lay on the ground. The shadow of two enormous high-rises fell over them. Paul looked up to the windows and desperately hoped that someone was watching. Someone who wouldn't be frightened to get involved. Someone who wouldn't close their curtains and turn away.

"Where are you taking me?"

Whatever their destination, they hadn't taken the precaution of blindfolding him. Wherever it was, he wasn't coming back from it.

"You'll find out soon, ya prick."

They began to walk along a pathway that started between the two high-rise blocks of flats, Bucky and Dunsmore on either side of him, the knife point pressed against his left kidney. They followed on through trees and bushes until eventually they reached the rush of the river. The angry torrent raged beside them as they continued along the snowy path. If the chance came and he threw himself in, would they still let Lena go? In those temperatures it would be over in seconds. Better than what awaited him at the end of the path. It didn't seem likely. Bucky and Dunsmore were close beside him, the knife jagging with each step. The snow was getting heavier and filled their footprints.

As they approached an iron railway bridge spanning the river, the pair flanking him began to slow. Paul lifted his head to see two figures standing at the entrance of the tunnel under the bridge. It was dark and the snow was obscuring his vision, but he could just about tell that one was bent over, holding his side, with the other tucked beneath his shoulder, taking his weight. Even from a distance, Paul knew who it was, though it didn't seem possible.

They kept going until they reached them. Without warning, Bucky and Dunsmore pushed Paul from behind and sent him stumbling to the ground. The cold snow soaked through his thin shirt. He was cold, colder than he'd ever been before.

Manny's half-dead breathing was laboured, his canines bared in agonised frenzy. His skin was the colour of ash. He was only upright by the sheer force of his will. Beneath his coat, Paul could see where someone had crudely patched him up, a blood-soaked bandage tight around his middle.

He should have been in hospital, but instead he stood there looking at Paul, holding his side, the blood seeping through his fingers. Every disjointed movement caused him obvious pain and his face was contorted in jagged peaks, but his eyes were unflinching.

The person shouldering Manny's weight was smaller. It took Paul a few moments to place the face. The partially healed gash on his cheek was the clue – Connor, the kid from the club. He suddenly remembered having felt as if someone was watching them in the pool hall earlier. There was no way Manny could have survived without immediate medical attention. Someone had been there. Someone who could identify Paul. And now he had an idea who. They'd known it was Paul from the second he ran out the door.

"I'm... going... to make you... suffer." There was a sharp intake of breath with every word Manny spoke. The others stood in obedient silence. "Terry!" he called out.

Paul followed Manny's line of vision to the tunnel entrance.

They all watched as Lena's small figure emerged from the darkness, cutting through the snow, head up, with slow, easy steps. White flakes clung to her black hair. She stopped still, looked at Paul in trance-like terror. Right behind her was a second figure. The skull face, the hollow socket: Terry. His hand was tightly squeezing her upper arm, holding her in place.

"Lena!" The shout erupted from Paul. He watched as she struggled against Terry's grip, broke free and ran to him.

Paul half ran, half crawled to meet her and caught her as she flew into his arms. The others watched. She rested her tear-streaked cheek against his chest, making damp patches on his shirt front, and he smoothed his hand over her hair. They touched each other lightly, as you would a wound. An eerie amber glow lit the sky as he tried to store the memory of every caress, every stroke of his fingertips. There just wasn't enough time to hold her how he wanted. Her body shuddered slightly on his chest and all he could think of was the time he'd wasted. His eyes misted with tears.

"I'm sorry, Lena. I'm sorry," he repeated.

She lifted her head from his chest and shook it, indicating *no*. Paul looked into her blanched face and hugged her close. "Paul…" But she couldn't finish what she was going to say.

Paul looked over to Manny. "You can let her go now. I've given myself up. I've done what you asked."

Snow was lying thick on the ground now. Terry, Bucky, Dunmore and Connor, who was still supporting Manny, had formed a circle around them. Spit dribbled from Manny's slack mouth as he stared at Paul with shiny eyes the colour of a stagnant pond with the light bouncing off it. "Boys," he said.

Bucky and Dunsmore started to close in on Paul and Lena and the pair huddled even closer. A struggle ensued as Bucky and Dunsmore tore them apart, dragging Paul to the side, leaving Lena alone in the centre of the circle.

Paul's face puckered. "You said you'd let her go!"

"That's not going to happen." Manny's voice was thin and reedy.

Clouds of white breath hovered over each of them. Paul's eyes flitted between them, looking ferociously from one to the next. Only Terry was unmoved; he'd seen women become casualties in war zones. It neither scared nor excited him. It was just another day on the field.

"This is your fault, Paul." Manny heaved and groaned, every utterance an exertion.

Lena's eyes were closed; she was speaking softly to herself, as if in prayer.

"Lena, run!" Paul shouted.

The knife pierced his back. The shock of it sent him to his knees, panting furiously. Speckles of blood darkened the snow. His hand went to his lower back and came back red. He looked up at Lena.

A blizzard blew wildly between them.

Behind her he saw Connor separate from Manny and begin walking towards her. His arms were raised, shaking violently, holding out a gun.

"Lena," Paul said. Her eyes opened and locked on his.

"Do it, Connor," Manny growled.

The gun shook behind her head. The look on her face was one of terror, although she couldn't see what was happening.

"Turn and shoot *him*, Connor," Paul said through gritted teeth. "Turn and shoot the bastard and it'll all be over. Shoot him!" Paul screamed as Bucky and Dunsmore wrestled him, covering his mouth.

"Don't even think about it," Terry said and trained a gun on Connor.

Connor saw it, but still his finger stalled above the trigger. Beads of sweat rolled down his temples as his hands shook, just as Paul's had when he'd held the bat above John's head. Connor was poised and ready, but still he couldn't pull it.

Paul watched Lena's arms reach out to him as behind her Connor lowered the gun and hung his head. In slow motion the limping figure of Manny closed in on Connor. With a new-found strength, adrenaline pumping through his body, Paul got to his feet and lumbered towards them. But there was nothing he could do. Manny reached out and took the gun from Connor's limp hand. Paul threw himself towards Lena just as Manny pulled the trigger. At the moment the chamber exploded loudly into the night, her body crumpled into Paul's arms. A thin red line trickled from her temple.

He fell to the ground and wrapped his arms around her lifeless body. The blizzard raged and Paul could no longer see any of the others, or hear them. Through the thick veil of snow, Manny grabbed him and whispered in his ear, "I fucking loved you."

Bucky and Dunsmore started to kick. Venting their own anger and frustration. Paul could feel his bones breaking, teeth smashing, head cracking, as he lay on the ground beside her.

He finally lost consciousness. The last thing he saw was her large eyes staring at him as the snow slowly covered her.

CHAPTER TWENTY-NINE

Annie looked at him with loathing. Paul jerked his head forward and chose a spot in the distance to stare at.

"She died. I survived," he said, staring listlessly at the water.

Annie was too numb to speak.

"When I woke up a week later in the hospital, my own mother wouldn't have recognised me," Paul said. "They left me for dead in the snow. But someone called an ambulance. I never found out who. I was brought back to life. Again."

The river sparkled beside them in the moonlight. Annie shivered as the temperature dropped in the damp shadows of the tunnel.

Paul went on talking. Talking and staring. Talking and staring. "I remember the first time I met Lena. She was fourteen. I thought she was sixteen. She stayed over at my flat and we talked for two days straight. About everything and nothing. All the deep things teenagers talk about." He smiled bitterly. "I remember telling her that you need to live your life free of fear. That that was the next best thing to immortality. That no matter what life threw at me, I was confident I could survive. And it gave me strength. I didn't understand then what I know now – that my ability to survive is my biggest weakness."

Tears stung Annie's eyes but she carried on listening.

"In the hospital I woke up alone. I had my own room. A policeman was outside guarding the door. But then a disturbance in another part of the hospital took him away and the nurse sneaked me in a visitor. Manny. He was in his hospital nightshirt and slippers, wheeling a portable saline drip alongside him. His skin was still grey but he was in better shape than I was. He told me they'd found John's body. That he knew I'd put them all at the scene. That if I didn't retract the statement and take full responsibility, or if I told them about Lena, he'd kill my son."

Paul took a breath and continued.

"Carmichael had done what I asked him to do that night. He sat with my family until morning, protecting Stacy and Jack. He'd stationed a patrol car outside the house. I'll be eternally grateful for that. But when he came to visit me, a few minutes after Manny left, I gave him a full confession. Said I killed John alone. No matter how much he pleaded and begged, I wouldn't say anything else. No matter how much protection he offered. I don't think he ever forgave me."

Paul inhaled sharply. "And so I went to prison. For John's murder. Which was right. Because, after all, I did kill the man. Stacy moved away with Jack after it all. I haven't seen or heard from them since."

"And Manny? He didn't try to get revenge? He didn't try to get even all those years you were in prison? For trying to kill him." Her face scrunched with scepticism.

"The opposite." Paul's voice was hollow. "He protected me. And when I came out, he was there waiting."

"You're still in contact with him?" Annie felt like she was

about to throw up. "What did he do with her body?" she said, through gritted teeth.

Paul's face took on an ugly sneer. "What do you do with an unwanted pussy? Put it in a sack and throw it in the river."

Annie stumbled where she stood. A screech tore out of her throat as she rushed at him. "Bastard!" she screamed, hammering his chest and arms with her fists. "Bastard! Why is he still living? Why haven't you killed him?"

"Because I don't care anymore," he shouted.

"What?" She stopped and took a step back, too disgusted to even touch him.

"I said, I don't care." His eyes blazed and for a moment she was frightened. "I should have ripped Manny's heart out and thrown it to the dogs. I should have stabbed him and waited till the last drop of blood trickled out of him. Should have taken a torch to his home and watched the flesh melt from his bones. I should have done the same to myself. But I haven't!"

Paul sank down onto the mud and looked up at Annie, almost pleading. "In prison I came close. So close. I got into fights. I tried to let them kill me, but at the last moment I always ended up fighting back. I tried overdosing, but could never quite take enough. When I got out, I even went to a bridge I'd heard of in Dumbarton. It's the place where dogs go to commit suicide. Since the sixties, over fifty recorded cases. They get to a certain point on the bridge and they just jump right over, apparently, crashing down to the rocks fifty feet below. I went there and I walked the bridge back and forth, waiting for the moment to come, for the impulse that sends even dogs over the edge. But it never came. Because, like I told you, I'm just an animal. I survive. That's all I do.

I'm lower than a dog. And I don't care."

Annie glared at him. She couldn't listen anymore. "Excuses, Paul. That's all that is. Excuses because you're a coward. That's all you are."

Paul hung his head, unable to meet her eye.

"You go to him tonight." Annie jabbed her finger at him. "And while you let him fuck you, I want you to look at him. I want you to look at him while he does it. Knowing what he did to her. What he did to you. And I want you to tell yourself that you don't care."

Paul pressed his face into his hands as tears streamed out of him. "I wanted it to be me. I wanted to be the one that died. I wish it had been me."

"But it wasn't." Annie spat at him and walked away.

EPILOGUE

A week later, Annie was sorting through her things in her living room. Sunlight and fresh air were streaming through her open window. The curtains flapped lazily in the breeze and a cup of tea was growing cold on the table. On the couch beside her was a cardboard box marked *Lena*. Inside were the few possessions Lena's landlord had boxed up from her flat after she disappeared: clothes, jewellery, perfume, toiletries. Alongside them Annie placed the cards and notes she'd received from Lena as a child, and the newspaper clippings she'd gathered over the years. All the clues she'd used to help piece together Lena's history. At the very top of the pile was a painting, done in acrylics, of a face that bore an uncanny resemblance to its subject, a face that until now she hadn't been able to bring herself to look at. Only now could she see the warmth that the painter had wanted to convey, the tenderness that had gone into every brush stroke. And she understood the love that had been shared. In that, she found comfort.

She hadn't seen or heard from Paul since she'd left him at the bridge. It surprised and shocked her to realise that she almost longed for his company now. He was the only one who understood what she was going through. Who shared her deep sense of loss. The task of finding out what had happened to Lena had filled her life. Now it was over, there wasn't much else left. All Annie felt was emptiness. She closed the box because she knew she had to. If she didn't, then Manny would have claimed her too.

She was going to go away for a while. She had no reason to wait around anymore. Lena wasn't coming home. In that sense, Annie had been released. She thought she'd start in Europe, then maybe go on to Asia. She'd always wanted to travel. And you couldn't live your life in fear – Lena would have told her that.

In the background the TV news was on, the noise and voices comforting, though she was paying no attention to what they were saying. But then a familiar name cut through her thoughts. She turned the volume up.

"Notorious Glasgow gangster Manus Munroe has died in unknown circumstances. Police say they are pursuing a person of interest."

Annie's thumb pressed the red button on the remote, flicking it off. She sat stunned, unsure whether to laugh or cry.

Her thoughts went to Paul and she knew what he'd done. She wondered where he was now.

In his hand he held a photograph of Lena. Sitting on a bench. Sixteen years old and full of life. Paul looked at it for a long time and smiled.

Finally she was with him again. She walked up behind him and hugged him, like she used to do. As he sat on the side of the iron bridge, his legs dangling over the edge, he knew there were things to be said, significant things. Secrets to be shared. Apologies. Explanations. He felt her warmth, smelled her scent as it all poured out of him. As he told her how much he cared. He could feel her breath in the wind as he leaned over the water.

In his final moment before he jumped, he saw her smiling face.

ACKNOWLEDGEMENTS

I would like to thank Lucy Ridout for editing *Take a Breath*. It is a better novel for all your insightful suggestions and revisions. Also to Jane Hammett for proof-reading the final version and picking up what we had all missed.

Thanks to my mum and dad, Danny and Una, for their continuing love and support and for being nothing like any of the parental figures in the book. To the rest of the Duffy clan, Oona, Fin and Connell, for reading early drafts and not laughing. To Dana for modelling so beautifully for the front cover. Thank you to Mark McGrory for his photograph and to Vanessa No Heart for her wonderful cover and interior designs.

I would also like to thank John Paisley for his advice and fact-checking of the police details. Thank you to Noreen Paisley, John Paisley and Siobhan Lynch for proof-reading and all their helpful feedback. Thank you to William McIlvanney for his kind words.

Finally I would like to thank my husband Jamie. For the countless hours spent reading redraft after redraft. For the endless discussions over every word and detail. For never growing tired or losing enthusiasm even when I did. If I were to list all the ways you helped me towards a final draft of this book it would fill a novel in itself. All my love always, best friend.

ABOUT THE AUTHOR

S.K. Paisley was born in Glasgow. She studied Law and English Literature at University of Glasgow before working briefly as a secondary school teacher. Her first draft of *Take a Breath* was started while living and working in London. She continued working on the novel while travelling around South America and finally completed it in Hamburg. The author currently lives in Amsterdam with her husband Jamie. *Take a Breath* is her first novel.

Printed in Great Britain
by Amazon